THE LEGEND AND THE LEGACY

To. Lisa

-2020-

Dick Damron

Bentley — Mazatlan

Dick Damron
THE LEGEND AND THE LEGACY

Quarry Music Books

The publisher acknowledges
The Canada Council for the
Arts and the Department of Canadian
Heritage for support of the art of
writing and publishing in Canada.
    The author has received no money
or assistance from these organizations.

ISBN 1-55082-193-8

Project Editor: Jim Brown

Design by Susan Hannah.

Printed and bound in Canada by
AGMV/Marquis, Cap-Ste-Ignace, Quebec.

Published by Quarry Press Inc.,
P.O. Box 1061, Kingston, Ontario K7L 4Y5 Canada.
www.quarrypress.com

CONTENTS

The Stories Behind the Songs

Every man's life ends the same way and it's only the details of how he lived and how he died that distinguishes one man from another.

—Ernest Hemingway

Ernest Tubb used to say, "It's nice to be important, but it's important to be nice." Dick Damron is definitely a genuinely nice man. In the business of sometimes pushy, abrasive people, Dick Damron has managed to retain a gentleness. He is a gentleman, a true "Canadian Country Gentleman," but he is also a gentle man.

— George Hamilton IV

Dick Damron has survived the ecstasy and the agony of country music to become a living legend, walking tall with that honor and with the humility that earned it.

— Walt Grealis

PREFACE

first met Dick Damron at a country music convention in the mid-1980s. After we had been introduced, Dick presented me with a large lapel pin bearing the slogan *Dick Damron Mystery Tour*. As I was pinning this badge onto my jacket, I remarked, "Great, when does it start?"

"You're on it," the genial, bearded Damron answered with a smile.

At the time I thought this witty. An effective promotional gimmick. However, as the days and years rolled by and Dick and I became friends, I realized he had not just been joking around. Dick Damron's life is music and the people who play, sing, and write it. At this point in his career, Damron had already won a wagonload of major national awards. He was Canada's Top Country Music Male Vocalist in '76, '77, '78 and '83 and Canadian Country Music Entertainer of the Year in 1985. He had charted five Number 1 Canadian Country Music hits, received seven BMI awards (as Canada's top songwriter) as well as Academy of Country Music Song of the Year awards for *Susan Flowers* (in 1976) and *Jesus It's Me Again* (in 1984) and been nominated for numerous Juno Awards.

He had also won Texas Proud Awards in '80, 81, 82 and '83 as Best Foreign Artist, Songwriter of the Year and Male Vocalist Of The Year. He pioneered Canadian country music tours of Europe with one-time CCMA president Hank Smith in 1972, and followed this up with his own tours from 1976 to 1989 playing to packed houses in large venues in Belgium, Holland, Germany, and the United Kingdom. He has entertained enthusiastic overseas audiences of Canadian, U.S., and Dutch servicemen. At the gigantic Wembley Country Music Festivals, Damron has shared the stage with Marty

Robbins, Ronnie Milsap, Don Williams, Donna Fargo, Larry Gatlin, Dottie West, Kenny Rogers, Moe Bandy, and Merle Haggard.

Since we met in 1986, Dick has also won Alberta Country Music Association awards for Entertainer of the Year (1993) and Album of the Year for WINGS UPON THE WIND (1993). He has been inducted into the Alberta Country Music Hall of Fame. He's also twice been named Artist of the Year by *Country Gazette* magazine distributed in Holland, Belgium, and Germany.

Equally important, Dick Damron's songs have been recorded by scores of other well-known country artists, including George Hamilton IV, Hank Smith, The Rhythm Pals, Orval Prophet, Carroll Baker, and Wilf Carter.

Although the many awards catalogue some of Damron's achievements, the "Dick Damron Story" chronicles the life of a starving songwriter who made it through persistence and hard work. No one put a silver spoon into Damron's mouth, nor was his career launched with hype or large chunks of dubious money.

Damron's first recordings were done in the late 1950s at the local radio station, CKRD Red Deer. *Gonna Have A Party b/w Rockin' Baby* and *That's What I Call Livin' b/w Julie* got a surprising amount of regional airplay. From that point forward, each step of the way was made by Damron himself, without a fanfare of corporate endorsement. No one "discovered" Dick Damron, either in rural Alberta or Nashville. Dick's first Nashville recordings, recorded in 1961 at Starday Studios, were put out as singles on Quality Records in Canada into a non-existent Canadian market. *Little Sandy b/w Nothing Else* and *Times Like This b/w The Same Old Thing Again* were released into a vacuum before national country music charts existed.

In February 1964 *RPM* magazine was first published in Canada, creating the first national chart for country music. Damron's records immediately began to show up on these charts, and by 1965, *Hitchhikin'*, from the 1963 Starday sessions, issued on RCA Victor, rose to Number 3. Dick's records climbed the charts without hype or payola, on their own merit. Damron's first album, THE NASH-VILLE SOUND OF DICK DAMRON, issued in 1965, brings together the '61 and '63 Starday Sessions. In 1965, Damron recorded again in Nashville at Bradley Studios. *The Cumberland* and *The Hard*

Knocks In Life were issued as singles on RCA Victor and these tracks along with others were collected in the 1968 album release DICK DAMRON.

However, success did not come overnight. Damron spent five more years writing songs and touring from Whitehorse, Yukon, to the Maritime provinces before he got his first big break. In 1967 he issued *Canadiana,* which was recorded locally and chronicled some slices of Canadian history for the Canadian Centennial. In 1968 he issued his third album, DICK DAMRON, which combined cuts from three Nashville sessions. Dick was also busy during these years producing records for other artists at Joe Kozak's Korl Sound facility in Edmonton. The most notable of these releases, Jimmy Arthur Ordge's recording of Damron's *The Cold Grey Winds Of Autumn,* won the Moffat Broadcasting "Country Record of the Year" award in 1967 and the BMI Song of the Year award in 1968.

Damron's first national and international impact as a recording artist and songwriter came with the 1970 release of *Countryfied,* a Number 1 hit for him in Canada, and a Top Ten hit world-wide for George Hamilton IV. During this period, Dick became a frequent performer on Canadian television shows like *The Tommy Hunter Show,* Peter Gzowski's *90 Minutes Live,* Ian Tyson's *Sun Country,* Ronnie Prophet's *Grand Ol' Country, The Don Harron Show,* and *Country Way,* the Family Brown's syndicated series. *Countryfied* became the theme for television shows hosted by George Hamilton IV in both Canada and in England. When TNN came along, Dick was one of the first to appear on the channel's *Wrap Around Nashville.*

The simple uplifting lyrics of *Countryfied* make it a natural for award show finales from coast to coast:

> *Well, I don't care who knows it, man*
> *I'm countryfied*
> *I love the countryside*
> *Like chicken, country-fried*
> *And I couldn't be a city-slicker*
> *Even if I tried*
> *I love the Country way of life . . .*

During the 1970s, as the infrastructure of the Canadian country music industry began to fill in, Dick Damron became known as Canada's own "outlaw" — a wildman on stage and a real entertainer, although you would be more likely to find him picking with the songwriters in the backroom than sitting around in the executive suites of the major label companies. And as the "family" of people who began to attend the annual Canadian "Country Music Week" grew, Dick was a much-loved figure, and his "Mystery Tours" were part of the legend-building. Along with The Family Brown and Carroll Baker, Dick Damron was a perennial award-winner. Again *RPM* magazine played a major part in the development of the Canadian country music industry when editor and publisher Walt Grealis began to build the "star system" machinery with the 1975 RPM Big Country Awards, which soon became the Academy of Country Music Awards and then the Canadian Country Music Association Awards, building to the first televised show in Winnipeg in 1986 and the first nationally televised awards show in Vancouver in 1987.

Many times I have enjoyed the ambience of an informal picking and singing session in Dick's suite at one of the convention hotels during Canadian Country Music Week. I learned that he treats everyone he has worked with or appeared with, equally, from the top-achievers to the musicians like Pete Drake, Buddy Emmons, Mark O'Connor, Fred Carter Jr., Mike "Pepe" Francis, Red Shea, Stewert Barnes, Sammy Taylor, Paul Franklin Jr. and Randy Scruggs . . . from the DJ's who spin his records . . . to the newest kid-on-the-scene who has yet to release his or her first single. As George Hamilton IV has remarked, "he treats everyone with respect and dignity, the little guys as well as the big guys. It is an endearing quality." And, although Damron has steadfastly remained independent, managing his own career, handling his own bookings, and maintaining artistic control of his music by paying for his own recording sessions and leasing his albums to labels (both major and independent), refusing to enter the political arena or hand over the reins of his career to any of the hundreds of managers, agents, promoters, or entrepreneurs who operate in the field — Dick is nevertheless respected by everyone in the industry. As his long-time

Nashville producer Joe Bob Barnhill writes, "I'm very proud to have been a part of Dick Damron's career, but more important to me — Dick Damron is my friend."

Over the years, I have joined the Mystery Tour in a variety of venues, places like Ivan Daines' Country Music Picknic (a rodeo and music festival in Innisfail, Alberta), south of the border down Mexico way in Mazatlan, backstage at awards presentations, and in Hamilton, Ontario in the majestic Anglican Cathedral, built in 1875, during the filming of the video for *Jesus It's Me Again*, where Dick was joined by Lisa Brokop, Sylvia Tyson, Cindy Church, Michelle Wright, Patricia Conroy, Stephanie Beaumont, Laura Vinson, Lyndia Scott, Tracey Prescott, Kelita and others who sang on camera, forming the prettiest country music choir ever assembled.

Following the 1989 landmark album THE LEGEND AND THE LEGACY, which yielded radio hits like the title track, *Ain't No Trains To Nashville*, *Wild Horses*, and *Midnite Cowboy Blues*, Damron has concentrated on gospel releases and instrumental albums. WINGS UPON THE WIND (The Christian Country Collection) was named Gospel Album of the Year in both Alberta and Texas, and was followed by TOUCH THE SKY (The Christian Country Collection, Vol. 2). The RCA/BMG vinyl release of the guitar instrumental album NIGHT MUSIC in 1988 was followed by a CD release MIRAGE, on ATI Records in 1992, which contains additional tracks.

Dick's 27 albums have yielded a bountiful harvest of timeless songs, 20 of which are issued on the BMG/RCA collection DICK DAMRON: THE ANTHOLOGY, the first in a series of CDs presenting the music of Canadian Country Music Association Hall of Honour members such as Wilf Carter, Hank Snow, The Family Brown, and Carroll Baker. This collection features many of Damron's best tracks, including a sparkling 1990 rendition of *Countryfied*, *Cinderella And The Gingerbread Man*, *High On You*, *Susan Flowers*, *The Last Of The Rodeo Riders*, *Cozy Inn*, *Mother*, *Love and Country*, *Tequila Charlie's*, and *One Night Stand* from the artist's Top Forty era, as well as the original version of *Jesus It's Me Again* (Song of the Year, 1984) and the newly-recorded video soundtrack.

When Dick Damron was inducted into the Hall of Honour on the 1994 Canadian Country Music Awards televised show, he stepped to the microphone and said, simply, "Hi, I'm Dick Damron, and I'm a survivor." Just what that has meant over the nearly 40 years of active duty in the country music field is colorfully described in this autobiography. The saga takes the reader from the Blindman Valley, in rural Alberta, to the music capitals of the world. Damron's often-cryptic comments point out that the working conditions and snares of music industry politics don't necessarily improve or change when you move from a country dance hall to a big city cabaret, from touring across Canada to touring in the U.S. and Europe. But this is not a searing indictment of the music industry; rather, it is an inspiring story of a country boy who gets lost in the music and survives to tell the story.

Dick Damron lives in Bentley, Alberta, where he was born and raised, and from where he ventures forth to play festivals and concerts. He spends his winters in Mazatlan, Sinaloa, Mexico, where he wrote this book.

— *Jim Brown, Project Editor*
Mazatlan 1996, Bentley 1997

CHAPTER ONE

All That Glitters...

THE LEGEND AND THE LEGACY

I WAS BORN A LITTLE BIT NORTH OF TEXAS
I'VE BEEN DOWN TO NASHVILLE, TENNESSEE
DEEP DOWN IN MY HEART
I'M JUST A LITTLE PART
OF THE LEGEND AND THE LEGACY

WITH MY SONGS I TRAVELED THIS WORLD OVER
PICKED GUITAR AND WAILED A LITTLE BLUES
DEEP DOWN IN MY HEART
I'LL ALWAYS BE A PART
OF THE LEGEND AND THE LEGACY . . .

© Sparwood Music

All That Glitters

I t was November 1985, and I was booked for a month-long engagement at the fabulous Desert Inn. The Desert Inn drew much of its fame from the fact that Howard Hughes had moved into the penthouse in 1966 and, instead of checking out at check-out time, bought the place, lock, stock, and barrel for $13,200,000. Howard Hughes died in 1976 on a plane bound for Texas from Mexico. But the Desert Inn was still owned by his Summa Corporation and our contract was with them.

I had performed in Vegas before, at the Palace Station and the Silver Dollar, when guitar pickin' buddies had invited me on stage to "sing a few tunes." And I had a booking waiting for me back in the late Sixties and early Seventies, but I could not get immigration papers to work there. When the National Finals Rodeo (N.F.R.) moved from Oklahoma City to Las Vegas in 1985, I called a few agents. They all told me Las Vegas was a "Top Forty" town. I explained to them that the N.F.R. was moving to Vegas and the city would be full of cowboys, Canadians, rodeo fans, and country music fans. My kind of people. They were unimpressed.

A few weeks later, I was in the San Francisco Bay area recording at Live Oak Studio in Berkeley. On my way home to Canada, I detoured back through Las Vegas from San Francisco. I had a brief meeting with Caroline Wallace, the Desert Inn's entertainment director, and in a few days the deal was signed. This was August. Little did I know that it would take until November, two days before our engagement, to work things out with U.S. immigration. Bobby Curtola, who was performing in Vegas at the time, came to my rescue and our papers came through only hours before our flight time. I will always be grateful to Bobby for that little miracle.

But that was all behind me now as we were touching down on the runway at McCarran International Airport. I would return every year for the next five years to perform at the Desert Inn during the N.F.R.

To play Las Vegas had always been a dream of mine. Just to be in the city that had hosted everyone from Willie Nelson to Bill Cosby, from Dolly Parton to Sarah Vaughan, and hundreds of names like Kenny Rogers, Frank Sinatra, and Elvis Presley. We were in the "Entertainment Capital of the World," not in one of the million obscure bars, lounges, clubs, and hell-holes I had performed in over the past 30 odd years. It was pretty big stuff for a kid from Bentley, Alberta.

Casino

Vegas runs the gamut from the 99¢ hot-dog-and-beer specials to the luxury suites that are comped to the players with credit lines of $250,000 and more. From the guy who throws a $50 tip to a dealer, to the weasel who screams at the change girl in the casino because the nickel machine swallowed up a nickel without showing a credit and demands a refund or he will call the supervisor, the manager, the cops, the FBI, or possibly the President! A weekend here is certainly like a weekend in Disneyland. Any more is like a lifetime. Adjust or die. Keep that sense of humor going all the time. Lose your so-called "sense of ha ha" and you are instantly on the outer edge of a nervous breakdown. It can be as awesome or as terrifying as you let it become.

It's kind of like getting an invitation to the marriage of Howard Stern and Ellen Degeneres, and not knowing what to wear. The ghosts of Howard Hughes, Bugsy Siegal, and Elvis all mix together in some strange kind of spirit world that swirls down the strip and hovers over Glitter Gulch (Fremont Street). If you have seen the movie *Casino* and had any trouble identifying the real people portrayed on the screen, you have never spent much time in Las Vegas. Tony is Nicky, Nicky is Tony, and Tony is Nicky. Rosenthal and Rothstein could be twenty-one-across on any airline flight magazine crossword puzzle. Don't ask the guy in the seat beside you — if he happens to be carrying a violin case. As in Hunter S. Thompson's *Fear and Loathing in Las Vegas*, you can fear and loath — or be feared and loathed — at the turn of a card or the roll of the dice.

I was living in Las Vegas at the Mardi Gras on Paradise Road in 1986 while performing at The Desert Inn when Tony Spilotro left his lofty position with the Las Vegas Mob to usurp power with the Chicago Boys. A few weeks later, he and his brother were found buried face-down in a shallow grave in an Indiana cornfield. And the move was on to fill the vacancy in Vegas. Names were bounced around on a daily basis in *The Sun* and *The Review Journal*, as well as on local television. The string of candidates appeared from all corners of North America, and their credits and background were printed as openly as if they were vying for a position on the local school board. A graphic picture of the big boys moving from their limos into a meeting at The Aladdin found its way into the pages of the dailies. Our driver at the time was an elderly man from New Jersey, who spoke with a perfect "Joyzee" accent. My drummer, Sammy Taylor, affectionately nick-named him Joyzee.

Joyzee kept us informed with a running commentary on the Spilotro story. Listening to him relay the info every night as he drove us to and from the Desert Inn was like watching Godfather III on TV with the picture tube blown.

Today, bag ladies and rag men and derelicts and thugs who hand out the "girly, girly" magazines along the strip are the product of a lot of people with bad ideas at the wrong time. There is a skinny little line somewhere between the human waste and the people who feed off them. As you walk by, a black woman shrieks, "Don't talk to *me* motherfucker. Jesus knows what you think!" My mind cannot even attempt to link the words in that statement. But this is Las Vegas and she is plying the oldest profession and it's a good 25 years since she was prime-time entertainment. She is 10 million light years from the 14-carat rich girls and their love-by-the-hour that is as close as your telephone. And all credit cards are accepted.

Sometimes I catch a cab up the strip to Fremont. It's an education just reading the signs as they fly by on the north end of the strip (Las Vegas Boulevard). There is an unending string of scary little run-down motels. One proudly claims, "Elvis slept here." Then there's "Graceland Wedding Chapel" and a hundred others: one proclaims, "Over 200,000 Happy People Married Here." Why are there so many pawn shops and bail bond signs and why are they side-by-side? And look there — right in front of the many-splendored Desert Star Motel — there's a whole fleet of patrol cars with red and blue lights flashing through the bizarre, late night Nevada light show. You can see a dozen cops with guns drawn and a half-dozen young blacks with their hands on the roof of a battered old Cadillac (with the front-end built up so high that the back bumper is dragging on the pavement). The cab driver doesn't even glance sideways. A few blocks later, I ask him about a new club in town that I have heard about. He turns his head slightly and sighs, "It must be a pretty nice place. It's been open for a week and they haven't killed anybody yet." In the immortal words of comedian Pete Barbuti, "They're not going to kill anybody in Las Vegas for eleven years! The desert's full."

The cabby drops me off at Fremont and I walk under the relative daylight of a million lights, down past Binion's Horse Shoe and The Las Vegas Club to the Union Plaza. I turn around and walk back up the other side of the street, past the Golden Nugget, The Four Queens, and the ever-present home of the Big Mac. I don't buy a watch from the guy with 20 watches on each arm. I don't try my 'free pull' for $250,000. I don't stop and see "The Gorgeous Girls of Glitter Gulch." I just give the one-armed man in the filthy, tattered "Jesus Saves" t-shirt a Canadian dollar and catch a cab back to the relative sanity of my hotel room, snap on the TV, and have a long, long shower.

Recently, Glitter Gulch received a multi-million-dollar dome of shining metal and lights and has been dubbed "The Fremont Street Experience." But beyond all this, I somehow managed to get "Lost in the Music," lost in trying to learn to be a better musician and a better entertainer. Traveling around the world, with a view from afar, Canada and Canadians always appear as great musicians but lousy entertainers. Most of us, I think, take ourselves far too seriously. If you can't laugh at yourself — well?

One thing about Vegas, there is a never ending stream of comers and goers. They come from every state in the union and every money country in the world. The trick is to find out where they are from and whether or not they are fight fans from Ireland or computer convention snobs. A word or two of recognition and you've got 'em. Sometimes, when the patter begins to out-weigh the music, the band gets a little sideways and can't seem to understand that it swings both ways. Very seldom is there a perfect balance between the pickin' and the patter. The trick, if it is a trick at all, is knowing when to entertain and when to shut up and play music. I'm not sure if one is born with it, but I think I have developed a strong instinct that seldom lets me down.

I learned a lot about the fine art of entertaining everyone in the building from masters like Roy Clark, when he appeared at the Red Deer Memorial Centre back in 1961, and from performing with the late and great Marty Robbins at Wembley Stadium in 1976. Marty not only entertained the huge crowd in front of him but also acknowledged the people seated behind him and around the perimeter of the huge complex as well as everyone backstage and in the wings. The other entertainers on the bill always gathered around to catch the shows and watch one of the masters touch everyone within earshot. Las Vegas was my opportunity to practice what I had learned at the Robbins and Clark "School of Entertainment."

The Winner's Circle Lounge was located at the north end of the Desert Inn, with the bar in the middle and the hotel desk off to our right. It seated about 275 people. However, when the hotel was busy or the main showroom let out, we had a few hundred extras around the outside railing of the lounge. And we entertained them all, including the waitresses, the bartenders, the bellmen, the change girls, and the entertainers from other shows.

We were warned from the first day that "if we were too loud or interrupted the dealers or the players in the casino, we would be history." Yet many dealers came by on their breaks during our late shows or on a slow night to request a song that they had heard us do. The security guards (in those days still carrying guns, night sticks, and wearing their brown military-style uniforms) became some of our greatest fans and always slipped me a word or a wink when the opportunity presented itself. Tie this kind of rapport in with the dynamite band I had put together, and we had a great show.

The band consisted of three regular members of Stoney Creek: Sam Taylor, Rob Warren, and Brian Richard. We added Myren Szott on fiddle and Ron Haldorson on steel guitar. We put the unit together in Canada and worked a few weeks at The Country Roads Saloon in Calgary and Cook County Saloon in Edmonton. We played five hours a night and rehearsed in the afternoons.

Instead of the usual country bar-band-of-the-week fare, I dug out the HILLBILLY JAZZ album of Vassar Clements and Doug Jernigan fame (in music circles) and the band learned *C-Jam Blues*, *Tippin' In*, and *Gravy Waltz* (a jazz classic by Los Angeles bass genius Ray Brown). Past experience had taught me to stay with my original music, so we did add *If London Were A Lady* and some of our mellower stuff. We later added Merle Haggard's *After Dark* and my own instrumentals *Trivial Pursuit* and *Las Vegas Nights* as well as *Sierra Madre Morning* from my guitar album. When people dropped by to catch the show expecting the straight, old country stuff, they were blown away with the jazz classics.

The other musicians playing the show rooms on the strip took note. When they found out that I welcomed them on stage and was not just there to exercise my ego, they showed up night after night to sit in on our late or late, late shows. Jamie Whiting (from the Ray Stevens Show, who played keyboards on many of my Nashville sessions) sat in at the beautiful grand piano on stage. Norm Carlson and Rocky Stone (from the Mickey Gilley band) sat in night after night. One of the greatest guitarists alive, James Burton (who has worked with everyone from Elvis to Emmylou), joined us on stage. And, as the nights went by, we had Ricky Solomon (from Reba's band) and some of her musicians who were killed in that horrible plane crash not more than a year later. Canadian fiddle players Tony Michael, Roy Warhurst, and Graham Townsend also dropped in from time to time, and Jeff Cook (of Alabama fame) picked and sang with us into one late Las Vegas night.

We had a steady stream of celebrities coming by over the years. People like Bill Cosby, Sammy Davis Jr., Bill Medley (of the Righteous Brothers), and Tommy Smothers (whom I met the next day in the Entertainment Director's office, and who praised our show while showing me a few "Yo Yo Man" stunts). This all made me feel like I was some small part of the entertainment world.

There was no cover charge at the show lounge where we performed. However, there was a "head count" done at every show. I was later told by Caroline Wallace that our show was great and our "counts" were exceptional. Over these five years, I performed for a total of seven months at The Desert Inn and sang the national anthem a number of times for the National Finals Rodeo at the 17,000 seat Thomas & Mack Center. I was determined to make the "Vegas thing" work for me and eventually end up in one of the show rooms, even if it was as an opening act for an American superstar. Then we would see where it took us from there.

I hired Norm Johnson, former head of Robert Goulet's RoGo Inc., to do publicity work for me, and over the years, I did every radio and TV talk show and was written up and reviewed by *The Sun*, *The Las Vegas Review Journal*, and every other entertainment rag in Vegas. One morning Norm picked me up at the Desert Inn and drove me to a local television studio to tape the early morning talk show. When we entered the green room, I immediately spotted Ronnie Hawkins' manager, Steve Thomson. Ronnie was appearing at The Sahara with Mel Tillis and was also guesting on the morning show. We watched Hawkins on the monitor, terrorizing Debbie Campbell as she tried desperately to interview him. When it came time for a commercial break, Debbie said, "We have one of your fellow Canadians coming up next. Do you know Dick Damron?"

Hawkins reared back in his chair and snorted, "I met Damron in Kingston Penitentiary in 1968. He's been in and out of every prison in Canada. You're not gonna let him on here are you?" Debbie forced a smile and went to a commercial break.

Flashback

Following those Desert Inn years, I returned to Vegas each year to take in the National Finals Rodeo and do a few guest appearances at the big opening celebration downtown on Fremont Street. The cowboy party that draws thousands into the city centre is known as the "Downtown Hoedown" and kicks off the ten-day N.F.R.

In 1993, I was back in Vegas for the N.F.R., but I was not playing any shows. It seemed strange to be there and not be involved in the massive bash that brings bands, musicians, and superstars into every casino hotel in town. Days and nights run together in this twenty-four-hour-city. By design, there are no clocks or windows in the casinos and time becomes non-existent. Frustration and confusion overtook me and I began gambling heavily and losing thousands of hard-earned dollars. When I finally came to my senses, my pockets were empty, my credit card was maxed-out, and the casino bank machine was smoking. As I headed across the crowded casino toward the elevator, music drifted through the din and clamor of the busy tables and money-hungry slots. I turned and made my way toward the familiar sound of country music. All of a sudden, I had a flashback to the great times we'd had playing at The Desert Inn.

So, I'm down here, but I'm not playing. And I'm feelin' kind of stressed out by all of this. Thinkin' "God, I wish I was going up there with these guys, even just to blow harp or something . . ."

I went back to my room and wrote a song using my little tape machine. It just wrote itself because the feelings were there. They just had to get out. That's what the song *A Hole In My Heart Without Jesus* is about. It's about being some place and feeling deprived.

THERE'S A HOLE IN MY LIFE WITHOUT MUSIC . . .

Which there was. And then, I wondered, "Why is it this way?" It was me that painted myself into this corner. I was there, but I wasn't performing. I felt this void. Then I sort of said to God, "Well, why is this the way that it is?" And I wrote: "There's a hole in my heart without Jesus . . ."

That's where that song came from. I think that if I'd done that song with a harder edge, with a full country band — if I'd been more commercially-minded about it instead of just putting it on a gospel album — and done that song with a full production, it could have been the kind of song that would have gotten a lot of country airplay. Everybody responds to this song, and I know they feel it.

THERE'S A HOLE IN MY LIFE WITHOUT MUSIC,
A PLACE THAT'S GROWN EMPTY AND STILL.
THERE'S A HOLE IN MY HEART WITHOUT JESUS,
I CAN'T FIND THE COURAGE TO FILL.

— *A Hole In My Heart Without Jesus* © Sparwood Music

I returned to Vegas in December of 1994 to perform at the 15,000-seat Grand Garden in the magnificent new MGM Grand Hotel. For the show, I had the luxury of working with producer Joe Bob Barnhill and a wonderful eight-piece band of studio musicians he had put together in Nashville. Artists on the show included Rodney Crowell, Ricky Lynn Gregg, Paulette Carlson, Mark Collie, John McEwen, Patricia Conroy, Doug Kershaw, Dan Seals, Confederate Railroad, Clinton Gregory, and many others. As I left the stage that night, I choked back the ominous feeling that this might be my final performance and the end of a ten-year love/hate relationship with Las Vegas. Pretty tough stuff for a kid from Bentley, Alberta.

(Top Left) *Dick performing the Canadian national anthem at the Thomas & Mack Center during the N.F.R. to 17,000 rodeo fans.*

(Bottom Left) *Dick with the Vegas version of Stoney Creek (left to right): Sam Taylor, Brian Richard, Myren Szott, Denis Larochelle, and Rob Warren.*

(Top Right) *Patricia Conroy and Dick Damron at the MGM Grand in Las Vegas, two of the first artists to perform at the new 18,000 seat Grand Garden facility.*

(Bottom Right) *The Desert Inn where Damron played The Winner's Circle Lounge from 1985 to 1989 during the National Finals Rodeo.*

CHAPTER TWO

Childhood Days

EVERY MOTHER'S CHILD

RICH MAN, POOR MAN, BEGGAR MAN, THIEF
WHAT WILL HE BE WHEN HE GROWS TO BE A MAN?
SUGAR AND SPICE AND EVERYTHING NICE
WILL HE FIND THAT SPECIAL ONE TO FIT HIS PLAN
TO HOLD HIS HAND
TO SHARE THE SAD TIMES AND THE HAPPINESS?

RICH MAN'S SON WITH SILVER SPOON
POOR MAN'S CHILD IN POVERTY AND LONELINESS
FROM THE CRADLE TO THE GRAVE
EVERY MOTHER'S CHILD PURSUES ELUSIVE DREAMS
OF ONE TRUE LOVE
TO SHARE THE SAD TIMES AND THE HAPPINESS

I'VE SEARCHED AND I'VE SEARCHED BUT I HAVE NEVER FOUND
THE LOVE THAT COMES TO EVERY MOTHER'S CHILD
AND FROM THE DARKEST CORNERS OF A LONELY TORTURED MIND
VISIONS OF A LONESOME DESTINY ARE RUNNING WILD
AND I KNOW, YES I KNOW, THAT I WILL NEVER FIND
THE LOVE THAT COMES TO EVERY MOTHER'S CHILD

Bentley and Birth

In the heart of the Blindman Valley, 12 miles west of where Highway 2 slices the province of Alberta up the middle, halfway between Calgary and Edmonton, lies the tiny village of Bentley. The Blindman River twists and winds its way south through the valley. Age-old spruce, poplar, and balm trees decorated with diamond willow, dogwood, and rose bushes cover the river banks on both sides. To the west the "Sunset" and "Medicine" Hills roll off into a never-ending horizon that has staged a million glorious sunsets. Miles upon miles of farmland, thousands of acres of cottonwoods, jack-pine, swamp spruce, and tamarack finally come to rest against the timberline of the eastern slopes of the towering Rocky Mountains.

In the early morning hours of March 22, 1934, in a small gray-stone house in Bentley, by the light of a kerosene lamp, I was pushed, kicking and screaming, into the waiting hands of my mother's sister, Florence (who had volunteered her services as a midwife). She carried me into the kitchen, where my grandmother had been anxiously awaiting the arrival of her youngest daughter's second child.

My mother, Mable Margaret Rombough, was of Irish and Pennsylvania Dutch heritage. My father, Ned Trobough Damron, had bloodlines that stretched back through Nebraska, Kentucky, and Texas, mixing proud Cherokee blood on my grandmother's side with early American whatever on the side of Grandpa Damron. (My dad's brother, Uncle Bud, was the proudest of our Indian blood, and always insisted that his great-uncle was the only Damron who amounted to a damn. He had been a prison guard in Kentucky and one night he got drunk and turned all the prisoners loose — our only claim to fame).

"Here," Florence said. "You take this damn thing. I have to take care of his mother."

I have heard this story told and retold a hundred times. Needless to say, it keeps one humble.

A few years back, when I performed at the senior citizens' home in Bentley, one of the ladies insisted on introducing me to the crowd. I told her I was sure they all knew me and that I knew most of them. But I granted her wish and she began.

"These days there are kids terrorizing the town with motorcycles and cars and trucks with no mufflers," she began. "I remember when 'Little Dickie Damron' did it single-handedly on horseback!"

When she had finished her introduction, I began singing my songs. Some listened and some related their favorite "Dickie Damron" story to the person next to them.

Runaway

From as far back as I can remember, I was always in trouble. And strange as it may seem, my very first memories center around something that became a large part of my childhood life and carried on into my early teens — running away from home.

At that time I was about four years old. My father was the high-school principal in Bentley, my older brother Bob had just started school, and my younger brother Howard and sister Lorna had not yet entered the world. Most of the other town kids were a year or two older than I was and were also attending school. So I spent most of the long days with my mother or playing out in the front yard.

It was a hot sunny afternoon. My father and brother were both at school. My mom was trying to have an afternoon nap. She tried to get me to crawl up on the bed and have a sleep, but I stood by the bed tugging at her hand, trying to get her to come outside and play. She fell asleep and I wandered out into the yard, down the street a few blocks and into a vacant lot behind a service station on the edge of town. There was an old grain hopper, owned by a local truck driver, stored there when not in use. In the fall of the year, it would be transported out to the local farms and loaded up with grain. The truck would back under it, the grain would be dumped into the truck, and then hauled to the huge grain elevators that stood alongside the Canadian Pacific Railway tracks in Bentley.

The hopper stood on four legs and had a ladder running up to the top. I played on the bottom steps for a few minutes and then climbed to the top of the 20-foot structure. It was all I could do to climb from one step to the other as the steps were about three feet apart. When I reached the top, I climbed over the edge and dropped inside. As soon as my feet touched the shiny sloped floor, polished from thousands of bushels of wheat, oats, and barley being dumped through it over the years, I slid down to the bottom where the sides went straight up. I was trapped and scared. I began crying and then called out. Again and again, I tried to climb from the bottom of the grain pit. After what seemed like hours of shouting, crying, and attempting the impossible climb, I fell asleep.

Meanwhile (as the story goes), my mother had begun looking for me. At first she casually checked the house and the yard. Then she called the neighbors to ask if they had seen Dickie, as I was called in my early years. By the time my dad and my brother, Bob, returned from school around four o'clock, the whole neighborhood had been alerted and my mom was getting more worried by the minute.

It wasn't long until everyone in town was involved in the search. They went up and down every street and alley, checking every nook and cranny, calling out to me. As the hours rolled by, everyone became more and more concerned and then the stories began — someone had seen a kid down by the river, someone else had seen me playing by the railway track on the highway. Maybe I was lost in the dense bush on the north side of town. There were dozens of stories and they were all checked out. The afternoon turned to evening, and as the sun began to sink behind the rolling sunset hills to the west of town, the concern was "How much longer should we look?" or "Shall we call it off until morning?" They elected to continue the search.

A teen-aged girl, who had served as my babysitter many times, joined the effort. When I awoke she was standing at the top of the ladder looking down at me and calling my name. In my excitement and confusion I can't remember how she managed to hoist me out of the hopper or get me down the ladder. By now it was almost totally dark. I was scared and crying. I wanted her to hold me or pick me up and carry me home, but instead she produced a willow switch and began striking me across the backs of my bare legs.

All the way up the street she switched me across the legs and shouted at me to get home. As we got closer to home, she told me that my dad was going to give me a licking. I began to cry again. When we came through the front door and into the house, my mom rushed to pick me up. I could tell she'd been crying. When my dad came on the scene, everything changed. He was always the disciplinarian — and this was the time for me to learn not to run away from home again. He took me into the bedroom. I was still crying. I then received one of his hour-long lectures, full of all sorts of threats and promises. When he left me alone in the bedroom and told me to go to sleep, I was a pretty unhappy kid.

I vaguely remember people talking about me running away from home. When you are a child, how do you explain that you were not running away ... that it just happened.

My grandfather bought me a beautiful big tricycle, and one afternoon I started riding down towards the Blindman River, west of town. It's downhill all the way, and in no time I was out of town and out of sight. By the time I realized how far I had gone and turned back, I was tired and it was uphill all the way back. Peddling the tricycle on the gravel road uphill became an almost impossible task. So I got off and tried to push it. Have you ever tried pushing a tricycle uphill on gravel?

By now the word was out: "Dickie Damron has run away from home again." However, it wasn't long until my grandfather came along in his shiny new '39 Chrysler. He picked me up, put my tricycle into the trunk, and took me home. This time I did get a real "licking" plus what was to become the standard multi-hour lecture that I received over and over for the next 15 years, anytime the slightest thing occurred that was not to my dad's liking.

The Other Side Of The Mountain

My grandfather used to sit in the big old rockin' chair in front of the handcrafted rock and concrete fireplace. He would rock back and forth, slower and slower, until he found the exact tempo, barely moving. The slow precise rhythm would mesmerize and hypnotize me as I watched him. His head would go back, his eyes would close, and just when I was sure he was sound asleep, he would say quietly, almost in a whisper, "Come here, Dickie."

I'd crawl up onto his lap and lay my head on his big old pot belly. He always wore a vest with the buttons done right to the top. He also wore a gold watch and chain. The watch was tucked into his vest pocket, and I learned to curl into the exact spot so that I could hear the watch ticking in my ear.

He'd put his arms around me and begin to sing in perfect tempo and harmony with the rocking and creaking of the old chair and the ticking of his gold pocket watch:

The bear went over the mountain,
The bear went over the mountain,
The bear went over the mountain,
To see what he could see

And all that he could see
And all that he could see
Was the other side of the mountain
The other side of the mountain
The other side of the mountain
Was all that he could see.

A Kid's Pony

I recall that while we were still living in town — we moved to the country the year I started school, so I must have been about five years old — my dad bought an old horse and brought it home for my brother and I to ride. He referred to it as a "kid's pony," which, in the local vocabulary, meant it was okay for kids to ride. I thought of a pony as a small horse, so when I saw this big 'pony' named Old Bess for the first time I was scared to death.

There was a story that Old Bess was the only animal to get out alive when a farmer's barn burned to the ground. For some reason or other, I kept imagining this old horse being killed in the fire. I would sit and watch her, tethered in the yard eating grass, and wonder why she was still alive when all of the other horses had died.

Dad would put my brother and me on her back and lead her around. After the ride, he let us pat her. I grew to love the aging horse. One day she tangled her front foot in her tethering chain, reared over backwards, fell to the ground and lay there. I was sure she was dead and I ran into the house screaming. My dad went out and untangled her. She got to her feet and was perfectly alright. But age and the cold Alberta winters finally caught up to her and she had to be put down to end her suffering. It took me a long time to understand what death was all about, and although it was only an aging old horse, it was the first time I had ever lost something close to me.

Playing With Fire

Not long after that, we moved to the farm about a mile north of town. When a town kid moves to the country, there are a million things to explore. Between my brother and me and the neighbors' kids, we were into something all the time. We smoked tobacco from the can of "Sweet Cap" that was always on the kitchen table at home. We smoked "tailor-mades" that the neighbor kids to the south stole from their dad, and "White Owl" cigars that the neighbor kids to the north acquired from the local grocery store. We smoked wild rhubarb stocks stuffed with dry leaves, and dry bark stripped from huge old balm and poplar trees rolled in newspaper. I always liked *The Rimbey Record* best, but some of the kids preferred the slow burning *Lacombe Globe* or the classier *Red Deer Advocate*.

Our farmhouse was painted a cream color with a red roof and white trim. It stood back from the other farm buildings and was completely surrounded by spruce trees, lilac bushes, and carrigana hedges. In the north-west corner between the house and the country road that ran into Bentley, there was a small grove of about 20 beautiful spruce trees growing close together and reaching high into the sky. To my grandfather, who had planted these trees when he built the house, this dense growth of evergreens was the perfect windbreak against the cold north winds that howled through the forty-below-zero Alberta winters.

In the summertime they provided a cool green shade from the late afternoon sun and a hideout for cowboys, Indians, and outlaws. No sheriff's posse or Texas Ranger could ever track us down. We would crawl on our hands and knees back into the thickest, darkest point and make camp.

One stifling hot afternoon, Hughie Blish, one of my grade two school chums, and I were "hiding out from the law," curled up on a bed of dry leaves with a blanket and an old cardboard box that served as our imaginary camp. He produced some cigarettes that he had lifted from his grandfather's general store in town.

I left camp, returned to the house and crawled up onto a chair in the pantry. I filled my pocket with big old Eddy's Red Bird matches and made my way back to camp. We lit up a cigarette and passed it back and forth.

Then we decided that real outlaws who are camped out and hiding from the law should have a campfire. We scraped together some leaves and dry needles from the spruce trees and struck a match. The size of the flame that flared up was two or three times what we expected, and it spread instantly into the dry grass and licked at the lower branches of the huge trees. We tried stomping on it, kicking at it, and then we panicked and ran through the dense bush towards the house.

By the time we reached the side of the house, my mother was on the back porch screaming at us. Someone had seen the smoke. But then the flames sprung up through the tops of the towering spruce trees and snapped and crackled and roared as the whole corner turned into a blazing inferno. She ran back into the house and phoned the Fire Department in Bentley.

My father and the farmhands were not around. We were helpless.

Then a miracle happened. The light afternoon breeze turned into a strong gust that carried the flames away from the house and back towards the road. The fire consumed everything in its path. Its new-found direction carried it out of the corner of the bush, through the dry grass, into the ditch and along the gravel road where there was nothing left to burn.

A few minutes later the Bentley fire truck arrived with a half-dozen men. They put out a few smouldering sticks, twigs, and patches of grass and stared in disbelief at the scorched spires and the section of bush that had burned to a crisp. Thank God the wind had turned it back from the house and farm buildings.

I think my folks were so thankful for the way things turned out that they just wanted to let it be. I remember a lecture on playing with matches, but I didn't get the punishment I deserved or expected. They knew how scared I was. Possibly they thought I had learned my lesson.

The Hanging Tree

It wasn't long 'til the outlaws were on the trail again, and this time "there was gonna be a hangin'!" My older brother, Bob, our neighbor to the north, Glen Wilton, and the Morison boys, Stuart and James, who lived about a half-mile south of us, had perfected the "hangin' tree."

It wasn't actually a tree. We threw a lariat rope over a high beam in the pump-house, put the noose around the victim's neck, and stood him up on a nail keg. We then gave the "outlaw" the loose end of the rope. It was simple — when we kicked the keg out from under him, all he had to do was let go of the rope and drop the two or three feet to the floor. The catch was that, when the keg went out from under you, natural reflexes made you hang onto the rope to keep from falling and you got hung. When that happened, we'd grab the outlaw and lift him up. The rope would go slack and we would all have a good laugh.

With enough practice and concentration, some of us could actually let go of the rope when the keg was kicked out. First-timers, however, always thought they could let go; but didn't. And a brief hanging was their punishment.

The next time Hughie Blish came to call, we made sure he was one of the outlaws and I was the sheriff. It wasn't long until he was caught robbing a train and we decided he should be lynched. We took him to the gallows and strung him up. When we tipped the keg out from under him, he began kicking so hard it took us a few seconds to get a hold of him and lift him up. He was turning blue and we couldn't pry his fingers loose from the death grip he had on the rope.

When we finally got him loose, we laid him down on the pump-house floor to let him catch his breath. It wasn't long until he sat up, complained of a stiff neck and a headache, and said he wanted to go home. He left for his mile-long walk back to town. We hoped no one would notice the rope burns on his neck.

About an hour later his dad drove into the yard, had a brief visit with my dad, and left. This time I got the licking of my life . . . and I knew why.

Merry-Go-Round

We couldn't always be cowboys, Indians, or outlaws. Sometimes we played on the "merry-go-round," which was actually an old wood splitter. It was built from a big wheel, poured full of concrete to give it weight, and had an axe head attached. When the belt and motor were hooked up, the wheel would spin. The operator just stuck one block of wood after another under the axe head when it came around, and it would split the wood. When the wheel was not hooked up, it sat idle with no motor or belt attached. The wheel would spin freely if it was given a good spin.

We tried different ways of riding the wheel, but nothing worked very well. Then we began perfecting a style. We would stand behind the wheel and loosen our belts. Someone would spin the wheel. When the axe head came around, we'd lean into the wheel and hook our belts on the axe head. It would lift us off our feet, carry us up and over the wheel and drop us on the other side.

At the slow speed, this became boring. We spun the wheel faster and faster. Then, with our belts hooked on the axe head, it jerked us off our feet, flung us over the top of the wheel and drove us into the ground on the other side. Now, this was fun!

We added further to this style. When we came off the wheel, we did a tumbling act into a sawdust pile about eight feet away. I never quite figured out why we didn't get killed, or why this never caught on as a circus act or an Olympic event.

The Flying Barn

On the north side of the pump-house, about 50 yards from our huge old cattle barn and out of sight of the farm-house, was a fuel stand. At any given time, there would be three or four 45-gallon drums of gasoline on this stand. Dad used this for the trucks, tractors and farm equipment.

When I was about seven years old, I was with Dad when he was fuelling up his old John Deere tractor. It was possibly the first time I had smelled gas. I loved the smell. When he drove away with the tractor I stayed on the fuel stand to play. I picked up the end of the hose. The pump was still in the barrel. I began smelling the gas first, just sniffing and then breathing deeply.

I had no idea what was happening. When I looked towards the barn, it was out of focus and seemed to be a long way off in the distance. I kept on breathing the gas fumes. Then the barn began to shimmer like a mirage and rose up about 20 feet from the ground. I ran to the house, crying out, "Mom, the barn's flying away!" Mom was not amused.

Don't try this at home, boys and girls.

The Train Trestle

As I grew older, the playground expanded. Bob and I would hike up to the junkyard, as we called it. It was actually the Bentley garbage dump. We would play there for hours, lighting fires and throwing any sealed cans and bottles into the fire, waiting for the heat to explode them. Some of the old wax and gas cans would go off like bombs.

There was a towering wooden trestle that the C.P.R. had built across the outlet. We played on it by the hour, climbing through the huge wooden beams just under the tracks and about 150 feet above the ground. The older boys would walk along the beams and the smaller kids would crawl across on their hands and knees. One scorching hot afternoon, we were climbing high up in the old trestle when a Canadian Pacific freight train came rumbling over the top. The aging trestle creaked and groaned and shook under the weight. We hung on for dear life.

After the screaming black beast blew its whistle and rolled on down the tracks, some of the kids were so scared they would not give up their hold on the bridge. It took a long time to convince them to let go and begin their climb back through the girders to solid ground. Still others wanted to find out the train schedules so they could be there next time the train crossed over.

A few years later, in the dead of winter on that same trestle, a young boy jumped from the tracks onto a snowbank to escape the oncoming train. The snow bank collapsed into the deep ravine, hurtling him to the bottom. When the town folk finally reached him, they found him buried under the snowslide. He was dead. Word spread through the village of Bentley, "Roy Cawston was killed at the trestle." This was a double blow to the family, as Roy's dad had died of a self-inflicted gunshot wound not too many years earlier. Now the widow had lost a son.

The first wave of rumors was bad enough. The second wave carried stories about how the kids placed rifle shells and shotgun shells on the tracks to be exploded by oncoming trains. True! The kids placed ties and railroad spikes on the tracks to try and derail the train. False! Sometimes we were caught playing in the middle of the trestle when the train came along and had to hang over the edge so the train wouldn't hit us. No comment! The 'Town Fathers' passed an unwritten law that we were not to be seen on or near the towering C.P.R. bridge. We obeyed this law for a few months.

We would spend long, hot summer afternoons down at the Blindman River, swimming, fishing, wading across the rapids, building rafts and floating down the river like Huck Finn. Then one scorching July afternoon on our way back from the river, Bob and I, along with Stuart and James Morison, decided to take the shortcut up the outlet, past the trestle, and across the fields to home. At the foot of the towering structure, we met with some 'town kids' from Bentley and began exploring some of the deep ravines that were created by the heavy snow run-off and the late spring rains. Suddenly we heard a rifle shot and a bullet smashed into the wall of the canyon, narrowly missing us. We were scared, but we thought it was just a single stray bullet from a hunter. Then another bang, and a slug kicked up rocks and dirt above our heads, sending a shower of dirt into our faces. The shots were getting closer. Then bang! bang! bang! Rifle shots rang out and the slugs bit into the canyon wall behind us.

One of the town kids, thinking he could run faster in his bare feet, kicked off his shoes and ran up the canyon, through the fence, and down the railroad tracks toward town. We decided just to stay down until the shooting stopped. Another round of five or six shots rained down on us. Stuart and I crawled on our bellies to the opposite end of the wash-out. We peered up over the edge. A shot rang out and a bullet almost took his hat off.

We had managed to get a quick glimpse of the sniper. He was perched on top of the trestle with the rifle to his shoulder. Then another round of gunfire rang out. The bullets whizzed overhead and into the dirt behind us. We ducked down and stayed down until the shooting stopped.

Later in the afternoon, we took turns looking up over the rim of the canyon. The gunman was no longer on the trestle. Then, on the road at the north end of the track, we spotted a truck pulling away. It was a blue 1949 GMC one-ton, with a long steel box and no stock racks. We recognized the truck immediately and headed for home to report the incident.

As we got closer to home, though, we decided to say nothing. After all, we weren't supposed to be at the trestle and we would all be in trouble.

Meanwhile, our town kid friend had run all the way back to Bentley. He arrived home screaming and in shock, his bare feet cut and bleeding from the gravel and cinders along the railroad. His parents called the police and they were waiting for us when we arrived home.

At first we denied it all. Then we admitted we had been shot at and then we reluctantly told them about the truck. We did not want, however, to tell them that we knew who it was. When we finally gave them a name, they got into their police car and left. We knew where they were heading when they turned north out at the road.

A few days later, we heard they had let the culprit off. He had a brand new rifle with a high-powered scope mounted on it. He convinced the police that he was a crack shot and that he was just trying to scare us.

Daredevil Dip

Many times our trips to the junkyard ended in trips to the doctor. It was not unusual for one of our gang to suffer cuts from some flying glass or severe burns from a fiery liquid that exploded out of some half-empty can. We were told time and time again not to play at the junkyard, but we always went back for more.

From the junkyard, the country road ran down over the hill to the north. At the bottom of the hill, it twisted sharply, crossed a narrow wooden bridge over the outlet, turned back to the left and climbed a few hundred yards up and out of the deep valley. The valley stretched from the sandy shores of Gull Lake, west to the Blindman River. Sometime in the past, this had been an outlet from the lake and flowed westward emptying into the Blindman. Now, it was little more than a trickle, with the exception of spring run-off or a heavy rainy season.

In the summertime, we played up and down the valley, laid in the sun on the south slopes, and drank from a cool spring that bubbled from the rocks and fed a tiny pool. The water in this pool was as clear as a mirror and as cold and clean as I have ever tasted.

In the wintertime, the outlet became choked with ice and snow. There were dozens of trails to ski, hills to toboggan or sleigh-ride down and, when the creeks flooded and froze, we would skate on the frozen ponds. Our favorite ski hill, "Daredevil Dip," was little more than a narrow cut-line running from the top of the south hill, down, down, into the outlet. It was tricky enough for the older boys, who were good skiers and had all the right equipment. We tried it in barrels, old discarded wash-tubs, or car hoods hauled from the junkyard. A good winter would usually provide the Bentley doctor with a little extra income from stitching wounds, setting broken bones, and dealing with dislocated shoulders.

Sometimes we would abandon Daredevil Dip and use the icy road instead. Tobogganing out of the deep snow of the dip and onto the glare ice of the road increased our speed of descent by ten times. We had been warned by our parents to stay off the road as oncoming traffic could not see us and the narrow bridge at the bottom of the hill would only handle one-way traffic.

On a cold blustery winter day, brother Bob and I, along with Stuart and James Morison, were riding the hill with an old sleigh my granddad had brought home from a farm auction sale. It was only large enough for us to ride one at a time. When my turn came, I lay down flat on the sleigh, gripped the wooden crossbar that acted as a primitive steering mechanism, pushed my parka hood back so I could see the steep drop of the long winding hill and hung my feet over the sides to act as an imaginary, and almost totally ineffective, braking system.

"Ready! Set! Go!" I hollered. Bob and James were on either side of the sleigh, pushing and running and trying to maintain their footing on the glazed surface. When they could no longer keep up, they gave a last push and I was launched. I was off and heading down the hill like a shot. I gained speed as I dropped over the brink of the hill and onto the steepest part of the ride. By now, I was completely out of control. I dragged one foot and then the other to try to keep the sleigh from leaving the road, going over the shoulder of the road and dropping off the narrow ledge.

The cold wind whipped my parka, stung my face and made my eyes water. I turned my head to the side and burrowed my face into my parka for a moment to avoid the chill. When I looked back at the road in front of me, there was a big red farm truck loaded to the hilt, just entering the bridge at the bottom of the hill. I was seconds from him and flying like a rocket. I let go with my left hand and double-grabbed the right side of the cross-bar. I pulled as hard as I could and swung both feet off the left side of the sleigh.

Miraculously, the little sleigh swung full right. I left the road and sailed through the air, over the edge, down the embankment and headlong through a tangle of bushes and willows that jutted up through the huge snowdrifts. And then I saw the rusty old barbed-wire fence almost buried in the snow. There was no way to avoid it. I closed my eyes, hugged the sleigh and, a split second later, I felt a searing pain as the barbed wire ripped through the back of my jacket and sliced open a long gash in the middle of my back, down the left side of my spine. And then the lights went out.

Prairie Skies

It wasn't always that crazy. Sometimes, right there in the middle of it all, a beautiful summer day would arrive, with all the magic fully intact. The blazing Alberta sun would dance across the prairies, slide over the silvery waters of Gull Lake and touch down in all its glory on my own little personal field of dreams — ten acres of lush green meadow stretching south across the gravel country road that led from the Damron farm to the village of Bentley. The green carpet was dotted with gopher holes, badger holes, and molehills. Although my dad had long since given up on raising butcher hogs and had turned to raising purebred registered Hereford cattle, my afternoon summer paradise was still affectionately known as the "hog pasture."

On any given summer afternoon when there were no Indians to

fight, no hangin's scheduled, and the Wiltons and the Morisons and my faithful companion Hughie Blish had more important things to do, I would venture out into the field away from the farmhouse and stretch out on my back with my face turned to the sun. I would spend hours watching a hawk trace lazy circles in the soft blue heavens . . . almost out of sight, then a long gliding descent, then climbing back up into the sky where he could lay effortlessly on the softness of the warm western wind.

I would drift off into late afternoon dreams. My wild, young imagination would carry me off on the perfectly formed wings of the massive hawk. Up and over the prairies, across the sky, behind the wispy white clouds that sometimes formed in the west, hung overhead and then disappeared over the dark edges of nowhere. I'd close my eyes and turn my head directly into the sun. The warmth of the sun would bathe my face and the bright yellow glow would make me squint even harder. I'd let my eyes open, but only enough to form two tiny slits. The light would dance and splash and spatter into a million little spears and then, just in time, just in the nick of time, I'd open my eyes wide enough to see the hawk, that magnificent flying creature, vanish into the center of the sun.

These were happy days.

In the early 1940s, something new and exciting appeared in our prairie skies. For a while, we forgot about the hawk and the gulls and the crows and the yapping black and white magpies.
Great new, yellow, flying machines took over the skies. They climbed, they dived, they rolled and maneuvered magnificently. The yellow Harvard Trainers were stationed at the Royal Canadian Air Force Base in Penhold, about twenty short air miles to the south. They were our new afternoon entertainment. We'd hear the roar of the engines and we would watch them until they were only tiny specks. Sometimes they would disappear completely and then appear again, falling, falling, falling without a sound. Then, in the distance, we'd hear the engine roar into life and see them loop and roll and dive.

This was serious training for Second World War aerial combat and most of these young trainers would soon be in battle, somewhere over Britain or Europe. To us it was our own private air show, and we loved it.

The Hired Hand

When a hired hand on our family farm took his life in 1944, I was barely ten years old. The man had shared the upstairs bedroom in our two-story farmhouse with me and my older brother, Bob.

On a cold snowy winter night, he slipped out of the house, made his way across the fields to an old abandoned building and there, in the cellar, he placed a bullet in his heart with my dad's .22 calibre Remington repeater. On that same thirty-below night, a chimney fire filled our house with smoke and soot, and the acrid smell of burning slag and cinders.

I can't remember who broke the news to us kids. When we returned from school that afternoon, the R.C.M.P. officers were investigating the incident. They sat at our kitchen table asking questions and taking notes.

When I found out what had happened, I was shocked and confused. The hired hand had worked for dad for quite some time and, in the evenings, he would sit in the living room and play dad's old fiddle. He only knew a few tunes and sometimes he would play the old traditional *Ragtime Annie* over and over by the hour.

I was afraid to go upstairs to bed that night. Every time I closed my eyes, I would see him sitting there playing the fiddle. *Ragtime Annie* echoed in my head until I thought I would go crazy. I don't remember my folks ever talking to me about it. I cried myself to sleep that night.

Some nights, I would hear my mother open the door at the bottom of the stairs. When she heard me crying, she would let me come downstairs and sleep on the big sofa in the living room. I would still wake up two or three times through the night and think that I saw him there in the shadows, where he used to sit and play. I was scared and I would call out to my mother. Sometimes she would say, "It's okay, just go back to sleep." Other times she would say, "You get to sleep or you're going back upstairs."

I just wanted to know that mom and dad were there in the next room. But they didn't seem to understand. It was a feeling I could never explain. As time passed, I got over it. But without anyone ever talking about the suicide or trying to explain it or counsel me, I had to come to my own conclusions. Although I never knew and, to this day, I still don't know what reason he had for taking his life. In my child's mind, his death was his means of escape.

There I was, only ten years old and my two alternatives to facing life were established: suicide or running away. Sometimes I think I am still running. But, after my teen years, a few adult years, and a handful of serious and semi-serious suicide attempts, I discarded taking my own life as an option.

There were two deciding factors. When my father died, I realized how much death hurt those around you. And when Roy Cook, my drummer and long-time friend, killed himself, I realized the futility of wasting a life to try to prove something to an uncaring world. I think this closed that means of escape for me forever.

Riding the Rails

When I was 14 years old, I ran away from home in the middle of November. My younger sister, Lorna, was given a note from the teachers to be delivered to my folks. It read, "Dickie has only been at school three days in September, two days in October, and one day in November." I bribed her not to give the note to our folks, but I knew it was only a matter of time until I would be in deep trouble.

So I just set off for school in the morning and hitch-hiked to the tiny village of Eckville, about 20 miles to the west of Bentley. I stayed in Eckville for a few days with some friends who had recently moved from Bentley. Then, on one of the coldest days of the winter, I left Eckville to hitch-hike on to Rocky Mountain House in search of a job in one of the camps.

I was heading out to the highway, where I could thumb a ride west, when I spotted a train pulling out of the station. I left the road, crossed the ditch, and ran through the knee-deep snow toward the grain elevators and the stockyard. The cold air burned my lungs and I could see my breath in the frosty air. I put my hand over my mouth and breathed through my cotton glove. I made it to the stock pens, ran up the ramp that was used for loading livestock and crouched down on the platform to catch my breath and wait for a boxcar on the slow moving freight train. The train was picking up speed now and the empty coal cars and cattle cars were moving by faster and faster. When I spotted a boxcar with an open door, I moved forward on the platform and crouched again. Then I sprung from the icy snow-covered platform through the door and onto the boxcar. I was bound for Rocky Mountain House!

I don't know why I was surprised to find that it was just as cold inside the car as it had been in the minus-thirty-degree weather outside. As the train picked up speed, the wind and the draft from the open doors made it even colder. Shavings, sawdust, and wood chips moved across the floor in never-ending spirals and I thought of trying to slide the heavy doors closed. Then I remembered stories of hobos being trapped when they rode the rails and I gave up on that idea. I found some cardboard and paper and bundled up in the corner.

I soon found out I had to keep moving or I would freeze to death. I danced up and down, swung my arms, and clapped my hands together to get my circulation going. I had learned that lesson well from years on the farm, surviving the long cold winter days working in unheated barns, granaries, and our old pump-house.

By the time we reached Rocky Mountain House, I was nearly frozen. As the train slowed at the first crossing and I realized we were entering the town, I jumped from the car into a snowbank, slid down the grade, crawled through the fence, and made my way up out of the ditch and onto the road. I flagged down the first vehicle that came along, and caught a ride for the half-mile or so into the center of town. When they dropped me off, I crossed the street and went into the David Thompson Hotel to try and get warmed up.

In the washroom, I ran the warm water over my hands and splashed it on my face. I ached all over. If you live in the south country or Mexico or any warm climate, you don't know how cold you can get without actually freezing. If you have lived in the outdoors in the great white north, or have walked five miles home from school in a blizzard long before the advent of the bright yellow school buses, then you know exactly what Robert W. Service meant when he wrote, "chilled right through to the bone."

When my face quit stinging and my eyes and nose quit running and the feeling came back into my hands and feet, I left the hotel and headed up the street. I had no idea where I was going or what I was going to do. I had not eaten since the night before in Eckville. It must have been close to four o'clock. When I got to the bakery, the smell of fresh baking made me realize how hungry I was. With not one cent in my pocket, I stood and stared through the frosty glass at the fresh baked bread and buns and the huge cinnamon rolls. When people passed in and out of the shop, the sweet aroma was even more intense.

I watched a woman come out of the back to wait on customers at the counter and then disappear back through the door into the kitchen. A plan began to form in my mind. I would wait until the last customer left the shop and, when she went into the back, I would push open the door, grab the closest thing I could reach and run like hell.

Then I heard a voice behind me. "Aren't you Dickie Damron?"

I turned to face two R.C.M.P. officers dressed in their huge buffalo coats and fur caps. One of them calmly said, "You'd better come with us."

I don't know how they could have possibly recognized me in my old black cowboy hat with both sides pinned up with two-inch safety pins, a brown cloth jacket, and my pants tucked into the tops of my cowboy boots.

They took me to the Club Cafe and bought me a large bowl of soup. One of them stayed with me and the other went to call my folks and let them know I had been found. I felt captured, but I was only a runaway kid who had been found. My parents arrived a few hours later. Instead of driving one of our old farm trucks, they had borrowed my grandfather's Chrysler for the trip to Rocky and back.

Dad drove, mom sat up front beside him, and I sat in the back seat. Not a word was spoken during the whole trip. I guess none of us really knew what to say. I stared out the window into the cold winter's night and watched the snow swirling up in front of the headlights of the oncoming vehicles. It was warm and toasty in Granddad's old car. I knew I would be punished when we got back, but deep down inside I was happy to be going home.

Horse Tales

As we grew older, we began living on horseback. My dad always had a large herd of cattle and 10 to 15 horses. We rode horses to work the cattle, move them to summer pasture, and round them up in the fall. The rest of the time we rode to school, to the lake, to the river, and would "ride into town" in the Old West tradition — just to "raise hell."

There was the time my horse reared in the street when Hughie Blish was trying to climb on behind the saddle and he fell to the gravel and the horse came down on him, breaking his arm and crushing his wrist. Then there was the Sunday afternoon horse race, when Stuart Morison, Lester Wenger, and I raced full tilt up Main Street on our high-headed cow ponies. At the crossroads, in the center of town, my horse swung north in front of the other two eastbound riders, and we collided heavily. We went down in the middle of the street in a pile of kicking, squealing horseflesh — three horses and their riders, with me on the bottom. Onlookers ran from the sidewalk to my rescue. They stared in horror at the deep gash on the side of my head, ground full of dirt and gravel, and the blood streaming down the side of my face. The collar and half of the shoulder of my denim jacket had been ripped away. The pain was intense. I thought I would pass out on the spot, but I made it back to the sidewalk and sat down.

A crowd gathered and everyone tried to convince me that I had to go to the hospital. The words of my old cowboy Uncle Bud kept ringing in my ears, "He hired out for tough, but he couldn't fill the bill." I had to show these folks that I was as tough as any 14-year-old kid could be.

I made my way down the street to the hotel, about a block away. A handful of people followed me into the washroom. I turned on the cold water tap and let it run until it was ice cold. The last thing I remember is splashing a handful of the icy water on to the open wound. The next thing I knew, I woke up in the Bentley Community Hospital with a doctor and two nurses working over me. They cleaned the dirt and gravel from my face, stopped the bleeding and stitched up the head wound.

The next morning, I crawled out of the hospital bed and peered at myself in the mirror. My God! What a sight. My face was swollen and discoloured. My right eye was almost closed. The little I could see of the eye was completely bloodshot. I found my clothes in the closet and pulled them on. I slipped out of the hospital without saying a word, and headed downtown to show everybody my battle scars. I went in and out of every store in town to make sure everyone could see me. When I got home, the doctor had called and my folks hauled me back to the hospital for another day or two of observation.

It wasn't long until I was back in the saddle again. Stuart Morison and I became known as "The Lone Ranger and Tonto." We rode up and down the sidewalks; we rode through people's yards and gardens. I rode my old black horse into Red Hughes' Pool Hall one night. We tried to get our horses into the Blindman Tavern a couple of times, but the bartender told us he'd kick our asses and I'm sure he would have. We had it coming. The townspeople always reported our craziness to my parents. Dad would say, "Goddamnit, boy! Some day you'll learn!"

Mom would say, "If you knew what your mother went through to bring one of you little bastards into this world, you wouldn't act the way you do." Amen.

(Top) *The main street of Bentley, Alberta, 1908.*

(Bottom) *The Damron family farm, with Gull Lake on the horizon, where Dick lived from age 5 to age 17.*

(Top) *Grandparents Clarence and Martha Trobough Damron with Dick's father Ned and his uncles Joe and Bud.*

(Bottom Left) *Dad's horse "Punk" plays dead for Dickie and Bob.*

(Bottom Right) *Dick's family outside their Bentley home in 1940, with Bob (left), Lorna (center), Dick (right).*

CHAPTER THREE

A Genuine Outlaw

JUST ANOTHER RODEO SONG

HE'S A HARD-RIDING COWBOY FROM OUT IN THE WEST
A GENUINE OUTLAW, NO KIN TO THE REST
HE'S WILD AND HE'S RESTLESS, THE RAMBLIN' KIND
AND I'M PROUD TO SAY HE'S AN OLD FRIEND OF MINE

HE FOLLOWED THE CIRCUIT TO THE BIG RODEOS
HOOKED ON A FEELING THAT GOD ONLY KNOWS
HIS LIFE AND HIS LEGENDS ALL STRUNG OUT BEHIND
AND I'M PROUD TO SAY HE'S AN OLD FRIEND OF MINE

HE'S OUT RAISING HELL, CASTING HIS SPELL ON THE LADIES
A GENUINE OUTLAW SINGIN' HIS RODEO SONG
HERE'S TO HIS HEROES, HE'S LOVED THEM SINCE HE WAS A BABY
JUST ANOTHER OLD OUTLAW WITH ANOTHER OLD RODEO SONG

HE'S A HARD-RIDING COWBOY FROM OUT IN THE WEST
HIS ROOTS THEY ARE PLANTED SOMEWHERE IN THE DUST
HIS LIFE AND HIS LEGEND ALL STRUNG OUT BEHIND
AND I'M PROUD TO SAY HE'S AN OLD FRIEND OF MINE

© Sparwood Music

What Do You Want To Be When You Grow Up?

When I was a kid, one of the most often asked questions was, "What do you want to be when you grow up?" I became convinced that some adults used this line just to let me know that I wasn't grown up yet — and that they were still in control.

In school, when the teacher asked the class this question, the girls all wanted to be nurses and the boys all wanted to be soldiers. My early school years were 1940-44. The Second World War was raging and there was nothing more important than to be a soldier.

When it came to my turn, my Grade Two teacher asked, "What do you want to be, Dickie?"

I went against the roomfull of potential nurses and soldiers and proudly announced, "I want to be a cowboy."

Every eye in the tiny schoolroom fixed on me, and the class let out a loud, "Ooh!"

I felt my face turn red and I felt the wrath of the teacher and the students. Under the weight of peer pressure I broke and quickly added, "I mean, when I get back from the war."

Cowboy Boots & Rodeos

When I was eight years old, I found an old cowboy hat three sizes too big for me and stuffed the hatband full of newspaper to make it fit. I always wanted a pair of cowboy boots, but never got them until years later. So I wore a pair of old rubber boots with the tops turned down and my pants tucked inside. When it was 90 degrees in July, my feet would ache until I could hardly stand it. But I wouldn't give up my "cowboy boots". When my folks tried to get me to take them off, I'd say I was going wading down at the river.

Dressing like a cowboy was only a small part of it. Bob and I used to make our way across the fields and through the barbed-wire fences up to the neighbors to ride steers. Dad had all kinds of cattle, but most were registered purebred Herefords and we'd have been killed if we were caught riding them. Even so, when the folks were away, we had our share of rodeos, both indoor and outdoor. But most of our steer and cow-riding and calf-roping events were held at the neighbors'.

One hot dusty Sunday afternoon, we made our way to the

Wilton farm north of our place. As well as a farming operation, the Wiltons ran a dairy and supplied milk to the town of Bentley, delivering milk door to door using a milk wagon pulled by an old white horse. On this particular Sunday, the folks were away, so it was rodeo time at the Wiltons'.

Their milk cows were as taboo as Dad's purebred Herefords. Still, there was a young waspy-looking, Jersey-cross steer with tiger stripes and spiked horns. He was wilder than hell and had never had a rope on him. We chased him around the farm for a half-hour, finally cornered him by the barn, and got a lariat on him.

We hitched an old binder-twine rope around his middle, and my brother climbed aboard. We turned that waspy beast loose and he literally exploded, leaping into the air, twisting and turning. Bob came down flat on his face in the dust. We screamed with delight. We'd found some rodeo stock — to hell with the purebred Herefords, to hell with the old Jersey milk cows.

Now it was my turn. I was a little scared, but I'd been the one playing the role of cowboy on a full-time basis, so I couldn't say, "No." I climbed aboard. Once again, the steer exploded. I managed to stay on top for a few jumps. Then he broke into a dead run and crashed through an old barbed-wire fence. He went through the fence and I didn't. My skinny little arm hung up on the rusty barbed-wire, ripping a six-inch gash from the inside of my elbow to my wrist. Bob and the Wilton kids came up behind me, laughing and cheering. They stopped when they got a look at my arm. Blood was pouring from the gash, and I was starting to pale.

They half-dragged and half-carried me to the cattle tank where the dairy herd drank and submerged my bleeding arm in the murky green water. "Don't tell Dad," I said, trying not to cry.

We didn't. I kept my shirt sleeves rolled down. But a few days later at the dinner table, someone noticed swelling in my fingers and stiffness in my arm. Dad insisted I roll up my sleeve. Mom almost fainted. In 15 minutes, I was at Doctor Henry's office and he was treating the infected arm, mumbling something about "crazy damn kids" under his breath. I still carry that jagged scar today. It traces a path down the inside of my arm from my elbow to my wrist.

It was my first major rodeo injury, and I continued on with the great desire to be a rodeo cowboy. I thrilled to the stories my Uncle

Bud told about the old rodeo hands he knew: Slim Watrin, Casey Patterson, the Thompsons, and his next-door neighbor, Cam Lansdell, who lived in the rolling hills west of Turner Valley, Alberta, just a few miles from my uncle's quarter-horse ranch. Cam was a winner and a loser of high degree. He traveled the country to rodeos far and wide and returned to his Turner Valley ranch between rodeos, sometimes sporting a championship silver buckle, an engraved saddle, or a shiny trophy. Other times he came home with a broken arm, leg, ankle, dislocated shoulder, or smashed knee. The slash on my arm paled by comparison, but it served as a kind of badge of honor in my yet-undeveloped rodeo career.

As the years rolled by, I began entering small amateur rodeos in Central Alberta. The first ever was the Buck Lake Stampede. My grandfather had two tiny log cabins nestled along the south shore of Buck Lake in the hamlet of Minnehik. My older brother Bob and I spent many a summer day at the lake with granddad and grandma before we grew old enough to become permanent employees on my father's farm, where taking a day off from the farm labor became a mortal sin.

We pulled into Minnehik in my dad's old blue '42 Chev pick-up, which granddad borrowed on a regular basis to make the 40-mile run up the gravel road that wound its way north past Forshee, Rimbey, Bluffton, Hoadley, Winfield, and west to our final destination. I suddenly spied a rodeo poster on the front of the battered Minnehik General Store and Post Office. The minute we pulled up in front of granddad's cabins, I jumped from the truck and made my way back to the store to check out the black and yellow poster: Buck Lake Stampede, Saturday, July 5th. Entries closed at noon on Saturday. As I surveyed the list of events — saddle bronc-riding, bull-riding, calf-roping, wild cow-milking, wild horse race — I spotted the event I was looking for: boys' steer-riding for 15-years and under. I was barely ten years old but I was ready to ride.

I read on, entry fee — $2.00; first prize — $20.00; second prize — $15.00; third prize — $10.00; fourth prize — $5.00. For the first time in my life, I would be riding in a real rodeo arena with chutes, judges, and timers. This was the real world of rodeo!

I hurried back to the cabin and announced loudly that the Buck Lake Stampede was coming up on Saturday and that I was going to ride steers. Granddad had some good news and some bad news for me: "You can go to the rodeo but I can't let you ride." I was excited about the rodeo but crushed with the thought of being at my first rodeo and not being able to ride. Then he added quickly, "Your mother would have a fit if she knew I let you ride."

Saturday morning, I was one of the first at the rodeo. The arena was full of bucking horses. The catch-pens at the back held the cattle for the steer-riding, calf-roping, and wild cow-milking events. The cowboys were gathering behind the chutes, unloading their gear, resining their riggin's, and limbering up. The great spirit of rodeo, that I still feel today whenever I am even close to a rodeo, swept over me.

I went straight back to the gate and entered the steer-riding competition. For my $2.00 entry fee I received a slip of paper that said "Dick Damron, Boys Steer-Riding" and a ribbon with the word "Contestant" printed on it. I shoved the paper into my jeans pocket, proudly tied the ribbon onto my hat-band so everyone could see I was a rodeo cowboy, went back to the chutes, and waited for my chance to ride.

After the bareback bronc-riding, wild horse race and a few other events, it was time for the boys steer-riding. The wranglers ran the cattle into the chutes and the chute boss called out the names and numbers. When I heard "Dick Damron, you're in chute number three!" I climbed up the wooden planks and stared down at the animal. I expected to see a 400 pound steer. Instead, I found myself looking at a big, old, rawboned range cow that would weigh in at a good 800 hundred pounds. I dropped my borrowed rope around her middle, and one of the rodeo hands tightened another rope around her flanks. I crawled down on top of the old cow and worked my hands in under my rope. They tightened it down. I dug in my spurs and nodded my head. When they yanked open the chute gate the rodeo announcer said, "Out of chute number three, our next contestant, Dick Damron!"

The old range cow spun sideways out of the chute, smashing my left leg into the gate. When she jumped high and to the right, my hands jerked out of the rope and I fell headlong down over her left shoulder and into the arena dirt. Dazed, I picked myself up and limped back into the chute.

A few minutes later I sat down to examine my left leg. It was scraped and bruised, but no real damage. When the rodeo was over, I went back to the cabin.

The next day when Granddad and I were walking down to the lake, he glanced down at me and said quietly, "Why didn't you *ride* that old cow?"

I didn't know he had gone to the rodeo. Nothing more was ever said about it.

Dreams of the Big Time

After that first real rodeo, I was hooked. I hit every rodeo within miles. My folks enjoyed taking in the rodeos and stampedes, but they were dead set against the idea of me riding. Mom was terrified. Dad would just say, "It's not a good idea," then tell me of every rodeo injury he had ever heard of. He would top it off with the chilling story of the death of world champion cowboy Pete Knight, when he was trampled to death by a bronc in Hayward, California, in 1937. Somehow these stories only made me want it more.

When we arrived at a rodeo, I would slip away to the rodeo office and enter the boys' steer-riding competition. I entered under the name of Jim Robinson and gave my address as Black Diamond, Alberta. The Black Diamond, Turner Valley, High River area of southern Alberta had produced a lot of great cowboys and one more would fit right in. With my folks seated in the grandstand, I would make my way around the arena and in back of the chutes. The first step was to borrow some equipment from the cowboys. Then I would find someone about my size, get a shirt and hat from him, and Jim Robinson was ready to ride. I pulled this off a few times and it got me through a couple of years of amateur rodeos close to home.

In 1949, I got my hands on a beat-up old G.M.C. pick-up truck and built a large "four by eight" plywood box on the back. Some say this was the first truck camper and we were way ahead of our time; others thought we were crazy sleeping in the back of a truck on the rodeo grounds. But it was free lodging. When our luck was down and we weren't winning in the rodeo arena, we would go down to the chuckwagon barns and the drivers would give us eating money for exercising the high-headed thoroughbred wagon horses. Life was good.

Dennis Anderson and I traveled together throughout the summer rodeo season. We were joined by a string of friends who dropped in and out of the rodeo scene. With Stuart Morison, Arnold Bergesen, Ted Atkinson, and Dennis' brother, Clarence, we hit the rodeo circuit and blazed a trail to Buck Lake, Leslieville, Rocky Mountain House, Benalto, Ponoka, Bearberry, and the Big Horn.

The first weekend in July, we rolled into Stettler in the heart of east central Alberta, only to find that we were too late to enter the steer-riding. Here we were at a rodeo, with nothing to do. We stood back of the bucking chutes with the cowboys who were entered, up and ready to ride. We talked it over and decided there were no other rodeos around within driving distance.

Just when we thought we had a lost weekend on our hands, Lady Luck touched down in the rodeo arena. "We got two bareback horses to go." A couple of the pro cowboys hadn't shown up and the stock contractor would pay ten bucks a head to ride these two bucking horses. No entry fees, no prize money. Just get on and collect your ten bucks. There was a horse named Prairie Chicken and one named Red Sails. We had our bull ropes for the steer riding but no bareback riggings. We borrowed riggings, gloves a half-dozen sizes too big for us, and almost everything needed to graduate from amateur steer-riding to professional bareback bronc-riding, or so we thought. The chute boss, whose job it was to keep things rolling behind the chutes, shouted at us, "God damn it boys, we haven't got all day! Get on 'em."

Dennis scaled the back of the chute and dropped down on Red Sails. It usually takes a rider a few minutes to get everything just so. The rigging must be set just right to suit the size and conformation of the horse and the particular wants and needs of each rider. The glove must be resined and worked into the rigging just right to ensure a solid grip. Many riders spend a long time behind the chutes tying on their gloves, wrapping wrists and elbows with tape and tensor bandages, strapping on shoulder harnesses, and wrapping their knees to protect old rodeo injuries. The chute boss and the arena director wanted to keep the rodeo rolling. They were paying ten bucks mount-money to ride these two bucking horses and they wanted us out there.

"Ladies and gentlemen, out of chute number four on a horse

called Red Sails, it's Dennis Anderson from Bentley, Alberta!" the rodeo announcer bellowed. Red Sails sailed out of the chute and lunged into the arena. The big reddish sorrel horse jumped and kicked down along the fence and, when the whistle blew, Dennis was still on top. The pick-up men moved in and rescued him. When he was safely on the ground, Harry Vold, arena director, stock contractor and owner of Red Sails, rode by with words of encouragement that he reserved for young up-and-coming cowboys. Dennis made his way back up the arena toward the chutes.

"And now, folks, another young Bentley cowboy coming out of chute number one on a great buckin' horse called Prairie Chicken. Here's Dick Damron!" The chute gate swung open, Prairie Chicken reared in the air, twisted out of the chute and jumped high into the arena. My only real riding experience had been steer-riding and amateur rodeos. Prairie Chicken was from the pro ranks. The absolute strength, power, and speed of the 1300-pound horse jerked me out of position on that first jump. He came down hard on his front feet and kicked high. My left hand came out of the rigging and my own 100 pounds of would-be cowboy was airborne. I slammed into the dirt flat on my back and Prairie Chicken flew over me and down the arena. I rolled over, slowly got to my feet, and somehow made it to the fence. I leaned against the wire, trying to catch my breath and thinking how the ten bucks would buy my gas to Calgary.

That night after the rodeo, Dennis and I and Jack Daines climbed into the truck and drove into town to the rodeo dance. I was stiff and sore from my flight on Prairie Chicken, and I never was much when it came to fancy dancin' . . . so, I hung out with the cowboys, drinking beer and smoking those big old rum-soaked and wine-dipped "Crooks" cigars. After the dance, we headed back to the rodeo grounds. By then, it was pouring rain. The little G.M.C. half-ton splashed through the streets and the windshield wipers slapped at the heavy rain.

By the time we got back to the grounds, we had decided to spend the night with Jack in the hayloft of the horse barn. Jack said a lot of the cowboys stayed up there — it was dry, the loose hay would make a good mattress, and the price was right. We grabbed our bedrolls and my guitar out of the back of the truck and headed for the barns. We slopped through the mud and rain and into the horse barn. We climbed the ladder up to the loft.

There were a dozen or more cowboys sitting around drinking beer and telling rodeo stories. The whole loft was lit by one tiny light bulb. We sat in the shadows and listened in awe to the stories the veteran cowboys told about the glory days of rodeo in Pendleton, Cheyenne, Fort Worth, Denver, and Calgary.

As the night wore on, someone spotted my guitar and the singin' and pickin' began. At first I felt a little uncomfortable. These hardened rodeo hands wouldn't want to hear some young kid singing country songs. But I had grown up singing all the old Wilf Carter songs, and when I swung into *Strawberry Roan* and *Pete Knight's Last Ride*, they loved it. I instantly became one of the gang. The hit of the night was yet another Wilf Carter song, *Headin' For The Calgary Stampede*. I must have sung the song four or five times that night. Little did I know then that one day Wilf Carter would record *The Last of the Rodeo Riders*, written by Dick Damron.

HE SITS ALL ALONE IN HIS OLD ROCKIN' CHAIR
A BEAT UP GUITAR IN HIS HAND
HE DON'T LOOK IT NOW BUT I KNOW SOMEHOW
HE ONCE AS A HELL OF A MAN

HIS HAIR IS ALL SILVER, HIS SIGHT'S FADING FAST
HE CAN STILL LOOK BACK 80 ODD YEARS
IN HIS SOUL THERE'S A PLACE TIME CAN'T ERASE
AND IT WON'T WASH AWAY WITH THE TEARS

HE ONCE WAS A SOLDIER, SHE WAS HIS QUEEN
WAY BACK BEFORE I CAME ALONG
IF YOU DON'T BELIEVE ME JUST SIT DOWN BESIDE HIM
AND LISTEN A WHILE TO HIS SONGS

HE'LL TELL YOU HIS STORIES, SING YOU HIS SONGS
HE REMEMBERS THE TIME AND THE PLACE

HIS BATTERED OLD HAT PULLED LOW ON HIS HEAD
SO YOU CAN'T SEE THE TEARS IN HIS FACE

HE'S THE LAST OF THE RODEO RIDERS
NOT THE WORST OR THE BEST. JUST A MAN
JUST A KID WITH HIS DREAMS OF THE BIG TIME
TURNED TO DUST IN IN THE SOUL OF A MAN

THERE'S A RODEO POSTER ALL FADED AND TORN
IN THE CASE WITH THAT BEAT UP GUITAR
AND THE GHOSTS OF THE MEM'RIES HE'S TRIED TO FORGET
FROM RIDING TOO LONG AND TOO FAR

FROM WINTER TO SUMMER. FROM SPRING UNTIL FALL
HE'LL TELL YOU IT WITH A SMILE
NOD HIS OLD HEAD. CLOSE THOSE GRAY EYES AND LAY BACK
AND DREAM FOR A WHILE

— *The Last of the Rodeo Riders* © Sparwood Music

The next morning, we loaded up the truck, pulled out of the mud and slop of the rodeo grounds, took Highway 12 west to Lacombe, and swung south to Calgary. We were headed for "The Greatest Show on Earth," the Calgary Stampede!

The little old G.M.C. purred like a kitten — it wasn't often she got to drive on pavement. She was used to the gravel road, the back roads and the dirt roads. As long as we kept her full of the used oil that we bought by the gallon from a local farmer and, as long as there was a creek, a river or a slough along the road where we could dip out a can of water for her leaky radiator, she was happy.

Dennis and I counted our money. With what was left of the twenty bucks we picked up in Stettler, we should have been able to pay our entry fees in Calgary and buy enough gas to get there. We pulled into a service station in Innisfail and bought $2.00 worth of gas. We hoped that would get us there. We didn't want to have to use our "Oklahoma credit card" that we kept shoved in the back of the truck carefully disguised as a length of garden hose and a gas can.

A few hours later we pulled into the Stampede grounds, made our way to the rodeo office and paid our entry fees. This was it. The big time! One of the greatest rodeos in the world. I was only fifteen years old. I thought my dreams had come true.

The Calgary Stampede

Calgary was big stuff. We were the "young guns" of rodeo and, even at fifteen, we had been to every rodeo in every one-pony town within hundreds of miles.

We had rodeoed in the rain in Leslieville, Alberta, and were trampled in the mud when old Bruce Cressman turned a herd of wild horses out of the catch-pen without a word of warning. We were backed against the wall in a Rocky Mountain House hotel room when three Indian cowboys, whom we had invited in for a beer, decided they wanted all our beer. One produced a crude hunting knife from his boot, one picked up our two cases of Calgary Horseshoe and Buffalo brand beer, the other yanked open the door, and all three backed out of our room and disappeared down the hall. We were too young to call the cops and report stolen beer, and we were too scared and shaky to want to play "Cowboys and Indians" in the darkness of the hotel parking lot.

We were too wild and crazy for the old-timers who would retaliate for the anguish we caused them by working us over in the arena. One time they yanked open a chute gate before I was ready; one time they ran Dennis Anderson, mounted on a bareback bronc, right into the narrow catch-pen. We were run through the fence at the far end of the arena, picked up off bucking horses by our collars, belts, and one time even by our hair. The pick-up man would just grab us, drag us off our horses, and drop us. "Save the horse and kill the cowboy."

One time, when Stuart Morison won some prize money in the calf-roping, we went down to the late night rodeo office in the local hotel lobby. The big old truck drivin' weekend rodeo cowboys, who also happened to be on the rodeo committee, politely told us, "You kids didn't win shit. Now fuck-off, if you don't want to get hurt." That's the only rodeo college we ever attended, but we knew we could handle whatever fate Calgary was ready to hand us.

We dragged our bedrolls and a blanket into one of the stock barns, strung the blanket across the front of an empty stall, and made camp. This was to be our home away from home, our Calgary Hilton, our rodeo headquarters for the rest of the week. Deluxe accommodation, three sharing (myself, Dennis Anderson, and Jack Daines) for a whole glorious week in Calgary. We drank hard, played hard, rodeoed hard, and chased every pretty pair of tight blue jeans that ventured into our territory. We were a little too young for the crowned head of Calgary Stampede 'queendom', but we could tell by the glances of the older cowboys that we made a lot of the right choices in our own age bracket.

There were a lot of high point rides that week, but we didn't do that well in the arena. I finished twelfth or fifteenth out of the dozens of riders from all over Canada and the U.S., but I left Calgary on Sunday morning feeling like a world champion cowboy. Life was so good that I hardly noticed the hangover and the smoke belching out from under the hood of my trusty G.M.C.

However, I was concerned about Dennis. He was stretched out in the back of the truck, bravely defending himself against a horrible bout of food poisoning. We made our way out of the city and headed north. I began to count off the towns: Balzac, Airdrie, Crossfield, Carstairs, Didsbury, Olds, Bowden, and Innisfail, on my way back up Highway "2" toward the relative simplicity, security, and sanity of the Blindman valley. Dennis would rest and recover in the warmth and beauty of the Sunset Hills.

Benalto

A week or so after Calgary, our next rodeo was in Benalto, a small village tucked away in west-central Alberta that hosts one of the oldest and longest running rodeos in Western Canada. Our performance in the rodeo arena that day was totally forgettable. None of us managed to place in the final standings and the only mark I received was a huge black and blue bruise in the middle of my back where a dirty old crossbred cow had kicked me after driving me headlong into the arena mud. It always rained at the Benalto Stampede.

After the rodeo performance, I hobbled back to the truck,

changed out of my mud-soaked clothes, and dug a pair of ragged jeans and my cleanest dirty shirt out of my rodeo bag. I pulled on my old, checkered mackinaw jacket against the chill evening air, stretched out on the seat of my pick-up truck and savored the throbbing pain in my back. After a while I slid off to sleep, feeling like some beat-up old dog that had crawled away to lick his wounds.

When I woke up a few hours later, I was so stiff and sore I could hardly move. Dennis Anderson, Arnold Bergesen, Stuart Morison, and a number of newcomers to our motley rodeo crew of would-be hard-riding cowboys appeared out of the darkness. Someone had got hold of two cases of that good old Horseshoe and Buffalo brand Calgary Ale and they were ready to party. The trick was to stay under 15 when it was time to enter the boys' steer-riding, and suddenly become twenty-one when it was our turn to enter a crowded tavern and purchase off-sale beer for the all-night parties that were a big part of our life on the rodeo trail. Most of us were only 15 or under, but someone had to turn 21 in a hurry whenever it was required, or we would have to face a dry party. And we weren't into that kind of recreation.

But the Calgary Ale was flowing that night. I climbed out of the truck and sat down on the running board. The rest of the gang leaned against the truck or a tree or hunched down in the darkness. It was too wet to sit on the ground. We drank, talked, partied, and relived the day's events in the rodeo arena.

The sounds of the midway with its rides and music and sideshow barkers drifted through the night air to our campsite. We were just down the hill and back in the trees a few hundred feet from the nightlife of a small-town rodeo. We made our way out of the camp and up toward the glow of the lights and the smell of the hamburgers, hot dogs, and onions frying at the food concessions. We loaded up on hamburgers and Cokes and set off to take in the sights and sounds of the midway. Dennis and Arnold and I hung together, with the rest of our crew straggling along behind. We passed the ferris wheel, the tilt-a-whirl, the merry-go-round, the pony rides, and another string of food booths. We were laughing, joking, and bouncing off each other. We had had too much beer and we were having too much fun.

In Calgary there had been a sideshow with some kind of creature in captivity. The barker had a spiel that we remembered from hearing it a hundred times: "Hey — go now. She's on the inside, she's big enough and strong enough to kill and devour a man." As we roared through the midway that night in Benalto, every time we passed a good-looking girl or group of girls we would holler outrageously: "Hey, hey! She's big enough and strong enough to kill and devour a man!" We were wild and crazy, but we didn't think we were doing any harm.

We ran into an old girlfriend of mine, a cousin of Dennis'. We had spent some time together, but nothing serious, I thought. For some reason, which to this day is still a mystery to me, she began screaming at me at the top of her voice. She called me every dirty rotten name in the book and a few that would not likely be in any book in those days. She gathered quite a crowd. I decided the best thing to do was keep on moving, so we spun off down the midway to a long tent that housed a string of gambling concessions. There was a crown and anchor, darts, a horse race, over and under, as well as a numbers game and a few others too numerous to mention. The long open front of the tent faced onto the midway and backed along a low wire fence and the Canadian Pacific Railway tracks.

We stood and watched the winners and losers come and go for a few minutes. There were a bunch of damn tough-looking "carnies" running the games. Dennis, Arnold, and I approached the numbers game; our crew crowded in behind. I began playing. I won a few, lost a few. Red the house won, blue I won. It was fifty-fifty and I was doing alright.

We had the board loaded up with all the money we had when suddenly the carny hollered, "Black! The house wins!" He swept all the money off the board and told us to get lost. Floyd Johnson, the oldest and biggest member of our group, objected. The carny reached under the counter and his hand came out clutching a claw hammer. He swung wildly and hit Floyd a glancing blow to the side of the head. We were immediately surrounded by the other carnies and told to fuck-off. We skulked away like a bunch of whipped pups, stopping only long enough to inspect Floyd's head wound. Luckily, it was not serious.

We stood for a while back in the distance and then a plan began to take shape. The tent that housed these games had one long common frame in front and a string of heavy iron stakes at the back. The whole frame was anchored to the stakes and tied back with a half-dozen ropes leading from the frame back to the stakes. We made our way to the other end of the midway, out of the rodeo grounds and back down the tracks behind their tent.

The ground, the grass and the underbrush were still wet from the rain, and we were soaked to the skin by the time we got to the back of the tent. It was pitch dark, but we could see the outline of the tent silhouetted against the lights of the midway. We climbed through the low barbed wire fence to the back of the tent. Carefully and steadily we worked each stake loose. Most of the stakes were made from old car axles and had been driven in with a heavy sledge-hammer. It was tough working them loose without moving the tent. When they were all loose enough to pull, but still in the ground, we took up our positions, with one or two of us on each stake. We whispered together, "One, two, three, pull!"

The stakes came out of the ground, the ropes came slack, and the long frame, canvas tent and all, fell over forward into the midway and landed in a crumpled mass. We were over the fence, out on the railway tracks and running full tilt into the darkness of the wet, July night.

We could hear the shouting, swearing, and screaming behind us. I could feel the pain burning in my back from my earlier injury, but we just kept running on down the tracks and into the darkness.

About four o'clock in the morning our party split up. I made my way in through the back entrance of the rodeo grounds, where the big trucks hauled the bulls and horses in and out. I rescued my pick-up truck from our camp and headed for home.

Dick Damron circa 1960.

CHAPTER FOUR

Music In My Life

GOOD OLD TIMEY COUNTRY ROCK'N'ROLL

BACK IN THE FIFTIES, WELL BLESS MY SOUL
THERE WAS ROCKABILLY ROCK
AND THERE WAS ROCK'N'ROLL
OL' CHUCK BERRY AND JERRY LEE
CARL PERKINS AND BOYS LIKE ME
PLAYIN' ROCK, ROCKABILLY ROCK

LET ME HEAR THAT GOOD OLD TIMEY COUNTRY ROCK'N'ROLL
I'VE SUNG SO MANY HURTIN' SONGS IT'S GOT TO MY SOUL
ORDER UP ANOTHER ROUND AND TURN THE LIGHTS DOWN LOW
PLAY ME A LITTLE BIT OF GOOD OLD TIMEY COUNTRY ROCK'N'ROLL

I LOVE COUNTRY MUSIC, I LOVE ROCK'N'ROLL
I'VE BEEN HOOKED ON RODEOS AND GOIN' DOWN THE ROAD
PICKIN' COUNTRY MUSIC GOT RIGHT TO MY SOUL
LET ME HEAR THAT GOOD OLD TIMEY COUNTRY ROCK'N'ROLL

SMOKED FILLED BARS AND HONKY TONKS ARE HOME SWEET HOME TO ME
RODEO QUEENS IN TIGHT BLUE JEANS, THAT'S WHERE I WANT TO BE
ORDER UP ANOTHER ROUND AND TURN THE LIGHTS DOWN LOW
PLAY ME A LITTLE BIT OF GOOD OLD TIMEY COUNTRY ROCK'N'ROLL

© Sparwood Music

Lost In The Music

There was always music in my life. My grandfather had a strange little banjo that had been converted from a five-string to a four-string. The fifth string had been removed and it must have been tuned to some kind of open tuning. He frailed it with his fingernails and thumb, and created a kind of chord rhythm that I could feel right to my toes when he played songs like *Froggy Went A-Courtin'* and *Oh Susanna!*. No matter how hard I worked on my father's farm, from the time I first learned to strum a guitar, my grandfather always delighted in telling everyone that I was, "no good for anything but playing that damned guitar." At that time, it used to hurt my feelings; but, looking back, it could well have been his way of bragging about his grandson without letting his pride show.

My dad played old-time fiddle tunes like *Turkey In The Straw*, and *Solomon Levi*. He would stand in the living room with his fiddle, and my mother would chord along on the piano. I am not sure that she enjoyed this style of music, as she had studied piano for 13 years and could sit by the hour and play through the thick folios of heavy classics. She was also a piano teacher and, at one time, had 50 weekly students.

Even with those early musical influences, nothing took hold of me until my Uncle Bud showed up with an old guitar and began singing the first country music I had ever heard. He would lay the guitar flat across his knees and use a kitchen knife as a bar to form the chords up and down the neck. The tuning "E, A, E, A, C#, E," formed a bright, ringing open chord, and I loved the sound as he sang *Be Nobody's Darlin' But Mine*.

I quickly learned that song, and struggled to figure out how to slide the bar up and down the strings. When I sang the song for my mother, she took immediate exception to the verse:

Mother is sitting in Heaven
Daddy has gone down below
Sister has gone to meet Mother,
where I'll go, nobody knows.

I was told not to sing that song anymore. This was pretty heavy censorship for a six-year-old boy. When the folks were away, I would pick up the guitar and sing that song over and over. Even though I didn't know why it was forbidden, I felt a wonderful sense of guilt every time I sang it.

I then discovered Wilf Carter and Jimmie Rodgers — and the strange phenomenon of yodeling. My grandmother used to buy me Wilf Carter song books. The neighbors had a wind-up gramophone and they played some of Wilf's old R.C.A. Bluebird Records, a moment I remembered in *The Wilf Carter Song*:

HE PAINTED HIS SONGS LIKE AN OLD WESTERN MOVIE
SANG FROM THE HEART, HONEST AND STRONG
FROM THE LAST RAYS OF SUNSHINE IN OLD ARIZONA
HE ALWAYS REMEMBERED HIS CALGARY HOME

(CHORUS)
I GREW UP AS A CHILD TO THE SONGS OF WILF CARTER
GOT MY FIRST GUITAR AND LEARNED EVERY TUNE
WHEN THE LAST COWBOY SONG IS ONLY AN ECHO
I'LL STILL HEAR WILF CARTER IN THE OLD PRAIRIE MOON

FROM THE GREAT ROCKY MOUNTAINS TO THE ALBERTA PRAIRIES
THE CALGARY STAMPEDE WHERE THE CHUCK WAGONS ROAR
WILF PAINTED HIS DREAMS AND THE LIFE OF THE COWBOY
LIKE OLD CHARLIE RUSSELL AND LOUIS L'AMOUR

FROM HIS HOME IN THE FOOTHILLS AT CROSSFIELD, ALBERTA
HE SANG OF PETE KNIGHT AND THE STRAWBERRY ROAN
IN OLD NEW YORK CITY THEY CALLED HIM "MONTANA"
BUT HE ALWAYS RETURNED TO HIS CALGARY HOME

— *The Wilf Carter Song* © Sparwood Music, 1997

My brother Bob learned to play the guitar much better than I. So, we began playing at local concerts and talent shows, with him strumming guitar and me singing. This was during World War II and some of the popular songs were *There's A Star Spangled Banner Somewhere, A Cowboy's Best Friend Is His Pony,* and *There's A*

Bridle Hanging On The Wall. But I never sang *Be Nobody's Darlin' But Mine* in public.

First Paid Public Performance

When I was 15, I formed my first band. My brother played accordion and guitar, my girlfriend played piano, and I sang and played guitar and fiddle. Our first paying job was playing for a dance at Lockhart, a little community hall about 15 miles out in the country from where I lived. For the next few years, we played every little country hall within miles. Our bookings consisted mostly of weddings, anniversaries, graduations, and local annual events.

Musically, we learned slowly, but our education on how to survive in the music biz had begun. We learned how to travel for miles to a gig, play all night, and not get paid. We learned about getting booked months in advance and being canceled out a few days before the gig because they had found a band that would do it cheaper. We learned about playing until four o'clock in the morning for a collection. When they passed the hat, someone else often kept the money. We learned about creative bookkeeping; playing for promoters on a percentage basis, where 50 per cent of 300 people, at one dollar each, equalled $42.35. And "Fuck-off, kid, if you don't want a broken arm." We learned . . . we learned . . . we learned. It was mostly a matter of money and experience: they got the money and we got the experience. The names and faces have changed, but a lot of these people are still around to help young musicians learn. Some of them are masquerading as agents, managers, festival promoters, record executives, and music publishers.

Back in the early Fifties, when we were putting together our first little family band, we rehearsed day in and day out for hours at a time. I don't know how my parents stood the constant racket that emanated from the living room and reverberated all over the small farm house. We were basically practising all the old-time music: waltzes, polkas, two-steps, schottisches, heel-toe polkas, square dances, and even the French Minuet. In those days, all of the dance bands in the area played all these types of tunes and we knew it would be expected of us. We were all kids — 14, 15, and 16 years old — and we knew all the old-timers in the area would be very critical of every tempo and every tune. We practised and we practised and we practised.

On a deathly cold night, we traveled to Lockhart in the rolling hills outside Bentley for that first gig. Everyone came bundled up in heavy overcoats and parkas. Some kept them on for the first hour or so. Others hung them on the few hangers in the cloak-room and, when there were no hangers left, a pile of coats and parkas was started on a table in the corner. Then most people would huddle around the wood heater in the corner that was stuffed so full of firewood, that it glowed cherry red from the intense heat. Twenty feet away from it you could freeze, so people would alternate between dancing and sticking close to the warmth of the heater. As the night wore on and more people arrived, the whole hall eventually heated up and the dance floor was jammed.

Most people enjoyed the music and would give us nods of approval as they passed by the stage. However, some would shout at us as they went by. One old-timer would say, "It's too fast!" Another would holler, "It's too slow!" Others would say, "It's too loud!" or "We can't hear you!"

But in the wee small hours of the morning, when we swung into an old-time waltz and the small sea of people locked into the 1,2,3 — 1,2,3 feel of the waltz beat, and the pulsating rhythm shook the old hall making the shiny hardwood floor creak and groan in sympathy, and sailed out into the thirty-below chill of the snow-white countryside — it was magic! And anyone in that tiny dance hall in rural Alberta who had enough rhythm in their bones to be able to walk and chew gum at the same time, knew it, could feel it, and loved it.

We were paid $15.00 for the whole band for the night. Out of this we had to pay for our gas, equipment rental, posters, and advertising. But we still considered our first-ever paid public performance a smashing success!

Our Little Family Band

Our little family band carried on for a few years. To keep from starving, I worked on my father's farm and took part-time jobs truck-driving, painting, and working on oil field exploration crews.

In 1954, Martha Evelyn Ohlson (longtime piano player in our

little band) and I were married. On May 9, 1955, my one and only child, a daughter, Barbara Jean, was born. The day after she was born, I realized I had to take some responsibility to become a provider. Running around the country playing small-time shows and dances for a dollar here and a dollar there would no longer make it.

It was a cold, rainy, late-spring day when I hitched a ride to Drayton Valley, Alberta. The Pembina oil fields were booming and I landed a job immediately with Brinkerhoff Drilling as a roughneck on a drilling rig. The job was immediate, but the first paycheque was still two weeks away.

I had often seen the towering derricks of the rigs off in the distance. By day they glinted in the sunshine, and at night you could see their lights for miles. The lights should have been a clue that this was a twenty-four-hour operation. Many times when they were setting up, tearing down, or when the relief crew failed to show, you were expected to put in a sixteen-hour shift.

The first day at the rig was hell. At 6:30 in the morning, the driller picked me up at the hotel, where I had spent a restless night trying to sleep sitting up in a chair in the lobby. I had no money for a room. We drove 20 miles west and south of Drayton Valley, slipping and sliding down the sloppy mud roads in his old pick-up. When we arrived at the drilling site, the rest of the crew headed for the change-house, where everyone climbed into heavy work clothes, rain slickers, steel-toed safety boots, monkey-face gloves and hard hats. I stood around in my cowboy boots, jeans, and a thin little brown cloth jacket. One of the roughnecks dug around and found a beat-up hard-hat and tossed it to me. We went to work.

For the next two weeks, I worked like a dog. The new guy at the rig gets every dirty job handed to him — and every trick in the book pulled on him. Instead of trying to train you, they capitalize on your ignorance of oilfield terminology and procedures, to make a total fool of you. You are expected to lift, carry, swing, shove, and move all kinds of heavy equipment weighing hundreds of pounds.

At first it seemed impossible to learn the names of every piece of equipment and to single-handedly move things that weighed over two, three, four, and sometimes five hundred pounds. But I learned by day, and at night we drove back to town where I spent another night sleeping in the hotel lobby in my mud-soaked clothes. I had no money and had virtually nothing to eat but the odd bowl of dinner soup. Sometimes I would slip into the bar and someone would buy me a beer. Within a week I developed a cold and terrible cough from the hard labor, very little sleep, no decent meals, and from the same mud-caked clothes clinging to me twenty-four hours a day. The diesel fuel and oil that soaked through to my skin caused so much irritation that I could hardly stand it. My co-workers offered no assistance. They seemed to delight in my misery, calling me a "god-damned weevil," a name used to describe a newcomer to the oil-patch. I counted the days until I could get my first check, get a room, have a hot shower, and buy some work clothes and a warm jacket.

I worked on the rigs until mid-July. Then one day a roughneck let a heavy chunk of chain loose. It swung a huge arc around the drill stem and struck me in the back of the head, behind my right ear. I woke up in the University Hospital in Edmonton with a hair-line fracture and an ear that felt like it was full of liquid.

A few weeks later I was back in the oilfields. I worked on a camp job on a drilling rig back in the Rocky Mountains, northwest of Calgary, Alberta. Within a few weeks, a driller had his thumb amputated when it got crushed between the kelly and the drill stem. A roughneck had the top of his head nearly blown off when a huge valve exploded in his face. In December, on a thirty-five-degree-below-zero night at four in the morning, the driller ordered me to take a pail of diesel fuel down and wash the pumps. I told him to "take this job and shove it!"

I loaded my wife and tiny daughter into my '40 Chevy and headed back to civilization. We wound down and around the mountain roads and through the dense forest. The narrow, bull-dozed trail opened into the valley and ran across the snow-covered flats. When we finally picked up the main road heading towards the highway, it felt like we were finally leaving the oilpatch behind. When we hit the paved highway and swung north, we began talk-ing about re-forming a band, finding musicians, and getting some bookings. It was close to Christmas, and we could possibly get a New Year's Eve gig. At least that would be a little sure money. We knew from past experience that January and February would be tough months, and that the below-zero weather of the cold Alberta winter would not make it easy.

We stayed at my wife's parents for a few days, while I located an old buddy who was willing to take me back to the mountains and haul my beat-up trailer out from the rig site. It was a hair-raising experience, snaking the trailer out of the mountains behind his Jeep.

(The Oil Company had towed the trailer in, back in September, before the heavy snowfall. Now we were on our own.) The narrow, bulldozed trail was choked with drifting snow and the steep mountain grades were covered in glare ice.

We finally arrived at my father's farm north of Bentley. It was thirty-eight-below-zero and the snow was knee-deep. We shoveled out a space to park the trailer, ran a power line over from the old house, and worked long into the night getting the oil heater fired up. Finally the eight-by-eighteen-foot trailer began to crackle and snap as the plywood and metal started to heat. The next day we covered the windows with plastic and banked the outside of the trailer with straw bales and snow.

This was to be our home for the next five years.

Getting a band back together was not easy. Most of the musicians we had worked with were working with other bands or had quit playing music to pursue a normal way of life. Red Deer was our closest city, and there we located Roger Dye, who played bass for me for the next seven years, and Ken Cave, a guitar player who also worked with us for a number of years.

We landed a Saturday night show on CKRD Radio in Red Deer. Although we didn't get paid for doing the half-hour show, it became the promotional key to enable us to pick up some bookings in the area. The late Fifties and early Sixties were still within the "golden era" of radio. People tuned in to our show on a regular basis. We played requests and dedications mailed in by listeners, which helped us establish contact with people all over central Alberta. Soon we were "in demand" to appear at shows and dances wherever the radio station was heard.

The Hoadley Story

There is a tiny country dance hall about 35 miles from where I live in central Alberta. Back in the 1950s and 1960s, it was a rough place. Most nights, there were fights of one kind or another. Farmers, truckers, loggers, and oil rig workers would congregate there after the neighboring bars in Rimbey and Winfield closed. They would arrive in pick-up trucks, logging trucks, farm trucks, and automobiles. In the immortal words of Robert W. Service, they were "dog dirty and loaded for bear."

Most of them drank the afternoon and evening away and would arrive around midnight, drunk and crazy, some with scores to settle with a boss or a co-worker — or with someone they had fought it out with the last time there had been a local get-together.

The nearest police were in Red Deer, a small city over 60 miles away, and they usually only showed up once or twice a year to crack down on drunk drivers. Policing the dance was up to the local hall committee. They had some able-bodied men and they meant to protect the women and children, the old folks, and couples who were there to dance and enjoy the local event.

The trouble usually started in the "stag-line," where all the men hung out at the far end of the hall, at the opposite end from the stage where the band played. The ladies sat along one wall, couples along another. It was not unusual to see a grandmother holding a sleeping baby while two or three youngsters hung by her side. Other ladies were in the kitchen preparing the midnight lunch.

The dance floor would be jammed with couples who danced the night away to all the old-time waltzes, polkas, two-steps, and square dances. But when a fight broke out, all hell broke loose. On one particular night, the whole crowd emptied out into the thirty-five-degree-below zero night and into the parking lot. The only light was from one little 60-watt bulb on the outside front of the hall above the door. We could hear the men shouting, hear the punches landing, and the bodies being slammed against cars and trucks.

The hall board members designated as bouncers did their best to keep the onlookers back from the battleground. Once in a while a woman would break through the crowd and go screaming into the middle of the siege to try and rescue a husband, son, or boyfriend who was receiving the beating of his life.

We stayed on the stage and kept playing. We had learned from experience that it would keep some folks in the hall who didn't want to get involved. We had also learned from a beating we had received at a small hall west of Sylvan Lake. That brawl had started when someone suggested that they shouldn't have to pay the 50¢ admission charge. They began beating up our ticket-taker and we left the stage to save her. The only thing that saved us was a tire iron produced by our bass player. He warded off a crew of eight goons from a Calgary Power construction crew who were bent on beating me up, my guitar player, and my 18-year-old wife who was seven months pregnant and still on the road playing piano so we could keep a band together and keep from starving.

Meanwhile, back at our Hoadley dance, we kept the music going as the fight continued. People pushed their way out of the hall until there was only a handful left inside. We stopped playing. I shouted into the microphone: "If you're here to dance, we're here to play. If you're here to fight, we're going home." Three or four couples edged back onto the dance floor, but nothing changed. I stopped playing and turned to the band. "Fuck it," I said, "let's get to hell out of here."

In record time we had our guitars, fiddle, bass, and our equipment loaded into my old station wagon. We had been parked at the back of the hall to give us access to the stage entrance. I could barely see through the heavy frost on the windshield. I wound down the side window and stuck my head out. The parking lot was jammed with vehicles and beer bottles were strewn all over. I was able to swing around the outside of the parked cars and head for the front of the hall.

By that time, 50 or 60 people had formed a ring on the road so the battle could continue in an orderly fashion. I could see the two contestants. Stripped to the waist, they were spattered with blood, and their breath was puffing frost into the frozen Alberta night. I shoved the gas pedal to the floor and laid on the car horn. The old station wagon swerved crazily, dug its way out of the snow-bound parking lot between the cars, and headed up over the shoulder of the road. The back tires screamed as they left the heavy snow and skidded onto the icy road.

We were only a few yards away from the crowd and bearing down fast. It was the only way out and I was not about to stop. I flashed the headlights, kept the horn blaring, and the gas pedal right to the floor. The first people to spot us flying up out of the ditch waved for us to stop. We kept on coming and then the crowd parted. People were running in all directions, shouting and screaming at us. A hail of beer bottles crashed against the rear of the station wagon as we crossed the country road and spun out onto the highway and into the night.

Strangely enough, there is a small sign that has hung in the Hoadley Community Hall for ages. It reads: "If you don't respect anyone else, for God's sake, respect yourself." I guess to some folks those are fighting words.

New Year's Eve

In 1958 my wife, Martha, and I were living in Bentley in that little matchbox-sized trailer with my two-year-old daughter. It was a bitter cold New Year's Eve, and even with the old oil heater belching and chugging and the stove pipe glowing cherry red, the trailer was still barely liveable. We had not managed to get a New Year's Eve gig (God knows we could have used the money), so we had gone to bed early.

In the middle of the night, we woke with a start. Someone was pounding on the door and we could hear voices and a motor running in the yard. The vehicle's headlights were shining directly in through the front window. I snapped on a light, pulled on my jeans, and glanced at the clock by the bed. It was almost midnight. My first thought was that someone was coming to have a New Year's drink. When I opened the door, three men pushed their way into the tiny trailer followed by a blast of thirty-below-zero air. I cautioned them to close the door and be quiet as my daughter was sleeping. They were all dressed in suits and were pretty well on their way to New Year's oblivion. They quickly explained that the Red Deer band, which they had booked, had failed to show up. They had a country hall packed with 300 or 400 hundred people at $10.00 a pop and they wanted us to rescue the night.

My first thought was to ask them why they didn't book us in

the first place. Finally, we agreed to go and play the rest of the night. Before we could do this, we had to get a babysitter, call our guitar player, sweep the snow and ice off my old wreck of a car, and wake up my folks so I could get my instruments and sound equipment out of their basement. We then had to load up and drive the 10 miles out to the country hall. When we got there, the place was jammed. Most of the crowd were drunk and most of them were in an ugly mood after waiting since 9:00 for the dance to start.

Only a handful greeted us as saviors of the night. The rest thought we were the band that was booked and that we were three or four hours late. As we struggled to set up our equipment and tune up our instruments amongst the clatter and noise, many people came to the front of the stage and cussed us out with all kinds of threats and insults. We finally swung into the first tune and the dance floor was soon packed. In those days, most dances ran from 9:00 'til 1:00 or 2:00 in the morning. We had not started until midnight, so we ended up playing non-stop until 4:00 a.m. After the dance was over, someone came up and tucked a small roll of bills in my pocket and thanked us for saving the night.

As I bent down to pick up my guitar case from behind the piano, I glanced at the roll of bills. $40! Forty dollars for saving them from refunding hundreds. I wanted to step out in the middle of the stage and throw the money on the dance floor, but I bit my lip and paid the band, loaded up and drove home in the 5:00 a.m., thir-ty-below-zero morning.

The next New Year's they booked another band. They didn't even call us. A rumor got back to us that they didn't book us back because we showed up late the year before.

Rockabilly Days

This country dance scene continued until 1964 and I learned a lot about dealing with people on a local level. Somewhere between 1956 and 1964, we made a long, slow transition from being an old-time dance band playing waltzes, polkas, and square dances to play-ing Fifties rock and roll. Tunes like *Long Tall Sally, Lawdy Miss Clawdy, Rave On, Corina, Corina,* and a ton of Buddy Holly, Buddy Knox, Chuck Berry, and early Elvis tunes for teen hops, graduation dances, and summer resorts. I rented the old Gull Lake Pavilion and we played there every Wednesday and Friday night throughout the summer months and on long holiday weekends. We played in Bentley every Saturday night and at the Varsity Hall in Sylvan Lake every Monday night.

Our old-time dance music gave way to the rockabilly sounds of Chuck Berry, Jerry Lee Lewis, Carl Perkins, the Everly Brothers, and the early Elvis Presley tunes. At that time, the band consisted of myself on guitar and vocals, Martha on piano, Roger Dye on bass, and Ken Cave on lead guitar. When we changed from the old-time music to the Fifties rock and roll, Ken Cave left the band and was replaced by Keith Bickerton. Keith played all the Ventures, Fireballs, and Champs tunes of the day, as well as the Duane Eddy guitar hits (*Rebel Rouser, Peter Gunn*, etc.). My younger brother, Howard, occasionally filled in for Keith, and became a great little guitar player. In those days, the fiddle seldom came out of its case and I only played steel guitar on the odd slow-dance. Originals such as *Rockin' Baby, Gonna Have A Party, I Guess That's Life,* and Bickerton's instrumental *Black Maria* became important tunes in our repertoire and gave us somewhat of an identity. My wife, Martha, perfected the piano sounds of Jerry Lee Lewis on the up-tempo rockers, and we worked Floyd Cramer's style into the ballads. We had a sound that worked, and although we were still not making much money, we were booked solid and worked steadily for the next few years.

Our Saturday night radio show on Red Deer's CKRD was taped on Thursday nights, so we had a full weeks' work, and although each gig only paid $10 or $15 each, we managed to scrape by and keep the band together.

In 1958, I was bit by the recording bug. I had written a few rockabilly songs which we played on our radio show and at our live performances. One night after our radio show, we stayed late and taped two songs, *Gonna Have A Party* and *Rockin' Baby*, in the tiny studio of the radio station. The station had a beautiful old grand piano and good recording equipment for that time. We had done the songs hundreds of times on our live shows, so the band was at ease with the tunes.

The tape turned out pretty good, so we decided to have records pressed. The tape was shipped to King Plastics in Cincinnati, Ohio.

They custom-pressed one thousand 45 r.p.m. singles on our own label. A few weeks later we were recording artists!

The record picked up a little airplay on some other radio stations in the area, and our horizons began to broaden. The miles became longer and the money got a little better. Then we were to experience our first taste of politics in the music business. Because we were considered to be tied in with one radio station, the DJ's at the other stations told us they couldn't play our record. Their management felt it would be promoting a band and a record that was associated with their competition. Some D.J.'s also pointed out that they didn't play Canadian records. In my naive young mind, I couldn't quite figure this out. I was Canadian, he was Canadian, the listeners were Canadian, the advertisers were Canadian, we all lived in Canada . . . but he was telling me "we don't play Canadian records." Some attitudes never seem to change.

We cut two more records over the next few years. After discovering the pitfalls of trying to promote and distribute our own records, we signed with Quality Records, who manufactured and distributed our records on a national basis. The first Quality Records releases were two more original songs, *Julie* and *That's What I Call Living*. They picked up some airplay across the country. It was exciting to hear that our records were being played in other cities and provinces.

People who liked this music knew that it was nowhere else to be found, and this helped to build our audience. When we recorded our original tunes and they began to show up on juke boxes and radio stations, we became "Fifties Rock Stars" in our own little world. There was a magic and excitement in those years that took a long time to duplicate. It also took 20/20 vision hindsight for me to realize this. Some of our old Fifties records are lodged in collectors catalogs, and every now and then, I get the odd phone call from collectors around the world, trying to track down the old 45 rpm singles that we recorded back in those days.

Around this time, I realized the limitations of using my own group in a small radio station studio. I then began to make plans to record in a commercial recording studio, with a producer and seasoned musicians. So, in 1961, I was off to Nashville, Tennessee, in the good ole' U.S.A. I returned two weeks later with my first professional recording session under my belt. The songs *Nothing Else, Little Sandy, Times Like These,* and *The Same Old Thing Again* were released on Quality Records over the next year.

First Pro Band

When Canada's antiquated liquor laws began to change, I moved from the country dance halls, Canadian Legion halls, community centers, and high school auditoriums to the bars, clubs, and taverns. It was the end of an era. About that time, my marriage came to an end and I began to pursue a career as a sideman with local Alberta bands.

The first hotel tavern I played was the Highway Motor Hotel in Edmonton. It was Edmonton's big annual celebration, known as Klondike Days, and I was playing steel guitar with Joyce Smith and the Tune-Smiths. Joyce had some very successful records out at the time. She had recorded in Nashville with Owen Bradley and all the top pickers of the day. The big American music trade magazines listed her among the best of the newcomers, and her records were getting solid airplay across the country.

The Tune-Smiths, at that time, included Rusty Campbell on bass, Fred Berg on lead guitar, and Al Brown, one of the funniest guys I ever worked with, playing great fiddle. Any time I played a steel guitar solo, no matter if it was great, mediocre, or awful, Al or Rusty would lean over and whisper, "Nice try, Steve." "Better luck next time." "Oh, well." Or, "Pick up your cheque, Harold." Sometimes, their comments were so funny that they would break me up 'til I couldn't play a lick.

With Joyce's popularity and the novelty of entertainment in the bars for the first time, there were line-ups at the door every night. If you weren't there by 7:00 p.m., you wouldn't get a seat. Our stage consisted of three or four sheets of plywood stacked on top of a bunch of the old-style wooden Coke cases. There was no stage lighting, no carpet, no curtain, and absolutely no acoustics. But the crowd loved it. They screamed and hollered and clapped to every tune. We felt like we'd hit the big time.

Not long after that, I put my own little trio together. My cousin, Danny Damron, played lead guitar and Jack Wensley, a native of British Columbia, played Fender electric bass. The first rural hotel we played was in Ponoka, Alberta. It was packed to the rafters. They brought extra chairs from the coffee shop and dining room into the bar, covered the shuffleboards so they could use them as tables, and the party was on.

Most of the bands in the area were dance bands and had no real show. I'd had the advantage of playing a few American nightclubs and doing a number of concerts with people like Skeeter Davis, Don Gibson, Little Jimmy Dickens, and Buck Owens. I had learned how to entertain people and we had a lot of comedy mixed in with the music.

After the first night, Russ Creasey, the hotel manager, got a call from the Liquor Board. "Tell Damron to clean up his show or we'll shut him down." The line they objected to was, "I don't want a mansion in Red Deer. I just want to shack up in Ponoka." We had to drop a lot of our show to keep them happy. Richard Pryor and Lenny Bruce would not have been proud of me.

Bluegrass Memories

I have always been a fan of bluegrass music. I picked up my first five-string banjo at the Calgary Stampede in 1961 after working the week in Calgary with Ernie McCulloch and The Golden Rockets. I was playing pedal steel guitar in the band and Slim Johnson, the guitar player, doubled on five string banjo. I fell in love with the free, open sound of the bluegrass tunes, and when Slim let me try out his banjo, I knew I had to have one. I bought a little old banjo for $49.00. That doesn't sound like much money by today's standards, since a good banjo can now cost a few thousand dollars. But I had only made $85.00 for the full week in Calgary, playing breakfasts, noon shows, and dances every night. By the time I paid for my drinks, food, and cigarettes, and the 49 bucks for the banjo, I didn't have much left to show for the week.

On the way out of town, I pulled into the Husky Truck Stop and filled my pickup with enough gas to get home. Back on the highway, I headed north to Bentley. I had both hands on the wheel, my hat tipped back, the gas pedal to the floor board, and my banjo propped up on the seat beside me. I was going home without a care in the world or a dollar to pay the rent or buy groceries for my wife and five-year-old daughter. I had had a "helluva week" playing music at the Calgary Stampede and I had me a five string banjo. As we used to say in the "Good Ol' Days", I was just as happy as if I was in my right mind.

I was crazy about that little banjo and I played it by the hour. I listened to every bluegrass record I could get my hands on and tried to copy the Scruggs' style of banjo, which had been developed by Earl Scruggs of the Flatt and Scruggs aggregation. Since I had already developed the thumb and finger pick technique on the steel guitar, playing the banjo came very easily to me.

It wasn't that long 'til I was able to get enough music out of the banjo to take it on stage for a few tunes. And any time there was a jam session, I played banjo instead of a guitar. A few months later, Ernie McCulloch hired me to play a club gig with him down in Washington state. During the entire trip, I sat in the back seat and played banjo. About the only three tunes I knew all the way through without stopping were *Cripple Creek, Sally Ann,* and *The Ballad Of Jed Clampett.* It must have driven everybody crazy, but they were nice enough not to say anything.

I played across the Prairies, through the Rockies, down through the orchards and lakes of British Columbia's Okanagan Valley, and on down to the State of Washington. Ernie drove, and his new bride, Lorna, and his brother, Howard the bass player, shared the front seat. Slim Johnson and his "Lady Vi" and I with my trusty "Five" huddled in the back seat. The back of the station wagon was jammed with musical instruments and suitcases. It was like a scene from some old Bonnie and Clyde movie.

Through the hot sunny day, the evening showers, the cool gray clouds of night, the banjo scored an endless soundtrack to it all.

Strangelove

I've almost lost count of the years I have played at the Calgary Stampede. I don't think anyone keeps stats on things like that, but I know it has been a long, long time, and it runs back into the late 1950s. I worked as a steel guitar player with Ernie McCulloch and the Golden Rockets, and with Harold Anderson's Calgary Ranch Boys. I played Legions and Elks halls and dance halls long before

Alberta allowed bands in bars. I played on the wagon seat of a chuckwagon in downtown Calgary. Orville Strandquist, one of the greatest old wagon drivers to ever race a four-horse team around the Calgary track (commonly known as the half-a-mile-of-hell), supplied the wagon. I supplied the music, and they served pancakes and bacon to the tourists and highbrow city slickers who passed by on Seventh Avenue.

When the liquor laws changed and the bar scene began to happen, I played at the St. Regis, the Westgate, the Sherwood Inn, the now-defunct Tradewinds, and many weeks at the Crossroads. In one day I would play the early morning "gin breakfasts" (where everyone was sloshed by 9:00 in the morning), the noon shows, the CBC afternoon broadcasts, then back to whatever bar I was playing, to play into the wee small hours. The Stampede used to be only six nights; today, it lasts ten days and nights. By the time it's over, if I really entertain and party and set the pace and give it all I've got, there isn't much left to give when the fireworks touch the sky on that final Sunday night.

In 1961, I played at one of Calgary's many fabled Stampede breakfasts at the Palliser Hotel. It was 7:00 in the morning and most of the guests were already blitzed from the gin and orange juice concoction they were serving up. Slim Pickens, who went on to star in *Dr. Strangelove* and dozens of other Hollywood flicks, was working the Stampede as a rodeo clown and bullfighter. After Wilf Carter's set, Harold Anderson and I picked and sang for an hour or so. Slim was called on stage and introduced to the crowd.

He raised his glass to the room full of early-morning stampeders. "I don't know which is worse," he said, "your liquor laws or your drinking habits. In Calgary, they pour you drinks as if they are trying to get rid of their booze — or get rid of you!"

Dick Damron's Cross-Canada Mystery Tour

Over the years, I have criss-crossed Canada from Victoria to Halifax, with stops in places such as 100 Mile House, Medicine Hat, Saskatoon, Boggy Creek, Thunder Bay, Gatineau, Moncton, and Peggy's Cove in, what we used to refer to as, the Dominion of Canada. I did it on planes, trains, buses, and the last wheels, if not the last legs, of every conceivable mode of transportation available to me at the time. Sometimes we'd hit Vancouver, Edmonton, Calgary, Regina, Ottawa, Toronto, Hamilton, London, Montreal, Moncton, Fredericton, and Halifax. For the first ten years of the "Dick Damron Mystery Tours," however, it was usually to places known as the "one horse towns," not really as unaffectionate as it may sound, but a term used to describe any city, town, or village that was smaller than the one we had just come from or smaller than the place we were then living in.

These "one horse towns" all had a Shell service station, a Bank of Montreal, a Ptomaine Joe's Restaurant, a newer motel along the highway, and a couple of older hotels in the center of town on Main Street. An old friend of mine, a great steel guitar player and former road warrior by the name of Al Gain, said, "You could always tell which hotel the band was playing in by the milk cartons and the roll of bologna in the upstairs window." Guitar player extraordinaire Dennis Larochelle nailed it on the head when he said, "A well-balanced diet for the road musician consists of eating from the four main food groups: sugar, starch, grease, and ketchup."

If we were west of Winnipeg and east of Calgary, the size of the town could also be easily judged by the number of grain elevators stretched along the Canadian Pacific or Canadian National Railway tracks on the other side of town. When there was a new band member on his "maiden voyage," someone would point to the elevators along the horizon of some windswept stretch of Saskatchewan highway and calmly say, "Look at all the whore houses." The new guy would immediately say, "Those are grain elevators!" Then we would come back with the old line, "They must be whorehouses! That's where all the farmers get screwed!"

A FEW CHUCKLES
A FEW TIRED SMILES
SOMEONE WOULD OPEN A BEER
LIGHT A JOINT
PASS A 26ER OF BACARDI
UP FROM THE BACK SEAT
THEN, MILE AFTER MILE OF SILENCE

When the boredom became too much to bear, someone would ask the age-old question: "Damron, when are you gonna get a radio in this fuckin' thing?"

There were a lot of "real good" musicians who couldn't stand more than one Dick Damron Mystery Tour, the mental and physical abuse that the road could deal out, along with irate phone calls from suicidal wives at home with the kids. Wives going home to their mothers. Wives going back to their husbands. Mothers going back to the kids. When we were out there on the edge of whatever, it was what kept us on the edge. Sooner or later we all felt there was no going back, until someone did.

In Kenora, Ontario, at the Kenricia Hotel on a cold November night in 1964, the wife of the drummer playing with the other band upstairs showed up unexpectedly on the weekend. She found her husband having a mad, passionate love affair with the "chick singer" from another band in town. She decided right then to end it all. She locked herself in their hotel room bathroom and laid waste to herself with a razor blade.

When we helped the drummer kick the bathroom door open, we were met with a horrible sight. We immediately called the doctor. He refused to come to the hotel, and instructed us to take her to the hospital, where he would meet us. We got her out of the tiny bathroom and onto the bed, wrapped her from head to toe in the sheets to try and stop the bleeding, then rolled her in the rest of the blankets, including the bedspread. We picked her up and headed for the door, only to come face to face with two R.C.M.P. officers.

One of the officers whisked the drummer off to jail. We helped the other officer get the woman to Emergency. An hour or so later (by now close to 4:00 a.m.), we were sitting in the hospital waiting room, anxiously awaiting word on her condition, when the first R.C.M.P. officer arrived with the drummer (husband) in tow. He had been locked in the local jail cell, where he had unscrewed the light bulb in the ceiling, smashed it against the wall, and slashed his wrists with it. He was bleeding like a stuck pig. The doctor went to work on him.

After being questioned by the R.C.M.P. officers for the rest of the morning, we finally returned to our hotel. I went to my room, had a shower, then popped two or three tabs of Valium washed down with a shot of Bacardi. I lay down on the creaky old iron bed and stared at the ceiling, trying to push the images of the night out of my mind so I could get some sleep. God, I hated this life!

The next morning, we loaded up and headed for the Rainy Lake Hotel in Fort Francis, then on to The Rocton in Atikokan, and next to the Shoreline Motor Hotel in what was the last throes of Port Arthur before it became Thunder Bay. We played two weeks in each of these places. Our last stop was to have been a further two weeks in Dryden. When we got word it had been canceled and that we could head for home at the end of the Port Arthur gig, we laughed and cried and danced. For the last few nights at the Shoreline, our show became so outrageous that they wanted to hold us over. We got off on a plea of insanity, loaded all our worldly goods into the old white stationwagon, and headed west.

Roy Cook, a native son of beautiful downtown Lethbridge, Alberta, a helluva drummer who worked with me for seven years and taught me more about music having a feel and a groove than all the Nashville studio drummers ever did, rode in the back seat all the way from the Lakehead across Manitoba and Saskatchewan through one of the worst December blizzards I can recall. By the time we reached Brandon, he'd downed two bottles of Bacardi. He drank another between Brandon and Lethbridge. He was talented and troubled. He had lost the sight in one eye in an auto crash, years before, and was slowly losing the sight in the other eye. We would lie awake at night in the dingy hotel room and quietly talk the hours away. Many times he talked and I listened. I loved him like a brother.

Back in the 1960s, when a southern Alberta rancher got sentenced to two years in jail for stealing cattle, butchering them and selling the meat, Roy (who always had a way with words), described it like this: "Old Hank got a deuce in the sneezer for operating a mobile butcher shop." Roy did a little time in the Lethbridge "Pen" himself. He said the Sally-Ann always gave the prisoners a 'sunshine bag' at Christmas time. "What's in a 'sunshine bag'?" I asked. "A pencil and a couple of fucking jellybeans," he replied.

Roy also told me how his mother had committed suicide when he was a child. She just walked out into Henderson Lake and drowned herself. I recalled painfully that, when I was a kid, my mother used to say, "I wish I was in Hell with my head shot off," and I would lay there in the dark with tears in my eyes and wonder what made women suffer the way they did.

A few short weeks later, I learned a little more about suffering when Roy Cook put a .38 to his head and ended it all. It's taken me a long, long time to come to terms with that. Sometimes I think I never will.

The day of Roy's funeral in Lethbridge, my brother Howard and I were driving to British Columbia's Okanagan Valley to play the Kelowna Regatta. It was a glorious day and the towering "Rockies" in the Rogers Pass seemed to comfort me and ease the pain of his loss and my guilt at not being able to afford to cancel the gig to attend his funeral. It was part of the price of scratching out a survival in the music business. I knew Roy would understand.

Howard and I talked about Roy and the not-so-good "good old days." Howard and Roy had also become good friends. Roy always pissed Howard off by constantly calling him "little brother." As we talked, my eyes filled with tears, my throat closed up and my heart felt like it weighed a hundred pounds. The mourning process was in full flight and my spirit was attending the funeral in Lethbridge that was going on that very moment. A spear of anger came to me through the hurt and sadness and I said to Howard, "You know, it was his choice! He talked about it for years, and now he's gone."

Roy could have been right there — in the back seat with his bottle of Bacardi, talking about Ramsey Lewis and Ray Charles and tapping out a jazz waltz or a bossa nova beat with a book of paper matches on his knee. He used to attach the jingles from an old tambourine to his drumsticks with wood screws about four inches back from the heavy end, and hold them by the light end. During his drum solo on *Caravan*, he would build an incredible intensity on the rim of his floor tom and then come off the rim with a long, descending roll to the sweet-spot in the center of the tom. The crowd always came to their feet with a standing ovation that lasted to the end of his solo. Club owners and hotel managers would invariably call me into the office and tell me to get rid of the drummer, "He's getting the crowd too worked up!"

On our second night at the Edmonton Inn we were told, "No more drum solos!" By Saturday night, we had a couple of hundred coasters piled on the front of the stage. Every one was a request for a drum solo. For our last song on our last night, we did *Caravan*, and during the standing ovation that followed, I gathered the huge armful of coasters off the stage and pushed my way through the crowd to where the manager was standing, threw the coasters in his face, leaned in nose-to-nose with him and said, "Fuck you!"

Roy and Howard are both gone now but we had a great little band and some of Roy's tempos and 'feels' still live in my music today.

The Downward Spiral

In 1969, I was living, or at least surviving, in the small southern Alberta town of Lethbridge. I had gone there in the first place because the old York Hotel in Lethbridge was one of the first places in Alberta to go with entertainment six nights a week.

The bar was packed every night and on the weekends there were huge line-ups. At closing time, nobody left without a case of beer under each arm. For our part in drawing and entertaining the patrons, we were paid the princely sum of $300-a-week for the whole band. Our rooms were supplied, but we paid for our meals and the few drinks we could afford.

Most of the time our meals consisted of toast and coffee for breakfast, a bowl of dinner soup with all the ketchup and crackers we could eat at noon, and a hot dog in the bar at night. Once in a while on payday, if we didn't have to save our money for gasoline for a trip to another city, we would splurge on the special of the day from the coffee shop menu. It was usually liver and onions, huge greasy beef sausages, or meatloaf. Because the city of Lethbridge is near the site of one of western Canada's first R.C.M.P. settlements (known as Fort Whoop-Up), these exotic gourmet meals were listed on the menu as "Whoop-Up Specials," and most of them were.

Another endearing feature of Lethbridge is that it rivals Chicago for the title of the Windy City. At least 300 days a year the wind blows like all hell. I have seen Coca-Cola signs ripped from the sides of old buildings, and people walking into the wind at such an angle that if the wind suddenly stopped they would fall down.

In our tiny upstairs hotel rooms, when it was thirty-five-below outside, it seemed like forty-below inside. The wind would raise huge bubbles under the linoleum floor and the old green blind would billow out about a foot from the window. After a long cold spell, the frost would be an inch thick on the inside of the windows. Besides the band, the only other people on our floor were a truck driver named Sandy and the Reverend Dr. Kik, who specialized in all sorts of "weird and wonderful" things (mostly abortions and venereal diseases).

I didn't have to be a corporation lawyer to figure out that playing these kinds of places would lead only to playing more of these kinds of places. I thanked God for the creative talent He had given me, and I spent most of my hours writing and rewriting country songs, hoping someday to find the one that would elevate me from this self-imposed state of shit and abuse.

At this time, the lady love of my life went back to eastern Canada to visit her children and her family, never to return. My drummer, who had been like a brother to me, shot himself. My father was dying with an unidentified form of lung cancer, and I was eating Librium and Valium like it was popcorn. I combined that with all the "Bacardi and Seven" that people bought me every night in the bars. I would laugh myself off stage, cry myself to sleep, and wake up in the middle of the night and take a few more pills.

One snowy, windy Easter holiday weekend when we were not playing music, the band members went their separate ways and I was left alone. The bass player and his wife had rented a tiny house in an alley a few blocks from the hotel. When they left for the weekend to travel back to their home town in British Columbia, they gave me the key so I could get out of the hotel for a few days.

From the time they left, with everything closed up for Good Friday, Easter Sunday and Monday, the depression and loneliness set in. On Sunday night, I couldn't handle it any more. I tried everything I could think of to snap myself out of it. I was broke, alone, and the downward spiral seemed endless.

The tiny house was a one-room remodeled garage, with crude plumbing and a gas stove which served as a cookstove and the only source of heat. In my desperation, and with no will to live, I snuffed out the pilot light, turned the gas wide open, and swallowed all the black and green Librium capsules and Valium that I had in my possession. I washed them down with a glass of straight Bacardi rum and lay down on the bed to die.

Two days later, I woke up in the mid-afternoon with my head pounding and ears ringing. My clothes were soaked with sweat. The pilot light — that I thought I had snuffed out — must not have gone out completely. With the gas turned wide open, the house was like a steam bath. Possibly, with my heavy use of the pills over the previous few months, my body had built up a tolerance to the massive dose I had taken.

I got myself together, climbed into my station wagon, and drove to a doctor's office a few blocks away. It was just about closing time. The nurse asked if I had an appointment and I said no. I waited while she checked with the doctor. Then she motioned me in. I related my story to the doctor and he wrote me out a prescription.

"Don't take any more Valium or Librium — just take one of these at bedtime," he said. "But never take more than one, or you'll never wake up again."

I thought this was a strange drug to prescribe to someone who was admittedly suicidal, but on my way back to the hotel I picked up the prescription at the drugstore. They were large gelatin capsules the shape of a football and were filled with a wine-colored liquid.

That night I took one and went to bed. I slept for a short while, possibly an hour, then woke with a start. My head was in a vice — a 500 pound weight lay on my chest, blood was dripping from the ceiling, and multi-colored lights were dancing around the room. I was hallucinating and terrified. The next morning, I flushed the rest of the prescription down the toilet. "Thanks a lot, Doc," I thought. "Now what the hell do I do?"

IN MY WRETCHED YEARS
SOMEWHERE BETWEEN THE BOY AND THE MAN
I CURSED THE LORD
FOR BLESSING ME WITH A TALENT
NOT BIG ENOUGH TO CARRY ME
THROUGH THE MOUNTAINS HE PLACED BEFORE ME
I WALKED ALONE
CRIED FOR HELP
PRAYED FOR UNDERSTANDING
AND TODAY I AM THANKFUL

FOR THE COURAGE TO WALK ALONE
THE STRENGTH TO HELP MYSELF
AND FOR SAVING ME FROM THE ANONYMITY
OF BEING FULLY UNDERSTOOD
AND THE MOUNTAINS ARE STILL THERE
THANK GOD

(Top) *The Musical Roundup Gang back stage at the Red Deer Memorial Centre in 1953. Left to right: Jimmy Brennen, Jim Ryan, Martha Ohlson, Bob Dye, and Dick Damron.*

(Bottom) *Live on CHCA TV (now RDTV) in Red Deer in 1960. Left to right: Martha Damron, Keith Bickerton, Roger Dye, Dick on National steel, and Ken Cave.*

Top: *Dick Damron & The Hitch Hikers at the Kopper King in Whitehorse, Yukon, where Damron appeared for 13 weeks in 1965. Left to right: Jack Wensley (bass), Dick's cousin Dan Damron (lead guitar), and Dick on Fender 1000 steel guitar.*

Bottom: *Dick and the CKRD Nite-Riders perform live at the Red Deer Fair in 1958, with Roger Dye on bass and Howard Damron on Fender Stratocaster.*

CHAPTER FIVE

No Trains To Nashville

AIN'T NO TRAINS TO NASHVILLE

BACKSTAGE AT THE RYMAN IN 1961
STANDING IN THE SHADOWS ALL ALONE
I CAME DOWN TO NASHVILLE WITH MY TWENTY-DOLLAR GUITAR
NOTHING BUT A POCKET FULL OF DREAMS

I WALKED THE STREETS OF NASHVILLE WITH THAT GUITAR IN MY HAND
WON'T SOMEBODY LISTEN TO MY SONGS?
COLD AND BROKE AND HUNGRY, I GOT BACK ON THAT TRAIN
THINKIN' GOD I MUST BE DOIN' SOMETHING WRONG

(CHORUS)
NOW THERE AIN'T NO TRAINS TO NASHVILLE ANYMORE
AIN'T NO TRAINS TO NASHVILLE ANYMORE
I AIN'T RODE THAT L'N SINCE 1964
AND THERE AIN'T NO TRAINS TO NASHVILLE ANYMORE . . .

THERE'S A DIGITAL COMPUTER IN THE OFFICE OF THE MAN
HE PICKS ALL THE MUSIC THAT WE'RE HEARIN' IN THE LAND
HE SAYS 94.7 OF THE TOTAL POPULATION DON'T WANT
SONGS ABOUT JESUS, COWBOYS, TRAINS OR HELL

YOU CAN'T AFFORD A VIDEO AND YOU AIN'T GOT A BUS
YOU AIN'T GOT FINANCIAL BACKING SON SO YOU AIN'T ONE OF US
THAT DIGITAL COMPUTER SAYS YOU'RE A LITTLE BIT TOO OLD
AND I SEE THAT BACK IN '55 YOU PLAYED ROCK 'N ROLL

© Sparwood Music

Starday Sessions

There were less than 20 people in the train's coach car of the Louisville-Nashville Line. Some read, some slept, but most of us stared out the windows into the darkness of the rain-swept Tennessee night. The old iron horse lumbered along the seemingly endless steel rails that stretched through rolling hills of the Southern countryside. One single headlight poked helplessly along the track, guiding the L & N through the relentless downpour of the torrential March rain.

Nashville's Union Station lay somewhere ahead of us. It was only another hundred miles or so. It seemed like thousands. But the thousands were already behind me. The L & N had carried me down from Chicago. The Northern Flyer of the Great Northern Railway had swept me across Minnesota, Wisconsin, and into Illinois. From Minneapolis-St. Paul on into Chicago, the ancient Soo Line stopped at every town, city, village, pillar and post between Winnipeg and Minnesota's twin cities. In Canada, the peoples' railway, the Canadian National, staffed by the most ignorant, arrogant, and obnoxious government employees available in 1961, had at least delivered me safely into Winnipeg on an all-night run from Calgary, over 800 miles to the west. The initial 100 miles from Lacombe, Alberta, to Calgary on the C.P.R. had been like a Sunday afternoon drive.

As I was reliving these first few days of my journey, the L & N slowed to a crawl and then ground to a halt. We were nowhere near any village, town, or city. If you stared long enough, you could pick out the odd tiny light off in the distance. We sat for hours. At daybreak, we could see that we were surrounded by water. The tiny lights we had seen off in the distance were in the upstairs windows of farm-houses, sitting in four or five feet of water. Because of the high grade that the railway tracks were built on, we were only in a few inches of water. By mid-morning we were underway, creeping along a few feet at a time, stopping to inspect the tracks for washouts, then moving cautiously along for another short distance.

By nightfall, we were through the worst of it and by midnight we rolled into Union Station in Nashville, Tennessee — Music City, U.S.A., the home of the Grand Ole Opry.

I picked up my guitar and suitcase and caught a cab. It was still pouring rain when we drove out of Union Station, hung a right on

Broadway, splashed through the Nashville streets, and pulled up in front of the aging James Robertson Hotel. It was midnight Friday, and I hadn't seen a bed since the previous Saturday night at home in Bentley, Alberta, Canada. God, I was tired.

The next morning I called my producer, Tommy Hill, at Starday Sound Studios in Madison. In a few hours, he picked me up at my hotel and we drove to the studio a few miles out in the country, on the edge of Nashville.

When we arrived at the studio, Tommy and I proceeded into his office and began working out ideas and arrangements for my upcoming recording session. Then he drove me back in to Nashville to the James Robertson. I went to bed early so I would be fresh and rested for the next day's session. Still overtired from my five-day train ride and excited about my first Nashville recording session, I could not sleep.

I got up, got dressed, left the hotel, walked over to Broadway and down to Tootsie's Orchid Lounge. Tootsie's is still a famous landmark. Its fame grew from the fact that although it fronts on Broadway, the back door entrance is right across the alley from the backstage entrance of the Ryman Auditorium, for years the home of the Grand Ole Opry. Many of the greats, like Hank Williams and Willie Nelson, hung out there between shows. Tootsie Bess, who is no longer on this earth, ran the establishment for years and was the benefactor of many a struggling songwriter.

On this particular night, there was only a handful of people in the place. George Jones' *Seasons Of My Heart* was on the jukebox. I stayed too long, drank too much and, at closing time, I made my way back to the James Robertson with a "Tennessee Belle" in tow.

I awoke in the morning with a splitting headache. The "Tennessee Belle" was in the shower. I reached for my jeans. My pocket was empty. All the cash money to pay for my session had been there the night before. Her purse lay on the floor beside the bed. I zipped it open and there lay my seven crisp, Canadian $100 bills. I took them out and slipped them back into my jeans pocket. A few minutes later, she came out of the bathroom, got dressed, kissed me good-bye, told me what a wonderful lover I was, and swung out the door thinking she still had my money in her purse.

An hour later, Tommy Hill picked me up and drove me back to the studio. When we arrived, the studio was filled with musicians setting up, tuning up, and checking sound levels. I was sick, sober, and sorry, and in no shape to do a recording session. But once the session got underway and the adrenalin started pumping, everything came off without a hitch. Willie Ackerman was on drums, Kelso Herston on lead guitar, Hargus Robbins on piano, Junior Huskey on bass, and Pete Drake on steel.

After the session, Pete Drake took me backstage at the Ryman Auditorium for the Grand Ole Opry. Between shows, we hung out at Tootsie's and I met everybody who was anybody in country music in 1961. The next day, I boarded the train for the long journey back to western Canada.

In 1963, I rode the train to Nashville again, this time with my younger brother, Howard, for company. I recorded six sides, issued as singles on RCA. Added to the first four, they became my first independent album release, THE NASHVILLE SOUND OF DICK DAMRON. In 1965, I made the trip in my white Pontiac station wagon.

Since that time, I have made dozens of trips, but all by air. Trips to record 20 albums, trips to appear at the C.M.A. International Show, or Fan Fair, or the Texas Proud Awards. But "there ain't no trains to Nashville anymore."

Soldier Of Fortune

In 1968, I was living in Nashville in a luxurious six-dollar-a-day room in the Sam Davis Hotel and walking back and forth to Music Row every day. It was one of the coldest and wettest winters in Tennessee history, capped off by the assassination of Martin Luther King in Memphis. The shock waves hit Nashville with an intensity that chilled the Southern city to the bone. I spent my days pounding on the doors of record companies and publishers and my nights confined to my hotel by the curfew that followed the assassination.

I had been on Music Row all day and, after walking back to the hotel in the late afternoon in the slop and slush of an all-night snowfall, I stretched out on the old iron cot in my room and fell asleep. When I awoke, I was starving. I left the Sam Davis and crossed the cold snowy street to partake of one of Nashville's many fabled chicken fried steaks. The smell of steak frying on the open grill of a sleazy little "dine and dash" made my mouth water. I sat down at the counter, but just as the waitress slid the $1.49 steak in front of me, the door to the grungy diner swung open and two of Nashville's finest entered. They ordered me out of the eatery and back to my hotel. I left the cafe and made my way back to the hotel to sit in the lobby. There was only a handful of people in the lobby and I decided that anything was better than going back up to the confinement of my hotel room. So I took a chair.

The only reading material on the battered wooden coffee table was a well-worn issue of the *Christian Science Monitor*. I picked it up and began thumbing through it. The word "Canada" jumped out at me and I began to read "Canada is messing with a dangerous man in Pierre Elliot Trudeau, a man whose visions range from slightly pink to a brilliant scarlet. A man whose dream is a French national socialist Canada." I laid the paper aside and took the elevator up to my dingy little broom closet. I felt lonely as hell and I wondered what was really happening to my country while I was away.

I sat down on the edge of the narrow cot. The depression and loneliness had sapped my creative energy just when I needed it most. I was scheduled to record the next afternoon at Music City Recorders.

I picked up my guitar and strummed a few chords. I wasn't very happy with the songs that I was set to record and I hoped there might be a spark or an idea that I could work into a song. I sat there for an hour or so, strumming chords, humming melodies, and trying words and phrases out in my mind. Nothing happened.

I propped my old D-28 Martin guitar up in the corner behind the door and stretched out on the bed. I felt like a prisoner in the sad surroundings of the narrow room. I stared at the bare light bulb hanging in the middle of the faded yellow ceiling. I thought about Canada and tomorrow's session. I thought about my songs and my insecurity, and I grew even more depressed.

I tried praying and meditating, and thinking and not thinking. I finally fell asleep on top of the covers with all my clothes on, but woke up at 5:00 in the morning and couldn't go back to sleep. It was going to be a long day. Just when I needed to be at my best, I knew I would be at my worst. I lay back on the bed and asked God to help me through the day.

My father had given me words to live by. They weren't original, but they rang in my ears many times just when I needed them most.

"Do the best you can, where you are, with what you've got." They'd helped me through adversity, along with the Rudyard Kipling poem, "If you can keep your head when all about you are losing theirs, and blaming it on you. If you can carry on when all men doubt you and make allowance for that doubting too." These words had helped me through many a time when a band mutinied, or agents and promoters put me in impossible positions where, if I hadn't kept my head and held on, I could not have made it through.

That day in the studio a young, hot-shot would-be producer had absolutely no control over my recording session. The musicians had a jam session at my expense. There were shots and rides and kicks and stops at the end of every line. There were chords thrown in that would make a jazz player blush, and arrangements no country music fan could even comprehend, let alone feel or enjoy.

On a break, I walked out of the studio into the Tennessee afternoon and stood there in the parking lot. I took off my hat and turned my face directly into the sun, hoping it would drain some of the tension and stress out of my body. I was so uptight. I knew I could never sing to the tracks that were being laid down. I was paying for the session with every last cent I had been able to scrape together in the last three years on the road playing bad-assed bars and living like a "road pig." And to top it all off, I knew that I would never be able to place this session with a record company. I just wanted to walk away from it all. But I fought back the tension and the tears, repeated the words to "If" over and over as a mantra, and returned to the studio to "do the best I could, where I was, with what I had."

The session was a disaster. I was embarrassed and nervous and I sang terribly. My money was gone and I knew the session would never see the light of day. That was in 1968. I lived to fight again, but I was so destroyed and intimidated that I didn't go back into a Nashville recording studio for five years.

In the meantime, I did some sessions in Edmonton and Toronto. When I returned to Nashville in 1973, I was convinced I would never record again. I just wanted to pitch my songs to Nashville publishers and have other artists record them.

When I walked into the offices of Beechwood Central Publishing on Music Row and met Joe Bob Barnhill, my life in the music business began to change. I knew that Joe Bob had a lifetime of experience in the music biz in L.A. and Nashville. We talked in his outer office for a few minutes. The conversation was easy and friendly.

None of the usual "Nashville bullshit" . . . "Oh, so you're from Hicksville up in Canada and you think you have some songs? This town is full of the best damn songwriters in the world. Hell, I got 15 songwriters on staff right now and they are all great. One of them got a song cut on a Buck Owens album back in '63 . . ." None of that! Just easy conversation.

We moved into his inner office. He closed the door and sat down behind his desk. "Let's see what you got," he said.

I knew he expected me to hand him a tape. Instead, I took out a few loose sheets of paper that I had scribbled my songs on, and asked if I could use one of the many guitars he had sitting around his office. Over the years, I found Joe Bob always had an office full of guitars. It always made me feel more at home than the usual stack of trade magazines, real estate brochures, and financial weeklys that adorn many other Music Moguls' offices. I flipped through my pages, trying to find one of my best songs. I thought he might only listen to one or two. I sang *Mother, Love and Country, Backstage Ladies, On The Road*, and *Lady-O*. He picked up one of the guitars and began strumming through the songs with me. A few minutes later, we took a little break and, instead of calling it off, he said, "What else you got?"

I knew from most of my experiences in Nashville that *that* usually meant, "I don't hear anything here. Do you have anything else?"

I sang a few more songs, and, finally, he said, "You've got some pretty good songs here!" Working with Joe Bob over the years, I learned that that was about the highest praise you could expect from him. I tossed his words around in my mind for a second and thought, "God, I think he likes my songs!"

"Who do you think we could get to record them?" I asked.

"Dick Damron."

We talked about it for a while and decided to do a demo session and record the songs with good musicians in a good studio and see how it all turned out. Joe Bob made a few calls and set up everything for early the next week. We spent three or four days working on the songs, doing charts, arrangements, and sequencing the songs in an order that would flow in the studio. Keep the ballads in there and keep the energy up with the uptempo songs. I learned a lot of things that seem obvious today, but are so simple and basic that many people in the music biz still don't have that 'feel'.

If you alienate the musicians or anyone on the sessions, you lose the feel and never get it back on that session. As well as the long days in the office, I worked long nights back at the luxurious Anchor Motel on West Broadway. It was hard to concentrate between the screaming sirens and the constant string of cabs picking up and delivering low-budget hookers to the sleazy motel. Sometimes, the action was punctuated by gunshots or the morning news that "Someone had been stabbed in 108."

On the day of the session, Joe Bob picked me up and we headed out to a little studio in Goodlettsville on the outskirts of Nashville. When we arrived, the musicians were already there, setting up, tuning up and getting levels. I met Gene Rice, a young engineer who worked miracles with the antiquated equipment. But some of the microphones that were considered obsolete in those days have become highly-prized and sought out by today's engineers as being far superior to some of the new, hi-tech mikes, which lack the warm and natural sound of their predecessors. I also met the musicians, Fred Carter Jr. and Pete Bordonali on guitars, Hal Rugg on steel, Jim Wolfe on drums, Tony Migliore on keyboards, and Steve Schaffer on bass.

We began working on the first song. Joe Bob came out of the control room and into the studio. He said quietly to the pickers, "Not as upfront and hard-driving as Waylon, and not quite as laid-back as Don Williams." At first, I was a little embarrassed and felt that the comparison with these superstars put me in a compromising situation. But as the session got underway, I realized that the man had created a niche for me. It worked for years.

We did two sessions back-to-back and the magic never stopped. Fred Carter Jr., who received a Grammy for his guitar work on *Bridge Over Troubled Water*, came up with some astounding acoustic guitar licks that I still use today. The "half-time feel" that carried on through many of my hit records was laid down by Jim Wolfe on drums. Many musicians in Canada will tell you that some of these records were the first by a Canadian artist to use that laid-back "half-time feel." You don't hear it used much today, but in those days, Joe Bob called it "the commercially-acceptable Dick Damron."

Gene Rice, Joe Bob, and all the pickers created a new career for me that night. After everyone was packed up, Gene made a rough copy of the tracks for me. It was already into the wee small hours and we were set to be back in the studio first thing in the morning to do my final vocal tracks. As we drove back into Nashville, we sat quietly. Joe Bob and I were both exhausted from the long but productive night. When he dropped me off at The Anchor, I mentioned that I would work on my vocals and be ready for the morning.

"No," he said. "You better rest your voice."

I said, "It's okay, I'll just sing the songs in my mind."

For the next few hours, I played the tape over and over, counting and marking bars, checking the structure of the measures in my phrasing with a few extra little notes where I sang too soft or too hard or lost my power or full voice. I knew I had a great session, and I wanted to live up to it. I finally hit the bed and slept with my clothes on, so I would be ready when Joe Bob showed up in the morning.

In the studio the next day, Gene set the levels with the tracks and my headphones. We tried a take. I saw Gene and Joe Bob nodding to each other in the control room. There was a moment's silence, and then Joe Bob said, "Come on in and listen. I don't think you can top that!"

"Singing in my mind" had paid off. We spent the next few hours doing the vocals and mixed the session the next day. The following day, I was on a plane to Toronto to play the tape for Marathon Records, a new independent label.

Everybody loved it and, in a few weeks, the first single *Mother, Love and Country* was released. It was an instant hit on almost every country music station in Canada. When it topped *RPM* magazine's country music Top Forty list, somebody in Nashville spotted the song on the charts and we had to scramble to come up with the money to pay the *demo session* off at full master scale.

Beechwood Music helped to raise half the cash (for half the publishing rights on the ten songs), and soon the SOLDIER OF FORTUNE album was released in Canada. It received rave reviews and was later released by Gordon Davies' Westwood Recordings in the U.K. to coincide with my first European tour, launching a whole new international career.

I returned to Nashville in 1976 to record the NORTH COUNTRY

SKYLINE album with *Susan Flowers, Waylon's T-shirt, Another Old Rodeo Song, If You Need Me Lord, North Country Blues*, and *Charing Cross Cowboys*. (*Charing Cross Cowboys* was written about the folks who hung out on Charing Cross Road in London and who sometimes showed up at our British concerts carefully disguised as country music fans, gunfighters and Confederate soldiers.) Joe Bob later produced LOST IN THE MUSIC, HIGH ON YOU, DICK DAMRON —HONKY TONK ANGEL, the guitar album NIGHT MUSIC, and THE LEGEND AND THE LEGACY, as well as my two Christian country albums: WINGS UPON THE WIND and TOUCH THE SKY.

Dick at T.J.'s (where The Ballad of T.J.'s *was born) during Fan Fair in 1980.*

The Stories Behind the Songs

THE BALLAD OF T.J.'S

One morning I read the following story in the daily *Nashville Tennessean*:

A Nashville guitarist was shot to death yesterday and four people wounded in a wild melee outside a nightclub — apparently because the bar's singer didn't know a requested song.

Homicide Lt. Sherman Nickens said three relatives drinking at T.J.'s bar asked entertainer Ge Haw to sing some of David Allan Coe's "laid back country material."

"They asked the singer to sing a song and he told them he was very sorry he didn't know it," said witness Robert Moore. "They told him to get off the stage and come outside and they'd teach him the song. The singer said he didn't want any trouble. Another man finally got them outside."

Moore said the shooting occurred a short time later when the band left the bar to go across the street to a restaurant. Police said they were approached by Donald Burton, 29, his wife Linda, 22, of Murfreesboro, and his brother Robert, 32, of LaVergne.

Police said Robert Burton allegedly opened fire with a pistol after band members allegedly brandished knives and slashed the Burton brothers.

Daryl Chapman, 30, lead guitarist of Haw's backup band, was shot and killed. Mrs. Burton said another band member, Wayne Kinkaid, 48, of Fairview, was wounded and the Burton brothers knifed.

The elder Burton was charged with murder and assault with intent to commit murder.

The headline read, "Guitarist Killed for Not Knowing Song." As I read the article, I envisioned Daryl Chapman lying in a pool of blood on Broadway in front of T.J.'s. Only a few nights before this, I had sat in the smoke-filled scum-bag bar on Nashville's "Lower Broad."

Never confuse the name "Broadway" in Nashville with the glamor of New York City's Broadway. Nashville's Broadway runs through the heart of old downtown Nashville and takes you out onto West End Boulevard. Lower Broad, as it is called, is a scant block from the Ryman Auditorium. It's lined with pawnshops, bad-ass bars where musicians play for tips, sex shops that peddle porno movies, a couple of guitar shops, Tootsie's Orchid Lounge, and Ernest Tubb's record shop. The streets are peopled with hookers, pushers, derelicts, singers and songwriters still holding onto some faded dream that sent them there from middle America.

At any given time, there could be a handful of tourists strolling the streets. Most of them are there because they were warned not to go there, and their natural curiosity lured them onto the scene. They walk the streets, stare through windows and open-doors into the hell-holes, and argue among themselves over whether it is safe to go inside. Most don't.

Police patrol cars constantly cruise the street. If you watch them drive by, you realize they are just making the rounds. The police seldom stop or leave the safety of the black-and-white chariots. They've seen it all, 24 hours a day, year in and year out. Their presence gives the tourists a false sense of security and they decide to go in for a drink and check it out. The time it takes to consume one drink, hear two songs, and experience the filth and degradation is well worth it. A few minutes later, they are back on the street, hailing a taxi and heading back to the safety of one of Nashville's better hotels. In the morning over coffee, they will tell their tour mates that they were down to Broad, and, it's really not all that bad. Their tour mates will tell them about the murder on Lower Broad that they saw on the late night tv news. And, yes, the police do actually get out of the black-and-whites. It has less to do with law and order and more to do with picking up the pieces.

Making a living playing these kind of bars is not really making a living at all. It is surviving 'til you get the big break. Almost every one of the "pickers" playing for tips in these "skull orchards" has a story for you. They used to play guitar with Willie. They wrote *Your Cheatin' Heart* and Hank Williams stole it from them. They are just playing there between road trips before they leave tomorrow on tour with Kenny Rogers. The tourists love these stories and can't wait to get home to tell the folks in small-town America that they had a drink with Willie Nelson's guitar player, and that they met the guy who really wrote *Your Cheatin' Heart*.

I laid the newspaper down, dug out a pen, took a napkin from the dispenser, and wrote *The Ballad Of T.J.'s*.

THE BALLAD OF T.J.'S

THE BARROOM WAS CROWDED AND THE BAND WAS GETTIN' HOT
WE WERE PLAYIN' IN THIS LITTLE DOWNTOWN BAR
WHEN THIS BIG OLD UGLY MAN
WITH A BOTTLE IN HIS HAND
WALKED UP TO THE BANDSTAND
AND HE SAID:

"PLAY SNAKES CRAWL AT NIGHT
OR I'M GONNA KILL YOU
PLAY OKIE FROM MUSKOGEE
OR YOU GONNA DIE
WE ALL WANT TO HEAR CRYSTAL CHANDELIERS
AND EVERY THING
OL' WAYLON EVER SANG..."

"WE DON'T DO REQUESTS
BUT SIR, I'LL DO MY BEST
TO PLAY MOST ANYTHING YOU WANT TO HEAR
THE BAND'S A LITTLE DRY AND BUDDY SO AM I
WE'LL PLAY 'EM, IF YOU BUY A 'ROUND OF BEER"

HE GRABBED MY OLD GUITAR
AND SMASHED IT AGAINST THE BAR
CAME AT ME WITH A BOTTLE IN HIS HAND
HE GRABBED ME BY THE COAT AND
WITH ONE HAND ON MY THROAT
HE LOOKED AT ME AND THIS IS
WHAT HE SAID:

"PLAY SNAKES CRAWL AT NIGHT
OR I'M GONNA KILL YOU
PLAY OKIE FROM MUSKOGEE
OR YOU GONNA DIE
WE ALL WANT TO HEAR CRYSTAL CHANDELIERS
AND EVERY THING
OL' WAYLON EVER SANG . . ."

© Sparwood Music

The background sounds on the recording were actually recorded live in that same bar. We took the tape into the studio and added it to the master recording. The background voices are a group of folks from Ottawa's Ramblin' Roads bus tour. If you listen closely, you can hear the voices of Hal Lee, Gerry O'Hara, and Bill Anderson of Canadian radio fame.

T.J.'s bar no longer exists. When I perform the song live on stage, I always tell the folks that the local improvement district "tore it down to build a slum."

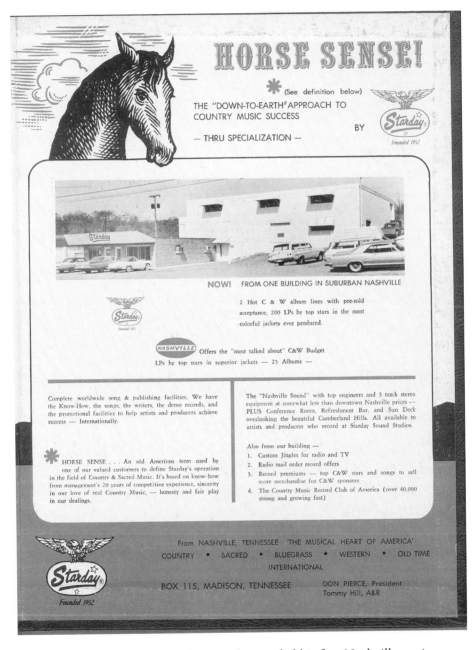

*Starday Sound Studios where Dick recorded his first Nashville sessions
in 1961 and 1963.*

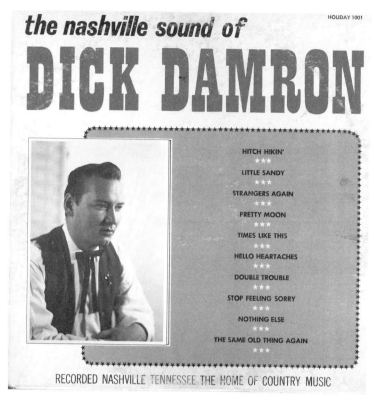

Cover of Dick's first album, 1965.

(Left) *Dick and his longtime producer Joe Bob Barnhill mixing* If London Were A Lady *in 1979 at Richey House.*

(Right) *Dick Damron at Joe Kozak's Korl Sound Studios, Edmonton, Alberta, 1968.*

108

Hangin' out on Nashville's Lower Broad outside the infamous Tootsie's Orchid Lounge (circa 1980).

During the 1970s some of the top names in Canadian Country stopped in to visit the CMA offices in Nashville. Left to right: Tommy Hunter, Don Grashey, Carroll Baker, Stan Campbell, Mike Graham, Dick Damron, and Barry Haugen.

Live at the Horseshoe Tavern, Toronto.

CHAPTER SIX

Lift Off

THE LONG GREEN LINE

ALL OF MY LIFE I'VE RAMBLED
FOLLOWING THE LONG GREEN LINE
TRYING TO MAKE A GREENBACK DOLLAR
BUT I NEVER SAVED A DIME
FOR A THOUSAND DAYS IN A THOUSAND WAYS
SEEKING FORTUNE'S GOLD
I NEVER GAVE A DAMN ABOUT LIFE
OR A PRETTY WOMAN TO HOLD
FOLLOWING THE LONG GREEN LINE
FOLLOWING THE LONG GREEN LINE
TRYING TO MAKE A GREENBACK DOLLAR
BUT I NEVER SAVED A DIME
FOLLOWING THE LONG GREEN LINE
FOLLOWING THE LONG GREEN LINE
ALL OF MY LIFE I'VE BEEN A HEARTLESS FOOL
FOLLOWING THE LONG GREEN LINE

Lift Off

Sometime in the early 1970s, I experienced lift-off. It's hard to pin-point, but my first feeling of any kind of recognition in the music biz came in 1968 with a Broadcast Music Inc. (BMI) Songwriter Award for *The Cold Grey Winds Of Autumn*:

THE COLD GREY WINDS OF AUTUMN
HAVE CHILLED OUR SUMMER LOVE.
I CAN FEEL THE WINTER COMING ON
AND THO YOU TELL ME OFTEN YOU'RE STILL IN LOVE WITH ME
I KNOW SOMEDAY I'LL WAKE AND YOU'LL BE GONE.

— *The Cold Grey Winds Of Autumn* © Glaser Publications

At this time, a number of artists began recording my songs. But my own recording career didn't really take off until the release of *Countryfied*, my first Number 1 record and a "Top Ten" international smash for George Hamilton IV.

I soon began to travel thousands of miles instead of hundreds. I performed on most of the major television shows, including *Tommy Hunter, Ronnie Prophet, George Hamilton IV, The Family Brown, Country Time*, the CBC Network show that originated in Halifax, and *90 Minutes Live* with Peter Gzowski.

Toronto became a focal point. I recorded there at the old RCA studio on Mutual Street with Gary Buck producing and all of Toronto's finest (musicians, not cops), pickers like Al Cherny (of the *Tommy Hunter Show*) and Red Shea (longtime guitarist with Gordon Lightfoot). On Sunday nights, I appeared at the "Boot Jamboree" held at the Locarno Ballroom.

I hung out in Toronto for a few weeks at a time and then flew back west to play the clubs and write songs. I wrote on planes, buses, in hotel rooms, backstage, and sometimes even on stage. As strange as it may seem, I can remember being on stage singing one song vocally and writing another one mentally. As soon as the show was over, I'd head backstage and copy the song down on whatever scrap of paper I could find. I never carried a notepad around with me. Somehow I felt that would be too premeditated and my songs might become jaded and contrived. It scared hell out of me later when I learned that some of the biggest chart songs of the day were contrived by two or three Nashville songwriters getting together in the back room of a publisher's office at 10:00 in the morning with a cup of coffee, a guitar, and a memo from their publisher: "A certain artist is recording at a certain studio on Monday morning. We need three up-tempo truck driving songs. We may have to give the artist a piece of the song and split the publishing with his label or producer, but see what you can come up with . . ." It blew my whole image of songwriting and songwriters and set me back a couple of years. I just knew that Hank and Willie and Lefty and Jimmie Rodgers and Wilf Carter hadn't done it that way and, goddamnit, I couldn't or wouldn't do it that way either.

As recently as 1991, at a songwriter's workshop/seminar in Vancouver, a roomful of young, aspiring songwriters were told that nobody should ever write alone. I had to bite my tongue to keep from asking the panel of publishers if that also meant that nobody should ever publish a song alone. You see, no matter how many writers there are, the publisher takes 50 per cent. The other 50 per cent is divided among the writers. This is not to say that a lot of great songs haven't been co-written, but a lot of the Hank Williams, Willie Nelson, and Kris Kristofferson songs will still be around long after the one-chart-wonders have faded into oblivion.

In 1973, I played the Horseshoe Tavern in Toronto. This was the big time to me. In Canadian country music, at that time, the Horseshoe was "it." The magic was there. It was so unselfish and so unpretentious. I went there to see artists and friends like The Family Brown and Colleen Peterson, as well as many of the Nashville names. One time when I played there, I followed Bobby Bare, and the week after Dottie West took the stage. In later years, Dottie West and I did the *Tommy Banks* television show together.

One week when I performed at the Horseshoe, I worked with Gary Buck's band, Loose Change, with Keith MacKay on lead guitar, Ken Near on steel, George Pasher on bass, and Roy Feener on drums. Gene McClellan came in to catch the show. I felt it was a great compliment to have a writer of his stature, who had written songs like *Snowbird* and *Put Your Hand In The Hand*, coming in to listen to my music.

DJ's from CFGM came in just to say "hello," and writers from the dailies came in to review the show. Walt Grealis of *RPM*, Canada's first music magazine, came in and reviewed the show. And just because we were all part of the magic. No media hype. No record company bash. No free drinks or freebees. It just happened. We were all in this thing together. But those days are gone forever, and nobody cares. Like Paul Harvey says, "Today in America, one gunshot is louder than a thousand prayers." We have lost our innocence. Motives have replaced our ability to dream.

Then the outward spiral began. Looking back, I can see it all. At the time it was all in a day's work. Things just seemed to follow that natural chain of events.

Rise And Shine followed *Countryfied* right to the top of the charts. Then I signed with CBS and *Long Green Line, Goin' Home To The Country, The Prophet,* and *Bittersweet Songs* all charted. Next came *The Cowboy And The Lady* on Broadland Records. Other artists such as Hank Smith had number one records with songs I had written. *The Final Hour, Sweet Dreams Of Yesterday,* and *Sharing The Good Life* all topped the charts. The late, great Orval Prophet recorded *Countryfied, Rise and Shine,* and *Eastbound Highway.* Other songs were recorded by Gary Buck, the Allen Sisters, and the Rhythm Pals (who were regulars on the *Tommy Hunter Show*). Lynn Jones charted with *Total Destruction.* R. Harlan Smith recorded *I Remember Love.* Everybody who was anybody was recording my material.

The Stories Behind the Songs

COUNTRYFIED

Countryfied is definitely the most commercially successful song I have ever written, and undoubtedly did more for my career than any other single song. It has been recorded by countless other artists around the world. It was used as a television theme and included in a number of compilation albums, including the READER'S DIGEST 20 ALL-TIME GREATEST COUNTRY SONGS, which put it into millions of homes in the U.S. and Canada. *Countryfied* has been recorded and released in almost every English-speaking country in the world, as well as Holland, Belgium, and Germany.

COUNTRYFIED

I DON'T CARE WHO KNOWS IT, MAN
I'M COUNTRYFIED
I LOVE THE COUNTRYSIDE
LIKE CHICKEN, COUNTRY-FRIED
AND I COULDN'T BE A CITY SLICKER
EVEN IF I TRIED
I LOVE THE COUNTRY WAY OF LIFE

I'M THE KIND OF GUY
THAT LIKES TO WATCH A RIVER FLOW
SEE THE GREEN GRASS GROW
FEEL A WARM BREEZE BLOW
HERE'S A LITTLE SOMETHING
I THOUGHT YOU'D LIKE TO KNOW
I LOVE THE COUNTRY WAY OF LIFE

© Beechwood Music

The first half of the song came to me in a flash one night as I was driving to a gig in Lethbridge. Months later, I was at Korl Sound Studios in Edmonton, a small studio owned and operated by

Joe Kozak, a cigar-smoking character, engineer, and a great friend who helped me through one of the toughest times in my life. I was recording songs for prospective artists looking for new songs. I knew *Countryfied* was not complete. At that time, I called the song *The Country Way Of Life*. I started singing the song with my guitar and, all of a sudden, it was complete. The words just rolled out as I sang.

I put *The Country Way Of Life* on tape and sent it to my publisher, Beechwood Music, in Toronto, Ontario. Back then, Gary Buck was heading up Beechwood Music, the publishing arm of Capital Records, and I had recently signed a songwriter's contract with them.

At that particular time, I was depressed, strung out on all kinds of prescription drugs, recently separated, and emotionally screwed up. I was sleeping on the floor in the back room of the small basement studio, playing the "sewer circuit," so named by a guitar player to describe the fleabag, slum hotels I was performing at in Edmonton. It was only a few months since my father's death and my drummer's suicide. I felt I was not far behind. I was writing songs like *The Final Hour, Escape,* and *The End:*.

I SEE THE SHADOW OF THE BRIDGE
BEFORE ME. A FEW MORE TORTURED
STEPS AND THE GOOD-BYE.
I HAVEN'T GOT THE STRENGTH TO LIVE
WITHOUT YOU. BUT AT LAST, THANK GOD,
I'M NOT AFRAID TO DIE.

— *The End* © Beechwood Music

I believe all those songs were on the same tape as *The Country Way Of Life*. When Gary Buck received the tape at his Toronto publishing office, he phoned and excitedly told me there was a "hit song" on the tape.

In the state of mind I was in, I found it hard to get excited. However, I was hoping that the "hit song" he was referring to was one of my negative, self-pitying suicidal ballads. Then, the whole world of country music would know how I felt. After all, wasn't that what songwriting was all about?

When he said the song in question was *Countryfied*, it took me a minute to get over my immediate disappointment and another minute to realize that the song he referred to as *Countryfied* was "Country Way of Life."

A few weeks later, when I was in Toronto to pick up my first BMI songwriter award for *Cold Grey Winds Of Autumn*, Gary Buck produced the recording session and I sang an acceptable, but uninspired, version of *Countryfied*. Within two months, it was released and made it to Number 1 on *RPM* magazine's National Country Music Charts. George Hamilton IV included it on his NORTH COUNTRY album along with songs by Gordon Lightfoot, Joni Mitchell, and Leonard Cohen.

When *Countryfied* was lifted from the midst of all those great songs by some of our greatest songwriters and released as the first single from George's album and again went to Number 1, my career as a songwriter sky-rocketed and the rest, as they say, is history.

TOP 50 RPM

COUNTRY

1	2	**COUNTRYFIED** Dick Damron-Apex-77110-J (Damron) BMI	MAPL
2	1	**ME AND BOBBY McGEE** Gordon Lightfoot Reprise-0926-P	MAPL
3	3	**FOR THE GOOD TIMES** Ray Price-Columbia-45178-H	
4	4	**YOU WANNA GIVE ME A LIFT** Loretta Lynn-Decca-23693-J	
5	7	**MULE SKINNER BLUES** Dolly Parton-RCA-9863-N	
6	6	**SNOWBIRD** Anne Murray-Capitol-72623-F (Maclellan) Beechwood-BMI	MAPL
7	8	**ODE TO SUBURBIA** Bob Smith-Apex-77112-J (Smith) BMI	MAPL

Backstage Ladies

The term "backstage lady" was refined from the rock and roll groupie thing, where most of the groupies were the younger, wilder, crazier, teeny-boppers, who screamed, cried, fainted, and then threw their panties and bras at their current rock stars. Backstage ladies in the country music field were usually older, more mature women, who hung around backstage after the show just so they could find out where the "action" was on any given night. The fact that many of our shows were in clubs and bars kept the age of these young ladies above the legal drinking age. Many of them were plain old country music fans or discarded wives and girl friends from the bands who had gone on before.

Although I have been credited or blamed with coining the phrase "backstage ladies," I am sure that it is only because of the fact that I wrote and recorded the song, and thus brought the term into wider use in country music circles. Not long after the song hit the charts, a young female country columnist in Ottawa changed her column in *Capital Country News* (now known as *Country Music News*) to "The Backstage Lady."

I LOVE THOSE BACKSTAGE LADIES.

THEY'RE THE BACKBONE OF OUR NATION

WHEN YOU'RE ON THE ROAD, THEY GIVE YOU CONSTANT INSPIRATION

SOFT AND SOOTHIN'. EASY MOVIN' WHEN YOU NEED SOME LOVIN'

YOU LOVE THOSE BACKSTAGE LADIES MOST OF ALL

THEY'RE HANGIN' OUT IN HOUSTON. STRUNG OUT IN L.A.

I KNOW THREE IN CALGARY AND TWO IN THUNDER BAY

BUT THE ONES I KNOW IN OLD T.O. GOT ALL THE COMBINATIONS

I LOVE THOSE BACKSTAGE LADIES MOST OF ALL

SO DRINK A TOAST TO ALL THE BACKSTAGE LADIES OF OUR NATION

AND ALL THE COUNTRY DJ'S OUT AT ALL THOSE COUNTRY STATIONS

WHO CAREFULLY TAKE CARE OF ALL THOSE LADIES THAT WE KNOW
'TIL WE GET A HIT AND GET BACK ON THE ROAD

— *Backstage Ladies* © Beechwood/Sparwood Music

I always promoted the cause at my shows with this little spiel: "Here's a brand new song I just wrote for all the ropers, dopers, users, and boozers and especially all the backstage ladies. I didn't want to call them groupies or snuff queens, so I just call them backstage ladies. Have we got any backstage ladies out there tonight? Say, yeah!"

A few voices would bounce back from the crowd.

"Have we got any ladies who would like to audition for the part? Say, yeah!"

Dozens and sometimes hundreds would scream, "Yeah!"

When my show was over, a few of the new recruits would make their way backstage and, as they say, the rest is history.

At the Tradewinds Hotel in Calgary during Stampede Week, a young wife had a spat with her husband and he took off and left her. She went to the hotel desk, told them she was my wife, and they gave her a key. Then she went up to my room. Later, when I returned to the room, she had taken her lipstick and written "Dickie Damron I love you" all over the walls and mirrors. Needless to say, the management was not impressed.

Another time, at the same hotel a year or two later, I loaned my room to a fellow musician and a new recruit. When she left the room, after the horizontal recreation, she took $6,000 of my hard-earned cash along with her. I remember a scary little incident when a backstage lady, on our first encounter, asked to use the phone by the bed. I thought she was calling her babysitter or a friend. "Hi honey," she said. "I'm spending the night with Dick Damron at the 'Cozy Inn'. I'll see you in the morning."

When she hung up the phone, I asked, "Who was that?"

"Oh, my husband," she replied. "We have an open relationship."

As the late-Sixties faded into the Seventies, the backstage ladies in my life changed completely, or maybe I just came to my senses or became a little older and a little wiser. Softer, gentler ladies entered and re-entered my life. "Backstage lady" took on a whole new meaning.

Always a Lady

The hospitality suite at the Inn on the Park, in Toronto, had been packed all night. People stood shoulder to shoulder, most with a drink in one hand and a cigarette in the other. This made it very difficult to carry on the music biz ritual of shaking hands with and slapping the backs of every male entering the room and hugging, kissing, and squeezing the opposite sex at every opportunity. The people stood all night, partly to circulate among the crowd and partly because there were less than a dozen chairs for the hundred or so people who had jammed into the room. But, hey, it was the once-a-year country bash in Canada, not yet known as "Country Music Week," but on its way and growing year by year.

The sun began to brighten the room as the crowd finally thinned to about a dozen people and the almost unbearable level of noise decreased. I spotted an empty chair and sat down for the first time in hours. I glanced at my watch. It was after five, and I was burnt out.

It could have been from the drinks and tokes earlier that afternoon, the few bottles of wine at the Awards Dinner, the 15 or 20 Bacardi and Sevens I had consumed in the suite, or the half-dozen trips we'd made to adjoining suites to do a joint or snort a line or two of coke. I'm sure it had nothing to do with the straight shots of tequila a guitar-pickin' friend of mine and I had done that afternoon, nor the afternoon delight I had experienced with the record company secretary, who swore she had always wanted to meet me.

It was time to get out of there. Then, across the room, I saw this lady. I had spotted her a time or two earlier in the evening. She was always with the same young man, so I quickly moved on to other prospects. But just as I noticed that she was still there sitting beside the same guy, she rose and walked directly toward me, sat down on my knee, and slid her left arm around my neck.

She was small, warm, beautiful, and reminded me of a miniature Barbra Streisand. When she spoke, I thought I would fall through the chair. In the purest Tennessee accent I had heard since my last trip to Nashville, she said, "I'm Linda and you're Dick, right?"

She sat on my knee for a few minutes, alternately sipping from her wine glass, puffing on a cigarette, and making small talk. Then she asked directly if I had a room in the hotel, motioned to her male friend to come over, and sent him down to get her bag from the car.

When he returned, she introduced him to me, said he was from Kingsport, Tennessee, and told him to call her at noon. She quickly explained that they were "just good friends." They had come up to Toronto from Tennessee a couple of years ago and went everywhere together. We shook hands and he said good-bye.

Linda and I made our way out of the suite and down the hall, bouncing off the walls and into the elevator. We got off on the wrong floor and stood there laughing as we waited for the elevator to come back.

Then we were in my room. She disappeared into the bathroom and I fell back on the bed. I must have dozed off for a minute. I woke with a start to see her standing by the bed. The first thing I noticed were the bare white feet, with toes slightly curled into the lush carpet. She had taken her hair down and removed the belt from her slinky dress. She was gorgeous and I was breathless.

When I reached out a hand toward her, she slowly stepped back, producing a bottle of wine in one hand. Opening the palm of her other hand she revealed a joint of marijuana. I raised up on the bed and kicked my boots off while she poured the wine and held out the joint for me to light. In the next few minutes we sipped at the Sauvignon, smoked the joint, laughing and joking all the time.

I lay back on the bed while she slipped my t-shirt over my head and fumbled to undo the big silver belt buckle that served to hold up my ragged blue jeans. When I realized she wasn't making much headway in her battle with the buckle, I ran my left hand down and popped it open with one easy motion of my thumb. She slowly slid my jeans down over my thighs, my knees, my ankles, and then I heard the buckle hit the floor.

She turned out the lights, opened the curtains and let the early morning sunlight fall across the room. She crawled up onto the big fluffy king-size bed and stretched herself full-length on top of me. I realized she had nothing on under the fine silky dress as I felt her warm, firm breasts and perfectly formed body pressing against me. She looked into my eyes for what seemed like forever and then she began kissing me on the lips. Her long dark hair fell down around me. I closed my eyes and breathed heavily.

I raised my arms and wrapped them around her with my whole body tingling and trembling. She raised her dress over me, straddled my hips, and lowered herself slowly. She moved up and down with the rhythm of a ballad. And so we drifted into the Toronto morning.

Hours later, the phone rang. She reached for it and sleepily said, "Thanks, Steve. Would you call J. Michaels and tell them I won't be in today?"

It was weeks before I saw Linda again. I was in Nashville, recording. I phoned and told her I could change my flight and come back through Toronto. She sounded excited and gave me her address. She lived in a small upstairs loft on Church Street. She had no doorbell so I was to throw stones or coins at the upstairs window and she would come down and let me in.

When I flew in to Toronto International, it was after midnight and pouring rain. I caught a cab to her address. I climbed out of the cab and stood in the rain with my guitar and suitcase, and began throwing dimes, nickels and quarters at the upstairs window. Finally one connected with a clink and the light came on. Moments later, we were standing in the downstairs hallway, clinging to each other, me in my sopping wet clothes, and her in her bare feet, panties, and bra. We stood that way for a long time, then made our way upstairs and into bed, where we drank wine, smoked a joint and made love 'til morning.

After that, we were together whenever I was in Toronto. She developed a real Dick Damron cult following, among them a hooker, a photographer, and one of her ex-boyfriends who happened to be a country music fan. They would go around to clubs and music business functions wearing t-shirts that said, "Waylon, Willie, and Dick Who?" When I played Regina, Winnipeg, Ottawa, or any place within easy flying distance, she would join me for Friday night and Saturday. On Sunday, she would fly back to Toronto and I would be on a plane to my next gig.

I was playing the National Arts Centre in Ottawa with Carroll Baker and The Family Brown. Linda flew over from Toronto and met me after the show. We went to the Chateau Laurier where I was staying, drank two bottles of wine, a bottle of white rum, and after stuffing wet towels around the hotel room door, smoked our brains out. We made love 'til morning, when she caught a cab to the airport.

I was drunk, stoned, and only half-awake when she said goodbye. I thought, "Shit, I need some sleep if I'm going to fly back to Alberta later today," so I took a few sleeping pills and crawled back into bed. A few hours later I woke up deathly ill. I couldn't raise myself up, so I rolled off the bed and half-stumbled and half-crawled to the bathroom. I was sick for a long time. Then I fell asleep on the cold marble floor and slept right through my plane time.

A few months later, I was returning from a grueling six-week tour of Europe. I phoned Linda from the ferry that ran from Dover, England, to Ostend, Belgium. I told her I was flying from Amsterdam to Toronto on my way back to Alberta and I would like to see her when I got to Toronto. She seemed strange on the phone but said to call her at work from the airport.

When the big 747 arrived in T.O., I rushed to the phone. After a few minutes, she explained that she had married a rich doctor with a family from a former marriage, and although it wasn't working out very well, she couldn't meet me. I said, "Okay. I'll check in at the Skyline and fly out tomorrow."

I picked up my bags and was on my way out of the airport when I glanced up at the Read-O-Gram. There was a flight to Calgary in about an hour. I went to the desk and managed to get on it. I checked in my bags, my banjo and my guitar, and was in the Departure Lounge when an announcement came over the loudspeaker: "Mr. Dick Damron, please pick up the white telephone."

It was Linda. "Where are you?" she said, "I'm waiting for you at the Skyline."

I told her I was on my way back to Alberta. We both talked and cried on the phone until they announced my flight.

I boarded Air Canada to Calgary and I never saw her again.

A BACKSTAGE LADY
IS ALWAYS A LADY.
SHE IS ALWAYS GENTLE ON YOUR MIND
SHE IS READY TO PICK YOU UP
AT THE AIRPORT
SHE IS READY TO DRIVE YOU TO THE AIRPORT
CELEBRATE THE GOOD TIMES
HELP YOU THROUGH THE HARD TIMES.
BE THERE WHEN YOU NEED HER
GIVE YOU SPACE WHEN YOU NEED IT.
SHE HAS THE CLASS TO MAKE
YOU PROUD AT THE AWARDS SHOW.
SHE WILL FLY HALF-WAY AROUND
THE WORLD IF YOU NEED HER
LOVE YOU FROM A DISTANCE
HER WARM, GENTLE
FEMININE SENSITIVITY CAN
SOOTH YOUR WOUNDED SOUL WHEN
NOTHING ELSE WILL WORK
SHE WILL HELP YOU DREAM YOUR DREAMS
SHE WILL KISS AWAY THE HURT
LOVE AWAY YOUR LONELINESS
HELP YOU MAKE IT THROUGH THE NIGHT
PHONE YOU IN THE MIDDLE OF THE MIDDLE
OF THE NIGHT FROM
THE OTHER SIDE OF WORLD
JUST TO SEE IF YOU'RE OKAY
SEND YOU AN ALBUM REVIEW FROM
HER LOCAL PAPER
AND MOST OF ALL SHE IS A KINDRED SPIRIT

*AND A FRIEND WHEN WE NEED EACH OTHER'S
FRIENDSHIP THE MOST*

— *Backstage Ladies (Reprise)*

Seven-Day-A-Week Bar Musician

A threadbare lime-green chenille bedspread. A battered old 19-inch black and white television with a bent and twisted coat hanger for an antenna. A toilet that won't flush and a shower that won't stop dripping. A window frame filled solid with bricks and mortar where there used to be a glass pane. Home sweet home for the road musician.

Along with these luxurious accommodations comes a double order of shit and abuse from the owner/manager/bartender of the sleazy old hotel. He's so goddamned miserable, he can't even stand himself. I guess he wasn't always that way. Maybe he got that way from spending his life running places just like this one. From getting punched in the mouth trying to break up barroom brawls. From getting hit on by his barmaids, puked on by drunks and fucked over by agents and bands and musicians that don't pay their tabs or their long distance calls when they leave.

He's quick to tell you that bands are the scum of the earth. Over the years, they have stolen everything that wasn't nailed down, wrecked everything that wasn't already wrecked in the band rooms. Burned down a club he owned in northern British Columbia. Screwed his wife and ran off with his teenaged daughter. There's not a helluva lot left of his so-called sense of humor. He hates bands, but disco's dead and strippers bring in a crowd of pimps and bikers and punks and whores who are sometimes — not always, but sometimes — run by big city operators who send out thugs to collect debts, settle disputes, and work people over when telephone threats won't do. He hates bands but they are, he thinks, the lesser of all evils.

Then some agent lies to him and tells him a better class of entertainment will bring in a better class of customer. That's when I show up. And the stage is set for instant replay and another magic moment in show biz.

Why did I take this gig? I took it because that's the way I do things. I took it because I had this week open. I took it because it paid $600. I took it because I'm Dick Damron and, even after all these years, I still don't know any better.

Dawson Creek, British Columbia, is located at mile zero of the famed Alaska Highway. At mile 49, the small northern city of Fort St. John stands in the heart of the British Columbia oilfields. In the early Seventies, drilling rigs, pipelines, gas plants, and the giant eighteen-wheelers worked day and night producing the black gold that created a wealth never before seen in that area. Roughnecks, truck drivers, and oilfield workers were making big money and they needed a place to spend it.

Two brothers bought an old bakery. They stuck a bar in one corner and built a rickety stage in another. This makeshift bar (known as "The Copper King" and often confused with The Kopper King in Whitehorse, Yukon) was a goldmine. The party never stopped. A week-long booking at The Copper King was like a month in any other bar. A two-week booking was an eternity.

I played The Copper King a half-dozen times during this period. Hank Smith, Reg Ault, Terry Lepard, and I drove the 500 mile skating rink from Edmonton to Fort St. John with all our equipment and four bodies jammed into Hank's aging Volkswagon hatchback and Terry's shiny new Pinto. We stayed at the luxurious Forty-Niner Motel at first, and later moved to "The Band House," carefully disguised as a slum lord's nightmare. Hank, with the insight of his German ancestry, affectionately named it "The Bunker." The name stuck until it burned to the ground one fifty-below-zero night a few years later.

There was a first-rate barroom brawl every night. When the bouncers ended up pushing half the crowd out the back door into the sub-zero sub-arctic night, they locked the doors to keep them from coming back in. There was a constant stream of "love affairs" between the bands, the barmaids, the bouncers, and the strippers. The club-owner's son was the local drug dealer. The R.C.M.P. were always at the club investigating "isolated incidences" and "inside jobs." The narcs were always at the band house checking out the band. When the local Curling Club decided to hire some of the dancers, strippers from The Copper King, to entertain at their Stag Night, the Mounties raided the party when it was in full swing. The girls were stuck on the first flight out of town and a number of the "party-ers" were charged with gross indecency. When the names of the locals were printed in the next day's newspaper, they read like a list of "Who's Who" in the northern city. The same City Fathers who were constantly trying to close The Copper King down became silent.

Too many all-night parties, too much creative book-keeping, and too many break ins and robberies (that were later found to be staged by the owner's son) eventually caused The Copper King to close its doors, forever. We were one of the last bands to play there, and I still have a bouncy little cheque as a souvenir of the night Hank Smith, wearing his beautifully-tailored white western suit, was tarred and feathered with Puffed Wheat and Grenadine. And the night the club-owners chased me all over the club with a long, shiny butcher knife from the kitchen, trying to cut off my shoulder-length hair, so I would look presentable on the *Tommy Hunter Show* the following week.

In those days the road warriors, those who scratched a meager living from the Canadian club circuit and criss-crossed the country in rusted-out vans and battered old yellow school buses, had a saying that you should never book a gig in any place that started with "Fort", "Saint" or "Prince." Fort St. John was a double "No, no." But, certainly, names and geography had little to do with it. Agents who booked bands-they-had-never-heard into places-they-had-never-seen always contributed to the nightmare of playing the "sewer circuit," as we called it back then.

But I loved them all. The guy who kicked down my hotel room door in Kirkland Lake and stuck a knife under my chin is every bit as dear to me as the guy who tried to pay me half my wages with Valium tabs out of the huge bottle in the office safe in a Toronto nightclub. And the bartender, who beat his wife senseless in an underground parking lot in Kenora, Ontario, is as much a favorite of mine as the jealous guy who stalked me with a rifle for three days. And the agent who did his best to get me canceled out of a week-long gig when I was 2500 miles from home with a five-piece band to pay is now gone — gone, but not forgotten.

First West Germany Tour (1972)

From the time when we first started playing small country dances back in the 1950s, there has always been magic in travel. The further we were away from the home town, the more freedom we felt. We played with a new-found energy and were almost always well-accepted by the crowds. As the years flew by, the circle widened to include every little town in central Alberta, and eventually to every province in Canada. In the early 1960s, there were the Nashville trips and a brief stint in U.S. nightclubs.

Our first shot at international touring came in 1972, when I joined up with Hank Smith, John Berg, Roy Warhurst, Elmer Tippe, and Paddy Smith for a swing through West Germany. The Young Canadians, a Calgary Stampede song-and-dance group, was also on the tour. We flew from Calgary to Frankfurt and covered the Autobahn from one end of the country to the other, playing Beer Fests, Wine Fests, Oktoberfests, and every other kind of "fest" known to "Germankind."

We played Frankfurt, Stuttgart, Munich, Heidelberg, Bingen on Rhine, Schlitz, and made a few side trips to places like Hank Smith's home town of Garmisch Partenkirchen, and the Dachau concentration camp. Our afternoon in the Dachau camp hung in my mind for a long time. Most of the memorabilia of the German war atrocities was perfectly preserved — the lampshades made of human skin, the torture machines, the ovens, the quarters that were designed for hundreds, and held thousands, as they awaited the "final solution." In the middle of the square stood a huge bronze statue depicting the pile of human remains discovered by the liberation forces. Arms, legs, skulls, and skeletons were piled high. And under it all, a plaque that read, "Let this be a lesson to the world of what can happen when too much power falls into the hands of the wrong people." I was amazed at the reaction of the members of our small group. There was shock, disbelief, revulsion and, if you can believe it, even justification. The phrase that still echoes in my mind whenever I think about that day is "Man's Inhumanity to Man."

The tour continued. We saw the beautiful Mosel Valley, the huge vineyards that have produced some of the finest wines in the world. It was hard to believe that this incredibly scenic country had staged World War II. I could still hear the old radio back home in the farmhouse at Bentley. Dad would never miss the late news. For an eight-year-old-boy, the voice of Lorne Greene speaking the names of German leaders — Hitler, Goering, Himmler and Goebbels — would echo eerily after I went to bed. I would lie awake at night thinking German tanks, Messerschmidts, and goose-stepping soldiers were in every dark corner of my upstairs bedroom. Now here in Germany, where road signs and city names would correspond with World War II memories, I would close my eyes and envision the guns and tanks rolling through the countryside. I could hear the gunfire and the bombs exploding all around me. Strangely enough, these visions were all in black and white. Then I realized that my source of reference was the black and white newsreel footage which we always saw after the cartoons and before Roy Rogers, Gene Autry, or Hopalong Cassidy took the screen in the Bentley Community Hall that served as our only theater two nights a week. When I opened my eyes and began watching that landscape unfold back from the Autobahn and the window of our speeding tour bus, I was again struck dumb by the beauty of that country.

We were taken to see the East-West German border. It was stunning. I somehow had expected to see a high wire fence and a helmeted soldier as depicted in *Stalag 17, Hogan's Heroes* and old World War II films. The demarcation line, as it was described on the sheet of paper that was handed to each of us, showed details of the excavation where the highway used to be. Electrically-charged fences, high concrete walls with gun turrets stretched along the top, all manned by groups of soldiers with huge machine guns trained on us. There were guard dogs leashed to a wire that allowed them to travel 90 feet up and down the base of the wall. They never stood still. Our guides cautioned us to be very calm, move slowly and to stay well back of the 15 meter limit. The piece of paper read, "Any waving, shouting or trying to make contact with anyone on the other side of the wall will be considered a provocation and you will be shot."

Today, the Berlin wall is history. I have no reason to return. The small boy will always see the black and white newsreel tanks, the guns, the soldiers, the concentration camps and the bodies. In my mind, I try only to remember the wine, the food, the friendly people, my music echoing in the town square, the courtyard of Heidelberg Castle, the streets of Bingen on Rhine, and the huge parades with thousands of people dancing in the streets as they made their way to the gigantic circus tents, where we played for their beer fest. They danced, laughed, consumed enormous amounts of the rich German beer, and clapped and screamed with delight to the sounds of our Canadian country music.

First U.K. Tour (1976)

As we broke through the cloud cover, a tiny patch of green sprang up from the Atlantic Ocean. The captain's voice, in that official airline tone, informed us that we were getting our first glimpse of the western coastline of Ireland. As every Irish song has told us, it is the greenest green you'll ever see. You have to use the word "emerald" to describe it . . . The Emerald Isle. A minute or two later, the heavy cloud cover surrounded us again, and the next time we broke through the clouds, we were making our final descent into Heathrow International Airport, on the outskirts of London, England.

It looked cold, gray, and uninviting. The fog, smog, and rain seemed to engulf us. Unlike the fluffy white clouds that we had flown through at our higher altitude, we were in the soup. As we came in low, I could see vehicles splashing along the motorways. They were jammed bumper to bumper and lined up as far as I could see from the window of the descending 747. Minutes later we touched down and began taxiing to the terminal. Eight and one-half hours in the air and an eight-hour time change left me feeling wrecked. Now I had to hope my guitar and banjo and luggage had all arrived with me . . . and that the guitar and banjo would still be in one piece.

My work permit had not come through in time for them to mail it to me. It was supposed to be waiting for me to pick up on my arrival. It had taken months of phone calls, sending documents back and forth, and general bureaucratic red tape to arrange the permit. I hoped it would be at the airport.

As I picked up my hand luggage, my hat, and denim jacket from the overhead compartment, a voice on the intercom said:

"Joseph Glenn Damron, please identify yourself to the purser." As I left the aircraft, the purser handed me a large brown envelope. At last and, just in time, I had my work permit.

I made my way down the long Heathrow hallways, on and off escalators, through doors, and down stairs. As I reached Immigration, I opened my work permit, ready to present it to the officer. He waved me through, not even looking at the document. I hesitated. "I have a work permit."

"You don't have any guns or dope, do you, mate?" he asked. He didn't wait for an answer, just waved me through. "Have a go, have a go."

The Mike and Margaret Story agency was promoting the tour, and John Carlton, who worked for them, picked us up at the massive airport and drove us through the traffic-congested streets of soggy old London town and north to Kettering.

My traveling companion, the lady in my life at the time, was Darlene Morray, a beautiful young lady with long, blonde hair, ragged blue jeans and a hippie attitude. She had come west from Toronto to Calgary to escape the wrath of Toronto's drug culture and a large dysfunctional family that had almost got her down. We had met in Calgary at the Stampede, where I was performing and she was working as a cocktail waitress. After a short, stormy relationship, we ended up living together for over seven years. This was my first major tour of the U.K., and her first time out of Canada. We had no idea what to expect or how to deal with it.

As we drove north towards Kettering, we talked with John, stared at the rain-soaked countryside, and nodded off from the lack of sleep. When we reached our destination, we were met by Dave Anderson, the guitar player with the band Colorado, which was booked to back me on the tour. As we transferred my guitar, banjo, and our luggage into Dave's vehicle, John handed me a tape and said, "This is for the band." I instantly recognized the tape. I had sent it over, six weeks earlier. It was a tape of all the music I would be performing on the shows. It had been sent to the agency to be forwarded to the band, so they could learn the songs. Dave confirmed my worst fears. The band had not heard the tape, nor learned any of my music. We had 200 miles to travel, no rehearsal time, and a show to do that night.

We arrived just in time to set up and do a sound check. With no rehearsal, I gave the band a list of the songs I would be performing, with the keys and the tempos marked beside each song. I told them I would start the ballads cold with my guitar and they could join in. The up-tempo songs I would count in and we would just vamp on the intros.

The show was horrible. Thank God it was a small crowd and no one really seemed to care. Not even the band. I found out how little they cared the next day when we finally did find time to rehearse. The tape was a studio copy of my Nashville sessions and they immediately dismissed it as "rubbish," a favorite British word used to describe anything they didn't know or understand. When a diminished or minor went by — or any chord they didn't know — they would look at the floor, look at the ceiling, adjust their amps, or make wisecracks amongst themselves. I realized it was useless.

I rewrote the show list with about ten of the straightest songs I could do. From then on, the show consisted of talking about songs, country music, Canada, the day's events, and doing those ten songs. Inside I was sick, sober, embarrassed, and dying a slow death. Outwardly I raised hell, and the more outrageous it was the better they liked it. Somehow we got through 26 shows in 26 nights.

From Land's End to John O' Groats, we ran up and down the motorways, seven of us jammed into the band's beat-up old Bedford van. It was cold and damp. The heater didn't work in the van and it never quit raining. About halfway through the tour, Gordon Davies, a tall strapping Welshman, owner and operator of Westwood Recordings, and his sidekick Tony Lee, convinced me I should go to Gordon's home at the Camp Farm in Montgomery, Mid Wales, for the night, and they would deliver me to the gig the following night. Gordon's Westwood record label had released my SOLDIER OF FORTUNE album to coincide with the tour, so we could pick up some more copies to sell on the road. We transferred our luggage from the Bedford van to Westwood's Volkswagen van.

It was just as cold and just as damp, but there were only four of us instead of seven. Darlene and I bundled up in the back with two or three old blankets that were used to cover the dozens of boxes of albums. We were off to Wales.

Tony Lee drove through the night. It was breaking dawn when

we passed through the British town of Shrewsbury, on to the west and across the border in to Wales. The Westwood van chugged up the narrow roads into the high hills. The roads I had traveled in Canada and the U.S. were built on high grades, with ditches on either side to carry away the snow and rain run-off. In Wales, it seemed like we drove in a sunken trench, with high stone fences and hedge rows on each side. We saw nothing except the hedge and stone walls flashing by the windows. In most places, the road was too narrow to pass or to meet another vehicle without pulling over against the side and stopping. But there was virtually no traffic at this time of the morning. And the old van moved slowly through the early morning rain and up the steep hills leading through Montgomery to the Camp Farm where Gordon lived and operated Westwood Recordings.

We were now about ten miles from Montgomery, and had been climbing, twisting and turning up, up and up. After passing through the tiny village, Tony swung the van to the right and almost stalled it on the steep grade. He geared down and we crawled the last hundred yards up the rocky driveway and in to the Camp Farm.

Darlene and I were so stiff and cold that it was an effort to crawl out of the van, drag our bags out of the back, and make our way into the huge old stone house perched on top of one of the highest hills in the area. Over the years, I have returned there many times. It's always raining. The huge spruce trees that surround the house are buffeted and bent by the strong winds that sweep through the Welsh countryside.

By now it was 5:30 in the morning. The night before we had had no sleep at all, as we had traveled with the band all the way from the south of England up to Great Yarmouth. Gordon showed us up the narrow steps and into a small, unheated bedroom. There was one tiny window, and the wind and rain beat mercilessly on the outside and howled through the inside. We closed the door, kicked off our boots, and crawled into bed with all our clothes on. We put the pillows over our heads, huddled together, and shivered our way to sleep. I had lost count of how many nights it had been since we'd had a hot shower and a warm bed.

Some time between 6:00 a.m. and 9:00 a.m. we managed to sleep. Then we were up and off to Birmingham. Before we left, we huddled around the "cooker," sipped a cup of strong coffee, and chatted with Gordon's wife, Gwen. We climbed into Gordon's shiny, almost new, Audi 5000. It had a heater and a radio. The heater even worked. The radio played BBC. We warmed up for the first time in days and listened to "the Beeb."

"Mrs. Bottomley of Stoke-on-Trent writes in: Our nine-year-old Cheshire cat, Cecilia, has not been at all well for the past few weeks and refuses to listen to your show anymore. Could anyone who knows what's wrong with Cecilia, please ring Mrs. Bottomley on 925."

"And it's nice to hear from Mr. and Mrs. Withers from Black-pool again. They write in to say they won't be able to write in next week, as Mrs. Withers will be traveling to Manchester to visit with her sister."

Meanwhile, Gordon had the Audi 5000 screaming down, down, down out of the hills, narrowly missing an old lorry that was parked by the side of the road. The hedgerows and stone fences flashed by at ten times the rate possible in the Westwood van. Gordon stood on the brakes, and a dozen or so woolly sheep made their way across in front of us. Then he jammed the gas pedal to the floor, and minutes later we were flying through a tiny village. I didn't dare look at the speedometer. I was too busy watching the locals scatter as we barreled down the stone street, across an old bridge, and back out onto the road.

"So, what time do we have to be in Birmingham?" I asked, hoping that we didn't have to drive this fast and he might slow down a little. He didn't slow down. As the days and nights whizzed by, I found out that the only time he slowed down, at all, was when he fell asleep and his foot slipped off the accelerator. I tried talking, not talking, turning the radio up, turning the radio down, asking questions, telling jokes. Nothing worked. He drove like a madman.

When Glory-Anne Carriere toured with Gordon, she sent me a postcard with one word on it: "Help!" When the Mercy Brothers toured with him, they nicknamed him "Sterling Moss." I understand they prayed every time they got into the Audi and kissed the ground when they got out. On a Dallas Harms tour, Gordon actually slowed down once. He got rear-ended. He used that as an example of what could happen if he drove too slow.

I prayed, listened to the BBC, ate Valium like popcorn, and lived through the whole damned nightmare. I may have forgotten to mention that Gordon's feet smelled like 35 pairs of old Russian army boots on a hot day, and that he chain-smoked the rankest, cheapest little cigars known to man. Every tour I said, "Never again." But the next year I thought, hoped, prayed . . . that it might be different.

We reached BBC Pebble Mill in Birmingham. We met Ken Dudney, proceeded into the studio, did a quick interview, played a few cuts off the SOLDIER OF FORTUNE album, and hit the road to Stoke-on-Trent, where I was performing that night.

It was my birthday, March 22, 1976. The venue was packed. The band did the opening, while I waited in the dressing room backstage. I had my guitar strapped on, my blues harp in my pocket, and was ready to hit the stage. The back door opened and the promoter stepped into the dressing room. "Don't go on, mate."

I looked at him questioningly.

"Don't go on, mate," he repeated.

"Why?" I asked.

"I can't pay you," he said. "The Sheriff seized the box office."

"But you've got a full house," I protested. "You can't refund their money. What are you going to tell them?"

"I'll just say you didn't show up."

I looked at him in disbelief. "I'm thousands of miles from home. They've paid for a show, I'm going to give them one, whether I get paid or not."

His tone changed. He shook my hand. "I didn't know you were that kind of a lad," he said. "I'll see you get your money before you leave the country."

I did the show. We loaded up our gear and drove off into the night. I never saw the man again.

European Tours

Beginning in 1978 our tours extended throughout Europe. At first, I was excited traveling to London or Frankfurt or Amsterdam, then driving all day and playing that same night in Birmingham or Munich or Oudewater. At the end of one leg of the tour, I would leave the band behind and catch a bus or a train, a ferry or a sky hopper across the

English Channel, pick up with another band in another country, rehearse our show, and do it all over again. Drive all day, play a show, get back in the van or bus and follow the white line through the night. Stop some place for breakfast at daybreak, or just grab a cup of coffee and a couple of chocolate bars and get back on the road. Sometimes we would get held up at a Dutch, German, or Belgian border crossing for hours. They would just wave us off to the side and we could sit there forever waiting for them to come and deal with us. Meanwhile, we would be going crazy because we had a few hundred miles to get to the next show and the clock was ticking away and the miles were not.

It was not unusual to go for two or three days and nights without seeing a hotel room. I tried to sleep in the van; I tried to sleep backstage between shows. After a few days, I'd get so tired that, even when we had a few hours to sleep, I'd lay down and stretch out. But sleep wouldn't come. I would just lie there and vibrate. When I closed my eyes, I would see headlights or road signs or white lines and I would snap awake again. I learned to pump multi-vitamins and Vitamin C, and keep a good supply of Tylenol for the headaches that developed from lack of sleep. A few tabs of Valium, Seconal, Surmontil, or whatever the doctor ordered seemed to take off the rough edges.

Once in a while, when we hadn't had a room or a shower for some time, we would stop at some roadside service station or whatever was available. I would strip to the waist and use a sock or a t-shirt as a wash cloth and my shampoo for soap and indulge in what was usually an ice-cold sponge bath. Then I'd splash on as much cologne, after-shave, and deodorant as I could find, and I was ready for another few days of the soon-to-be-infamous "Dick Damron Mystery Tour."

The only things that kept us going were the enthusiastic crowds. It certainly wasn't the money. The promoters collected thousands and paid us hundreds. It was just like when I was a kid with my little hometown band — *they* got the money and I got the experience.

Near the end of one particular string of 40 one-nighters in five different countries, I suddenly realized that I was the only one still standing. I had worked with four different bands, burned out three drivers, and worked for five different promoters. And I still had five days to go before we could cross the channel back to England and I could catch a flight back to Canada.

One night in West Germany, I was backstage waiting to go on. I was tired and sick and feeling weak. I stepped out the back door of the huge auditorium and gulped the cool night air. I hoped it might revive me and give me the extra strength I needed to do my show. It had just started to rain. I felt a few drops hit my face and the cool soothing effect was wonderful. I took off my old black hat and turned my face up to the rain. I stood there alone in the dark and let the big drops pelt down on me. I felt sick and tired and burnt out, and I wanted to cry. I had been up and down and over and under and around, in so many circles in the past few weeks, that I had totally lost my center of gravity.

I remember talking to myself and saying right out loud, "Jesus Christ, what am I doing to myself? *What in the hell* am I doing to myself?" I just wanted to walk away into the night, away from it all — the band, the show, the promoter, the whole goddamned thing. What difference would it make? Would anybody really give a fuck? That's it, I'll do it, I'll just go find a little hotel somewhere and have a hot shower and go to bed and sleep for three days and nights and, when I wake up, I'll go to Frankfurt and buy a ticket home.

Then from inside the auditorium I heard the band start the long vamp intro to *The Long Green Line* . . . I pulled my hat on, ran in the back door, up the stairs and out on stage. I was soaked to the skin. I picked up my guitar, walked up to the mike, and screamed at the crowd, "Good evening, jolly fun-seekers! I'm your friendly local neighborhood long-haired hippie weirdo country and western cowboy singer, part-time snake charmer and the illegitimate son of Adolf Hitler. Are you ready to party? Say yeah! Are you ready to party? Say yeah!"

The crowd answered, "Yeah!!!"

"All right," I said. And the party was on.

The crowd was in awe. The band was in shock. They played their asses off. We gave no quarter and took no prisoners.

Only four more days and I could go home.

Learning To Kill People

The crowd at Southport was on their feet screaming for more. We had laid waste to the place. The J.D. Band was hot. Jeannie Denver had done a great show. Pete Nelson had opened the concert for us with his off-the-wall comedy. When I hit the stage, I was ready. And it was about time.

The first tour in 1976 had been a learning experience. I went back in '78 and did the U.K. from one end to the other. In 1979, I felt I had a better understanding of the British country music scene. The J.D. Band had my music down. By this time, I had three albums released over there, so all my music was not totally obscure.

Most importantly, I had found out that I could do exactly the same show as I did any place else in the world and they loved it. Of course, I changed a few names and places so the British crowd could identify with the one-liners.

"Good evening, jolly fun-seekers! Live and direct from the Best Little Whorehouse in Texas, I'm your friendly, local, neighborhood, long-haired hippie weirdo, part-time snake charmer, and the illegitimate son of Margaret Thatcher. I'll be here raping, pillaging and plundering until five o'clock in the morning. Can you all stay 'til five in the morning? Say 'yeah'!"

The crowd screamed back "Yeah!"

"Are you ready to party? Say 'yeah'!"

"Yeah!"

Then I sang an up-tempo country rocker called *All Nite Country Party*. Did a Wilf Carter yodel that I turned into a ten-minute production. Told the crowd that this was the low-budget portion of the show, brought to them by Black and Decker Instant Home Vasectomies, Colonel Lingus Kentucky Fried Chicken, British Airways and Honda Kick-Start Vibrators. Explained that when I yodeled, I didn't sound like Wilf Carter, or Slim Whitman, or Keith Manifold — I sounded like a cross between Margaret Thatcher, Pierre Trudeau, a Saskatchewan coyote, and a retarded turkey.

Then I would introduce my magic Wilf Carter yodeling hat and explain that, when I placed the hat on my head, it instantly transformed me from a "long-haired hippie weirdo" into a "yodeling cowboy." Before placing the hat on my head, I would look inside under the hat band and then say to the band, just loud enough for the audience to hear, "How the hell did that get there? I thought we smoked it in Birmingham!" Then I would do the yodel and people would fall out of their chairs laughing.

Sometimes the band would laugh so hard they could hardly play. The music ranged from *Jesus It's Me Again* to *Sex, Drugs and Booze*, from *If You Need Me, Lord* to an outrageous version of *Up Against The Wall, Rednecked Mother*. I even did a radio commercial in my best radio announcer voice: "Hi there, Buckaroos! Does your mouth taste like the bottom of a buckin' chute after a hard day at the rodeo? Do them barrel-racers back off when you say 'howdy'? Try Gene Autry Cowboy Mouth Wash! And now, back to music!"

I had stolen this line from world champion cowboy Larry Mahan and "Captain Crunch and the Deep Cross Cowboys" when I had played The Nugget with them in Reno, Nevada. I played some bluegrass tunes on the five-string banjo. Nothing obscure. Stuff like *Duelling Banjos*, the theme from *Bonnie & Clyde*, and *The Ballad Of Jed Clampett* from The Beverly Hillbillies television show. I played some blues harp for them and gave the band a chance to jam. By the time we closed with *One Night Stand*, I knew I had finally got my British show together. I had gone full circle.

After trying all sorts of different approaches, I was right back to what I had done for years in Canada and the U.S. It was the real thing, and they knew it.

Jeannie Denver and I sold albums and signed autographs while the band loaded the instruments and all the gear into the van. Gordon Davies, "our fearless leader," collected the money and we hit the road for the long drive to Dover. We arrived just in time to board the ferry to Ostend, Belgium.

It was a six-and-one-half-hour voyage across the English Channel. The water was rough and we bounced off the walls in the narrow aisles as we made our way to the cafeteria, the bar, the duty-free shop, and finally flopped into the big chairs in the television lounge to ride out the cold dark night and one of the roughest crossings we had ever experienced. We got very little sleep. A voice on the intercom informed us that we would be docking in a few minutes. We made our way downstairs to the vehicles in the belly of the ferry. It was dark and damp. The diesel fumes from the giant intercontinental transports burned our eyes as they ground slowly up the ramp and onto the docks. We climbed into the van and followed them through the dockyards, through Belgian Customs, and headed for West Germany.

It was not yet daylight and a heavy fog pushed inland from the coast. The headlights of the van sent feeble rays of light into the darkness but did little to brighten our path. The magic of the night before, in Southport, had long since worn off. We were tired and stiff from sitting all night while the ferry pitched and tossed and rolled its way across the channel.

Gordon drove. We were back to driving on the right side of the road again, after a month of running up and down the motorways and all over the British, Welsh and Scottish countryside on the left-hand side. It felt strange to be meeting the traffic on the opposite side of the road, and the dark choking fog around us made it even more scary. In an hour or so, dawn began to break and the fog thinned and broke into small patches. So many times before we had headed north up the coast for the Dutch portion of our tour. This time, our route would take us through Belgium and into West Germany to the Canadian Forces bases in Lahr and Baden Solingen. By mid-morning, the sun was streaming in the windows of the old Bedford van and I could feel the warmth through the window. We stopped for petrol and coffee and a quick trip to the restrooms, crowded back into the van, and pulled back onto the highway. We crossed the border into Germany and a few miles later we were on the Autobahn. The only speed limit was the floorboard of the old blue van. We had two shows to do that night at the Centennial Club in Lahr and we would just make it in time to set up, do a sound check, and hit the stage for our first show.

There was a sparse crowd for the first show and everyone assured us that the second show would be packed. It was. Jeannie opened the show and got a warm, but reserved, response from the crowd. I was tired and burnt-out. I knew I could not handle a long night and a dead crowd. I hit the bar, downed a couple of Bacardis, and went backstage to await my introduction.

When the MC began his intro, I caught the band's attention from the wings and said, "Let's really smoke this thing." I hit the stage and counted "One, two, one-two-three-four!" and we fired headlong into *The Long Green Line*. The increased volume and energy caught the crowd's attention. When we finished the opening song, I shouted, "Hello Canada!" The crowd was all Canadian servicemen, their wives and girlfriends. I kept on top of them.

"Hello, British Columbia! Hello, Alberta! Hello, Saskatchewan!" By the time I got to the East coast, the crowd was screaming and we laid it on them. The show went great for the first half-hour. Then an officer came on stage. "We have a complaint!"

What the hell? I thought — we're up here bustin' our ass to give them a show and they've got a complaint? I looked at him, expecting the worst.

"The band's not drinking enough!" he said.

Five bottles of champagne were then delivered to the stage, followed by a dozen tiny green bottles of Jagermiester, a rare German drink that smells like Vick's Vatronal, tastes like Buckley's cough syrup, and kicks like tequila. We began knocking the drinks back, making a production out of every drink. We drank a toast to everybody and everything from here, there, and everywhere. We played some tunes, sang some songs, and drank and drank and drank. They kept bringing more booze to the stage and the whole show turned into one big party. Jeannie Denver came back on stage to sing with us.

Gordon Davies had just returned from a trip in to Lahr to secure our luxurious accommodations for the night. I was sure we would be at the Hilton, the Sheraton, or the Rhiengau, as we had not seen a hotel room or a shower in three days. He joined us then and picked up an acoustic guitar. We swung into the "high-class" portion of the show and did *The Rodeo Song, Up Against The Wall Rednecked Mother*, and *It's Hard To Say I Love You When You're Sitting On My Face*. The crowd went berserk. This was just like any old Canadian tavern on a Saturday night. How much closer to Canada could we have brought them?

Then the first casualty of the night occurred. Allan Holmes, affectionately known as "Sugie" (longtime drummer, small in stature but with a huge capacity for Newcastle Brown Ale), succumbed to the great amount of alcohol contained in the weird and wonderful concoctions he had consumed. He slowed to a stop, fell backwards off his drum stool, and lay there on his back with his legs in the air like a dead budgie. Kevin Thistlewaite, former guitar player with the White Line Fever Band, and one of the newest members of the J.D. Band, laid down his guitar, slid in behind the drums and picked up the tempo. The show must go on.

We played and drank and drank and played; took three encores and a standing ovation, and finally just left the stage and ran for cover. We stayed backstage in our dressing room and waited for the crowd to thin out. A few soldiers made their way backstage with more beer, wine, Jagermiester, and still more bottles of unidentified European booze. The soldiers helped us load our gear back into the van behind the club. We took turns leaning against the wall and throwing up in the canal. George, our spare driver and part-time roadie, was curled up in the back of the van. Out cold. We piled the gear around him, under him. and on top of him. He didn't seem to mind. We said our good-byes, squashed into the Bedford, and fought for seat selection close to the windows. It was only a few miles until we pulled into a deserted alley and Gordon Davies led us up the backstairs to our rooms at the "Davies Hilton," cheerfully disguised as two small adjoining rooms with one tiny bathroom. The seven of us took up positions on the bed, on the floor, and in the rickety old chairs. "Sugie" and George slept in the van. They didn't seem to mind. Most of us spent a sleepless few hours. The bathroom was busy all night. In the morning we were sick, sick, sick — sober, sober, sober, and real sorry.

We loaded up and struck out for Baden Solingen to do an afternoon show and two evening shows. It was Canada Day on the base and they were ready to party. We were ready to die.

Two guys showed up from the Canadian Forces Network to do an interview. We found a small room backstage. They turned on the tape machine and started asking questions. I told them the tour was going fine. Everything was wonderful. It was a great life out on the road. That seemed to satisfy them and they left with a copy of my NORTH COUNTRY SKYLINE album, promising to play it forever.

The afternoon show went fairly smooth. "Sugie" was suffering and so was his drumming. George was still sleeping in the van. It was cold and uncomfortable, but he slept on. That night, between the first and second shows, we went down into the bar and found a table. We ordered up a round and sat back to pass the time until our second show. The bar was wild and crazy — the soldiers were wilder and craziers. It could have been Fort St. John, B.C., Kirkland Lake, Ontario, or the Eastgate in Sault St. Marie. Only the names had been changed to protect the nation. Anyone in the room could easily have gotten off on a plea of insanity.

A drunken soldier staggered over to our table. He was built like a bull and moved with all the grace of a cement truck. I knew he had something on his mind. He ignored everyone else at the table and zeroed in on me.

"Hey, Damron! Is this all you do . . . bum around the country playing music?"

"Yeah," I replied.

"That's a pretty useless fucking life," he said.

He kept badgering me and, a minute or two later, I countered in self-defence, "Well, what it is you do?"

"I'm learning how to kill people!" he roared.

Every eye at our table swung in his direction as he crouched into some sort of military killer stance.

"Do you know how much pressure it takes to ram your fingers up under a man's rib cage and rip his heart out? Can you break a man's neck with your bare hands without making a sound?"

I glanced at my watch and said to the band, "I guess it's time to do our last show."

We got up, went backstage and left him standing there.

After the show, we loaded out and headed back across Germany and Belgium to catch the ferry at Ostend. Another long drive and another sleepless night. Maybe it would have been easier simply to learn how to kill people.

One year, on the November 11th Remembrance Day holiday, I was driving across southern Saskatchewan on the Trans-Canada Highway. There was a special broadcast on CBC radio to mark the day. The announcers were interviewing veterans of the First and Second World Wars, officers, soldiers, sailors, and airforce men. The last man to be interviewed had been a deserter. When he was asked why he had deserted, he answered in a cracked, age-old voice, "I thought if there weren't no soldiers, there wouldn't be no war."

The Stories Behind the Songs

MID-NITE FLYTES

The British Airways 747 lifted off the runway of the massive Heathrow International Airport, circled up through the heavy overcast spring sky over the cold, gray expanse of foggy old London, England, and headed out over the Atlantic Ocean. I tried to make myself comfortable and relaxed during the eight-and-a-half-hour flight to Chicago, where I had a brief stopover and a connection to Nashville with Delta Airlines.

I glanced around the cabin of the huge aircraft, hoping to spot some empty seats. If I could find two or three seats side-by-side, I could stretch out and try to catch some sleep. No such luck. It was a full flight. I was totally burnt out from almost 40 one-nighters in England, Scotland, Wales, Holland, Belgium, and Germany.

When you are on an overseas flight that eats up hour after hour of flying and takes you through numerous time zones, the last thing you want to do is try to figure out what time it is at home, what time it will be when you arrive at your destination, and what time it will be by your human clock which will still be set on European time plus the eight-and-a-half-hour flight. Jet lag, somewhat like the common cold, has been researched and written about for years. There is no known cure. What works for one person does not necessarily work for another. It was daylight when I left London and would still be daylight when we touched down at Chicago's O'Hare airport.

Why *Mid-Nite Flytes* sprung into my mind, I'm not sure. It must have had something to do with the confusion of my human clock. The first line of the song: "I can't sleep on mid-nite flytes, so I just sit / and try to write a song for you," leaped into my mind and I searched for a pen and something to write on. It has long been my experience that, if you don't get a song down on paper or tape, it will be gone as fast as it appeared. I found a pen and used the back of the baggie supplied by all airlines. It's not especially designed for songwriters, but it served the purpose and, I'm sure, I am not the first or the last writer to utilize this service. The rest of the song came to me in a rush and I copied it down as fast as I could.

MID-NITE FLYTES

I CAN'T SLEEP ON MID-NITE FLYTES
SO I JUST SIT AND TRY TO WRITE
A SONG FOR YOU
A SONG THAT I CAN SING YOU IN MY MIND
I SIT AND STARE OUT AT THE RAIN
AND WATCH THE CLOUDS ...

WATCH THE CLOUDS
GO DRIFTIN' THROUGH MY MIND

IT'S A LONG, LONG WAY FROM LONDON
TO CHICAGO, ILLINOIS
747 CARRY ME
GOTTA CATCH THAT DELTA
FLIGHT DOWN TO NASHVILLE, TENNESSEE
AND I HOPE SOMEBODY'S
WAITIN' THERE FOR ME

SEEMS LIKE I SPEND HALF MY LIFE
SITTIN' ON A MID-NITE FLYTE TO NOWHERE
OR SOMEWHERE I HAVE NEVER EVER BEEN
FLYIN'S JUST A FANTASY TO COUNTRY BOYS
AND FOOLS LIKE ME
FLYIN', TO SOMEWHERE I WON'T EVER
BE AGAIN

© Sparwood Music

The verses tell you what I was doing and feeling, while the chorus of the song is almost a recital of my flight itinerary: "It's a long long way from London to Chicago, Illinois. / 747 carry me. / Gotta catch that Delta / flight to Nashville, Tennessee, / and I hope somebody's / waiting there for me."

Two days after I arrived in Music City I was in the studio with my producer, Joe Bob Barnhill, working on my HIGH ON YOU album. The song *Mid-Nite Flytes* was recorded as an album cut and later released as a single on RCA records. It was far from being a smash hit, but it grew to be a favorite song of a lot of fans. People who are fliers and travelers identify with the feeling.

My flying experiences began when my brother Howard and my cousin Danny were working towards getting their pilot's licences. They both became commercial helicopter pilots, and I flew with them many times when they were putting in their hours in private training planes. But my first hair-raising experience was a 1965 flight with a Canadian bush pilot. We flew in a Cessna 185 from White-horse to Watson Lake (in the Yukon) and back. On the return flight, we lost all radio contact and dipped down through a blinding snow storm to follow the Alaska Highway back through the rugged north country. I never quite got over that one, and I haven't flown in a small plane since.

When I graduated from living on the highway and began flying commercial airlines, my first flight was from Calgary to Nashville via Billings, Denver and Kansas City. The old jet-prop Electra jumped and bounced over the Rockies and I realized, for the first time, that not only birds flapped their wings. As I stared out the windows at the peaks and valleys below, watching the big, silver wings rise and fall with each pitch and roll, I couldn't believe how far the wings flapped and I began seeing flashes of newspaper headlines with black and white photos of the "Plane Crash in the Mountains."

When I arrived in Nashville, I was wondering about the possibility of taking a bus or even a train back home. The five or six day endurance test did not appeal to me, and after spending a few weeks in Nashville recording and pitching songs, my urge to get back home far out-weighed my fear of flying. The flight back to Canada was smooth and uneventful.

I soon became a "frequent flyer" to the point of absolute boredom, though not without a frightening moment or two. I have experienced bomb scares in Denver, Calgary, and Heathrow Airport. On a late-night flight from Toronto to Edmonton an absolute crazy man was seated across the aisle, four rows behind me. From the time we were airborne, until we arrived in Edmonton, he mumbled, talked, and later screamed at the top of his lungs about "having a bomb," constantly threatening to "Blow this fucking thing out of the air!"

Flight attendants tried to quiet the raging fool. When that didn't work, the Purser, and then the Captain, came back and tried to calm him down. I'm sure they did everything and followed every procedure in the book. However, when that didn't work, they told him the R.C.M.P. would be waiting for him at the gate in Edmonton. This only enraged him and he began screaming, "I have a gun and I'll blow those fucking Mounties away! I'm not afraid of those useless bastards."

When we arrived, two Mounties immediately came on board and escorted the man off the plane. In the arrivals area, there were another half-dozen police officers waiting. The maniac slid to the floor and, when he refused to get up, they dragged him out through the baggage claim area. While he was being dragged away, he screamed, over and over again, "I'm not leaving 'til I get my fucking guitar . . ." Meanwhile, I was waiting for my guitar, and when it came around on the carousel, I was almost afraid to pick it up. I thought that some of the Toronto passengers, who had just deplaned and who were waiting for their luggage, might think that I had some connection to the guy. I waited until most of the passengers left before I retrieved my guitar and flight bag and headed home.

Then there was the time we lost cabin pressure on an early-morning flight from Nashville to Detroit, and the time I flew from London to Chicago and arrived too late to catch an aged DC-10 which exploded minutes after take off, killing everyone on board.

One stormy afternoon, I flew from Nashville to Indianapolis, just in time to witness the aftermath of a tornado that had uprooted trees, ripped the roof off of a car dealership, and dumped it on top of a huge lot full of cars, while devastating a small area of the Indiana city. I have often wondered how close our flight path and the path of the tornado had been that afternoon.

When we lost power on one engine of a giant 747 over Scotland, I thanked God it had not happened out over the Atlantic. We spent about 48 hours in Glasgow being shuttled back and forth from Prestwick Airport to the hotel. Many of the passengers became irate and did not seem to realize the alternative to the mere inconvenience we were being asked to endure.

Flying in the 'Great White North' is another thing. When it's the middle of a stormy winter's night and you're looking out the window of your plane watching a crew de-icing the huge silver wings, it's kind of like watching some one doing your windshield. You want to holler and tell them that they missed a spot, before the old Military Hercules lifts off for Fort Churchill and takes you to another C.B.C. Northern Services concert. (Didn't I hear an announcement at the Winnipeg airport that there was a Northwest Airlines flight leaving for Tampa, Florida at about this time . . . is it too late to get off this thing and change my ticket?)

Why does the Late Night News in your hotel room, the night before you fly out, always seem to carry vivid footage of another airline disaster? I no longer read my horoscope in the morning paper in the departure lounge. I don't need to be told, "It's a bad day to travel." Janis Joplin once said, "Flying is like being pushed through a tube from one departure lounge to another." I used to have a line in my show where I proudly announced that the winner of our "door prize" would get two weeks in the "Departure Lounge of his or her choice," anywhere Air Canada flies.

Over the years, I have actually grown to enjoy flying and I have enough Delta Sky Miles to fly to Pluto and back, but the phrase "final descent" always makes me uneasy. Some airlines have changed it to "final approach." Ahhh . . . that's a little better.

Once, as I watched a plane making its descent at the far end of the runway at Mazatlan's International Airport, I commented to a young Mexican standing next to me, "I wonder if that's Delta?" A few seconds later, he replied, "Wait and see how many times it bounces . . ."

The Stories Behind the Songs

IF LONDON WERE A LADY

In the spring of 1979, we were nearing the end of the European leg of our seemingly never-ending tour. We had covered England, Scotland, Wales, Holland, Belgium, and Germany. We were back in the U.K. for our last few dates.

When we received word that the theater where we were to perform that next night had burned to the ground, we made plans to take in the George Hamilton IV concert in Oxford. George, being the gentleman that he is, left passes at the box office and provided Gordon Davies (my tour manager) and me with the best seats in the house. Halfway through the concert, George introduced me to the audience and then performed *Countryfied*, telling the audience that I had written the song for him and that my current tour was so hot the venues were burning down before we could play them. The response was tremendous.

Later in the show, George did a song he attributed to Scottish singer Moira Anderson. He told the crowd that, "if Scotland were a lady, she would look just like Moira Anderson." What a beautiful thought! It stuck in my mind for hours, but I had no idea that the seed had been sown for one of the prettiest songs I would ever write.

A couple of days later, when I was in London for a few hours waiting to fly to Chicago and on to Nashville to record, the thought changed to *If London Were A Lady*. I had been walking along an almost-deserted street. It was foggy and a drizzling rain had me soaked and chilled to the bone. A few doors down, I discovered a small pub. I entered, ordered a cup of coffee, and removed my rain-soaked jacket. By the time the waiter returned with my coffee, I had taken a paper napkin from the dispenser and had begun to write *If London Were A Lady*.

IF LONDON WERE A LADY

IF LONDON WERE A LADY
I KNOW SHE'D BE AS PRETTY AS THE CHELSEA MORNING SUN
I'D HOLD HER CLOSE AND KISS HER
AND THANK HER FOR THE KINDNESS SHE HAS SHOWN
IF LONDON WERE A LADY
I'D TAKE HER CHILDREN WITH ME FOR A WHILE
SO THEY COULD SEE THE STILLNESS
AND FEEL THE WARM REFLECTION OF HER SMILE

AND IF SHE CLOSED HER EYES
SHE COULD SEE TEN THOUSAND MILES
AND KNOW THE REASON WHY
I'M GROWING OLD
AND, IF LONDON WERE A LADY
SHE'D BE A PERFECT LADY
A PERFECT LADY, SOFT AND WARM TO HOLD

© Sparwood Music

The song came to me full-blown, words and music. I wrote the words as fast as possible before they could slip away, and prayed that I could remember the melody long enough to get back to my hotel, dig out my guitar, and get it all down on tape.

Within an hour, I was listening to the song being played back on my Sony Walkman. I liked the "L" sound of London and Lady and, I felt that I had captured the feeling of the city. Every city in the world has a distinct feel. Toronto, Vancouver, Chicago, Las Vegas . . . no two cities have the same personality. To me, this was as British and as London as it could possibly be.

The next day I flew to Nashville, checked into the Hall of Fame Motor Inn, caught a few hours sleep, and met up with my producer, Joe Bob Barnhill, in his office in the Faron Young Building. This was to be the fourth album we had done together. I began singing him the songs that I had written for the album: *Dollars, All Nite Country Party*, and *We've Almost Got It All*. When I began singing *If London Were A Lady*, he stopped me. My first thought was, "Oh no, he doesn't like the song. And, I feel, it's one of my best."

Then he said, "You know how to make this song a smash country hit? Change it to *If Nashville Were A Lady*."

In my mind, I rejected the idea. But anyone who has spent any time in Nashville, knows that the Nashville music moguls consider Nashville the absolute center of the universe. So, I began to sing the first lines:

IF NASHVILLE WERE A LADY
I KNOW SHE'D BE AS PRETTY AS
THE CHELSEA MORNING SUN.

We both broke out laughing. It wasn't a Nashville song. No one was robbing a liquor store. There was no one lying in the street on Broadway. The police sirens weren't screaming in the night.

The next day we recorded *If London Were A Lady* at Richey House Studio in the CBS Building. Joe Bob produced, Jack Gilmour engineered. The musicians included Tony Migliore on piano, Weldon Myrick on steel, Pete Bordonali and Steve Chapman on guitars, Clyde Brooks on drums, and Bobby Dyson on bass. The song is included on the 1980 RCA album HIGH ON YOU.

(Above) *Dick kicking back in hi.*
wooden shoes, Zjwndrecht, Ho
1980.

(Top Left) *Live in the courtyard*
Hiedelberg Castle, West German
1972 with Elmer Tippe, Roy
Warhurst, Dick Damron, Hank
Smith, John Berg, and Paddy Sn

(Middle) *Dick with former pres.*
of the Dick Damron Fan Club,
Glenys Bowell, and Westwood
Records CEO and Mystery Tou
manager, Gordon Davies, circa

(Bottom) *Damron with leading*
Country artists Roger Humphrie
Kelvin Henderson backstage aft
Damron's Bristol concert.

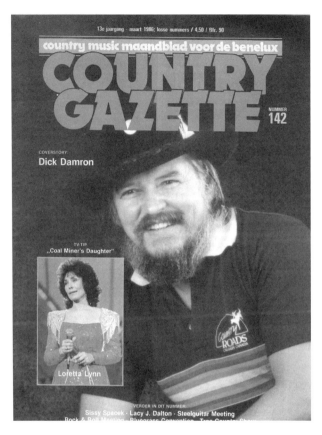

(Above) *The readers of* Country Gazette *in Europe voted Dick Damron Foreign Artist of the Year in 1986 and 1987.*

(Right) *Dick on the cover of Dutch Country Music Festival program in Uden, Holland.*

(Top) *Dick Damron at the Wembley International Country Music Festival in England where he appeared with Marty Robbins, Merle Haggard, Kenny Rogers, Dottie West, Carl Perkins, Don Williams, Donna Fargo, Tompall Glaser, Dave & Sugar, Carroll Baker, and many others.*

(Right) *Saturday afternoon jam at Toronto's Country Music Store.*

Lost In The Music

LOST IN THE MUSIC

LOST IN THE MUSIC, STONED ON A SONG
SEARCHIN' FOR FREEDOM TO FLY
I FEEL THE MAGIC LORD
I CAN TOUCH THE SKY
SEARCHIN' FOR THE FREEDOM TO FLY

HIDIN' IN THE WIND WITH MY CIRCLE OF FRIENDS
HOOKED ON A FEELIN' IN MY SOUL
LOST IN THE MUSIC, STONED ON A SONG
SEARCHIN' FOR THE FREEDOM TO FLY

© Sparwood Music

The Paradise Knife And Gun Club

For years and years, I watched the scenes unfold on a nightly basis in the "Paradise Knife and Gun Clubs" of the world — the tiny little "hole in the wall" clubs, bad-ass bars, honkytonks, watering holes, skull orchards, piss tanks, beer parlors, taverns, cabarets, and a thousand other names that would take forever to mention. They were all different, so different that they were all the same.

I was caught in the middle. I loved them and I hated them. There were nights of musical magic when everyone in the establishment was into the music and the band and the songs; there were nights of pure hell that would make the Devil cringe or dance with glee at the very prospect of a new load of loyal subjects ready and willing to join him at any given moment. I kept telling myself I was just there to play my music. I was writing songs and scratching every nickel together to pay for another recording session. Somehow I always had faith that the next song would be a hit and the next record would top the charts. Then I would fly off into the distance, leaving this whole scene behind, and play concerts and tv shows and sell records and win awards.

All that was a million Light Years away. I tried to convince myself I was a silent observer, and so I observed.

I was in a small club in Sandy, Oregon, on June 19, 1979 when a truck driver, big enough to burn diesel, beat a half-dozen Mexican migrant workers almost to death. I was still there, terrorized, when one of the "walking wounded" returned to the club later that night and drove a shiny steel blade into the diesel-burner's gut. I was working with "Hawg Wild," a Portland-based country band, and they warned me not to go to the washroom, the parking lot, or even a dark corner in the club, alone. I wasn't too sure that it was any safer on stage, but maybe the fact that there were five of us up there and we were all drunk, stoned, and crazy would help to keep the drunk, stoned, and crazier crowd at bay. No such luck.

About midnight, a beer bottle sailed out of the crowd across the dance floor and shattered against the stage. The glass sprayed the front of the stage — nothing major, a tiny piece of glass in the back of my hand that barely drew blood, an inch-long gash on the inside of the battered old cowboy boot on my right foot, and a small slash where the neck of the bottle went through the grill cloth of an old Fender amp. Hell, we never even stopped playing!

Later, when we were having a toke in the parking lot under the Oregon moon, one of the pickers suggested that we should start playing gigs for nothing and just collect danger pay. (A few years later, at the Ranchman's in Calgary, Alberta, I actually paid danger pay to Gordie Merrill, one of my all-time favorite fiddle players. But that's another story.)

We still had one more glorious night at Toni's in Sandy, Oregon. Saturday night is the big night in the honkytonks of America "friends and neighbors," and the night of June 20, 1979, was no exception. We made our way into the club through the smoke and the noise and the smell of stale American beer. No one had cleaned the diesel-burner's blood off the floor; it was now just a dark spot on the filthy old carpet. No one had bothered to sweep up the fragments of broken glass on the stage.

I had driven up from Portland with Jamie Isonhood, one of the greatest keyboard players I have ever worked with. At the afternoon rehearsals, he sounded like the best studio musician on the planet. He had worked sessions in Memphis with the "big boys," and he could do it all. But by the time we had smoked our faces off, drunk a few dozen shots of whatever brand of tequila, rum, or whisky was available, sucked back Southern Comfort in honor of Janis Joplin, Lone Star beer in honor of Willie Nelson, and lit up on whatever happened to be the Saturday night drug of choice . . . we were ready to hit the stage. We sounded like Star Wars Revisited.

The band smashed into the "vamp-'til-unconscious" intro to *The Long Green Line*. Tony screamed into the mike: "Ladies and gentlemen (the overstatement of the night), live and direct from Canada, make welcome Dick Damron!" I hit the stage, strapped on my guitar, and we vamped for another thirteen-and-a-half bars, more or less — at least until the groove was there and my guitar began to sound like it was part of the band.

I walked up to the mike and instead of the usual, "Thank you very much, friends and neighbors," I screamed: "Fuck you very much, friends and neighbors. Live and direct from the night depository at the sperm bank in beautiful downtown Portland, it's Uncle Dick and his Electric Grandmother with another five hours you probably won't care for . . .

"We are going to immediately raise you to a higher level of total indifference. At midnight, I'll be doing my high-classed country porn section of the show. We'll be doing *The Rodeo Song, Up Against The Wall Red-Necked Mother, It's Hard To Say I Love You When You're Sitting On My Face,* and a song I wrote for Dolly Parton called *I Just Got Over Him And Now I'm Under You.* Can you all stay 'til 8:00 in the morning? Say 'yeah'!

"Take off your clothes, light your hair on fire, walk across the ceiling on your lips, these are the good times. Are you ready to party? Say 'yeah'!"

By now the crowd was screaming, the band was still pounding out the vamp intro and I launched into the song: "Following the Long Green Line . . ." The party was under way.

After the first song, I screamed into the mike, "Is everybody doin' alright? Say 'yeah'!" They screamed, "Yeah!" I screamed, "All right!"

I had struck a nerve. I had found the lowest common denominator. We were the honkytonk heroes of the night. After every song I taunted them. "Did you bring the drugs? Say 'yeah'! Did you bring the Tequila? Say 'yeah'. Is there anyone here who's never been to Canada? Is there anyone who hasn't screwed Margaret Trudeau?" And the night went on. They partied and danced and drank, shot up in the washrooms, toked up in the parking lot, and had so much fun they almost forgot to have their regular Saturday night brawl.

Long after midnight, when I did my famous Wilf Carter impersonation, I asked if we had any Wilf Carter fans. If we had any Slim Whitman fans. Then I screamed at them again.

"How many people want to hear me yodel? Say 'yeah'! How many people don't want to hear me yodel? Say 'yeah'! How many people really don't give a shit? Say 'yeah'!" The place exploded, and I launched into my yodel.

When the gig was over, we packed our gear and were in the parking lot loading up Jamie's old van for the trip back into Portland. I was feeling kind of smug. I had found the secret. Just entertain them. Give them such a party and such a good time that there wouldn't be any brawls, or shootings, or knife fights.

Then the whole parking lot exploded into a mini-Viet Nam. We could hear women screaming, punches landing, and bottles breaking.

We could see shadowy figures entering, re-entering, and being dragged out of the circles back to the de-militarized zone. We climbed into the safety and the darkness of the old Ford Econoline, lit up a toke, passed it around, and sat there observing the drama unfold in the half-light of a four o'clock Oregon morning. When the ambulance and the Highway Patrol cars began to arrive, we backed slowly along the far side of the club and, without turning on our headlights, managed to drive through the ditch. We came up on the wrong side of the highway, made our way to the end of the median, pulled a U-turn, flashed on our headlights, and headed for Portland.

When we pulled up in front of my motel, there was a chunk of cement split out of the sidewalk, the chain-link fence was flattened and a little blue Chevy car was half-submerged in the swimming pool. The band dropped me off and I made my way up the narrow stairs to my room.

The next morning I woke early, suffering from too many self-inflicted wounds. The booze and drugs had my head throbbing like a jackhammer. I looked out the window. The fence was still down, the car was still in the pool, and now there was a police car and a tow truck in the parking lot. I packed my bags, picked up my guitar, called a cab and headed for the airport, ready for the instant replay that night in another club, another town and another time. On the plane, I spotted a picture of the car in the pool on the front page of the morning paper. I read about the wife and the husband and the fight and how she floor-boarded the car. It jumped the sidewalk, went through the fence, and into the pool. She had been charged with Dangerous Driving and Public Mischief. "What the hell," I thought. "It's not my wife or my car, and tonight I'll be a long way from here, at the Rodeo Lounge in Indianapolis, Indiana. It will no doubt be the same movie, just a different scene, different actors, different town." I dropped the newspaper and stared out the window of the 737 at the fluffy white clouds for a moment. The glare was too much for my bloodshot eyes and my throbbing head. I lay back and tried to relax. I cursed the prospect of a four-hour lay over in Denver, and wished I had a direct flight to Indianapolis so I could get some sleep. Who in hell books these gigs anyway?

I do. I do.

I'VE SUNG SOME SONGS 'BOUT RODEOS AND PLACES I'VE BEEN
PICK UP TRUCKS AND OLD TIN CUPS AND DAYS WHEN MEN WERE MEN
I'LL LAY EVEN MONEY ON A FRIEND OR TWO OF MINE
IF YOU CARE TO SPIN THE BOTTLE ONE LAST TIME

WHEN SATAN SPINS THE BOTTLE ON THE FINAL JUDGEMENT DAY
THE LOSERS FALL BESIDE HIM AND THE WINNERS FADE AWAY
IT'S TOO SOON TO MAKE A DIFFERENCE
TOO LATE TO CHANGE YOUR MIND
WHEN SATAN SPINS THE BOTTLE ONE LAST TIME

— *Satan Spins the Bottle* © Sparwood Music

Country Music Festivals

In 1976, a new phenomenon surfaced that helped to get us out of the
bars for at least a few weekends every summer. I am credited, blessed,
or blamed with one of the first outdoor Country Music Festivals. Ten
miles west of beautiful downtown Bentley, the Medicine Lodge Ski
Hill seemed to offer a prime spot to stage an event such as this. I
booked some bands and built a stage at the foot of the hill, so the
whole hill could be used as a natural grand stand. We promoted the
show locally and nationally. We drew about 3,000 people. About
2:00 in the afternoon, the old Alberta sky opened up and we had a
two-hour downpour. People ran for cover, the bands dragged their
instruments and equipment in out of the rain. The sound company
cleared the stage without somehow getting electrocuted. Somebody
robbed the concession booth. The big-breasted gals had a "wet t-shirt
contest." A naked drunk streaked down the hill through the mud and
crashed into the stage. A couple of drugged-out crazies tried to climb
the towering ski hill with a Land Rover and flipped it over and over
and over . . . down the hill to where the crowd had been, minutes
before. The Red Deer Rent-A-Cops, my feeble attempt at security,
sent someone from where they were huddled in the relative safety of
the ski lodge to ask if they could go home.

I reached in my pocket, counted out the few hundred dollars we
had agreed on and said, "Tell them to fuck off. It's all history."

That was the first Dick Damron Country Music Festival. That same 1976 August long weekend, Ivan Daines held his first Country Music Picknic at the Daines Ranch, just north of Innisfail, Alberta. Ivan's Picknic has survived it all and still runs every year. I have played it almost every year along with Ronnie Hawkins, Pam Tillis, Michael Martin Murphey, Ian Tyson, and just about every Western Canadian country artist you can name. The second annual Dick Damron Festival, in 1977, was a mild success. But the next year, I closed the gates forever. A wild and crazy rock and roll concert at the same site got out of hand and everyone in the area laid the blame at my doorstep, even though I was thousands of miles away touring Europe at the time. Everyone was convinced that if it was a festival in the Medicine Hills, it must be Dick Damron's. Most of them had their minds made up and I bowed out quietly.

Today, the "put-up-a-stage-in-a-cow-pasture syndrome" runs rampant. Some are successful for a few years and some are not. I played one, a while back, just west of Edmonton. It was poorly promoted, poorly attended, and nobody got paid. Word got around in music circles that the entertainers had lost a lot of money. Not long after that festival, I was playing a club in Edmonton, when a man appeared at my table during a band break.

"You Dick Damron?" he asked.

"Yeah."

"I hear you had a little problem with a promoter."

"Yeah."

"What would you like to happen to this guy?"

I gave him a questioning glance. He went into a slow monologue, quietly mentioning broken arms, knee caps, collections, beatings, or the "full treatment."

"It was only a few thousand dollars," I said.

"Oh, I thought we were talking about real money . . ." And he was gone.

Since that time, I have played dozens of festivals from Vancouver Island to Indiana's Hoozier Hills Festival, from the Rocky Mountain Jam to the Gatineau Clog, from the giant international festival in Wembley, England to the tiny North Country Fair in northern Alberta. I have played the gigantic Big Valley Jamboree in Craven, Saskatchewan. And I was also involved with the Cattle Country Jam at Brooks, Alberta for a number of years. There are always a lot of unknown commodities, including mother nature's contributing factors. But when all the pieces fit, there is a magic that can seldom be duplicated at a club or a one-nighter. And that is what we are all shooting for.

A Shattering Experience

In 1976, *RPM* magazine's "Big Country" awards were staged in Edmonton at the shiny new Plaza Hotel. The hotel was a block north of Jasper Avenue and only a block or two from the 97th Street drag. I had already taken in a number of BMI songwriter award shows, Juno Awards shows, and numerous other music business events in Toronto and Nashville. This was the first time an event of this kind had taken place in Alberta.

Charlie Russell, a country DJ from Woodstock, N.B., Jake Dole, a singer/songwriter/producer from Vancouver, and I decided to form an instant welcoming committee. We had partaken of a few shots of booze and were flying at an altitude that would scare anyone afraid of heights. I took the elevator to my room and returned with my trusty Gibson five-string banjo. Charlie and Jake came up with a couple of acoustic guitars, and right there, on the spot, we formed the world's newest country band.

We began playing in the lobby and then moved outside onto the sidewalk directly in front of the hotel entrance. When the guests began to arrive, we started pickin' and singin' all the old up-tempo bluegrass tunes we could think of. Taxis and limos pulled in from the airport with artists, producers, songwriters, record company executives and all sorts of music business people. A smattering of guitar pickers, fans, innocent bystanders, and backstage ladies also began showing up for the country music bash of the year.

As the night wore on, a steady stream of country music people continued to pour in. We kept on pickin' and singin'. Around midnight, the traffic slowed and we spotted a local derelict staggering down the opposite side of the street. When he heard the music, he stopped and listened for a minute, then made a B-line across the street to where we were playing. He was loaded and ready to party. He hopped up on the sidewalk and began his own original style of the *Red River Jig*, dancing forward, backward, and staggering sideways all at the same time. The crowd clapped and cheered. The attention spurred him on to even greater innovations in his exotic search for perfection of this rare and unusual style of choreography.

Then it happened. He danced backwards through one of the huge plate glass windows and crashed into the plush lobby of the Edmonton Plaza. The huge, high-backed, overstuffed chairs and sofas, the green potted plants and the perfectly manicured carpets were showered with the shattered glass. And there, in the middle of it all with a huge gash in the back of his head, lay the fancy dancer.

Onlookers and hotel staff ran to his rescue. Someone called an ambulance. They wrapped his head with a towel and placed him on a stretcher. When the ambulance arrived, the attendants slid him into the back. He turned his head slowly, looked at us standing around with our guitars and banjo still in hand and, in a slow, drunken voice said, "Don't quit playing, boys! I'm gonna be right back."

Now in the music business and, especially, at this kind of an event, there is an unwritten law: "If you haven't heard a good rumor by noon, start one." When other guests arrived and saw the gaping hole where the huge plate glass window had been, they started asking questions and got a lot of strange and varied answers. By morning, the stories had grown out of all proportion. The morning edition of the *Edmonton Journal* casually reported the incident as "Dick Damron's Shattering Experience."

Disco Sucks

At the height of the disco craze, I caught an early morning flight from Nashville on up to Detroit. I was dog-tired from virtually living in the studio day and night, putting the finishing touches on my HIGH ON YOU album. At the Detroit airport, I hailed a cab. A slightly-built black man, about 45, with short, gray chin whiskers and a battered old "Blues Brothers" hat, picked me up.

I crawled into the back of the cab with my guitar and flight bag. I was traveling light.

"Where to, man?" he asked.

"CBC Television in Windsor."

"Right on," he said. "You a guitar player?"

"Not really," I replied. "I'm a country singer."

"I used to be the best damned horn player in Detroit City," he said with pride in his voice. "But them damn discos got me drivin' cab."

Then his voice changed to the sad, defeated tone of a slave in an old Southern movie. "I ain't complainin', man. The mob's runnin' them things."

I sat quietly for the rest of the ride. We made our way out of Detroit and across the bridge toward the Canadian border. A light drizzle of rain pelted down from the gray, Michigan morning. The steady rhythm of the windshield wipers slapped away. I almost nodded off. I stared out the window through the iron girders, to the river below. My eyes closed again. The black man with the chin whiskers and the battered hat was on stage, his horn pressed to his lips. The spotlight seemed to shine right through him. The band wailed off in the distance but the horn was right there, big and bold and beautiful.

He is the best damned horn player in Detroit City, maybe in the whole country. Those fucking discos! I thought. Here I am, flying all over the country, cutting records, doing television shows, making money and, he's driving cab. There ain't no justice.

Drug Wars

I guess most people would relate drug wars to Colombia, Panama, Mexico, or even the streets of a number of North American cities. The real human drug wars, the ones that rage inside the users, addicts, and even your average garden-variety casual weekend party druggies, are what it's really all about. No matter if it's marijuana, cocaine, speed, L.S.D., booze or any of the hundreds of prescription drugs, lives are devastated.

Quite possibly the key word is "control." Everyone thinks he is in control, and, in the beginning, I think we are because we make the initial choice — or choices — to try this or that. It may be because of stress, curiosity, looking for a way out or a way in to any one of a million different situations. At first, most of the mind-bending drugs will create escape from all your problems and will heighten your pleasures. However, once you are on the roller coaster, the "fun" begins.

I hesitate to call it a roller coaster for several reasons. First, because it is one of the most over-used metaphors used to describe the drug situation. And second, because a roller coaster can only go as high as its highest point of construction, then back down to its lowest point. The track remains the same and the roller coaster cars merely follow that same track over and over in a never-changing pattern.

Once you enter the bizarre world of drugs, you go higher than you have ever gone before and come back down just a tiny bit lower than you have ever been before. You can almost immediately feel the sensations of the enormous highs in light, color, sound, sex, or anything else you may be experiencing at the time. But I don't think you notice that tiny difference in the distance that you come back down. The only way to get back up is to use more of what took you up there in the first place. Then you come back down just a tiny bit lower and lower and lower, into the pit of depression, paranoia, lack of confidence, and finally total devastation of any and all safety valves in the human emotional system. Then your personal drug war has begun and the winner loses all.

Growing up in the 1930s and 40s, I knew nothing about the outside world. We had no television, seldom did we see a newspaper, and the old battery-powered radio was always in need of batteries. In the late 1950s, when I joined up with a big city band for a stint as a steel guitar player, I was a country boy and a "babe in the woods." Suddenly, I found myself in the midst of a world I knew nothing about. There was a hot guitar player with the band who had been around and who had toured with many of the big-name country stars of that era. He had a saying, "as useless as an empty benny bottle on a Binion tour." Binion was a promoter of some repute during this time.

It wasn't long before I learned that "bennies" were tiny white Benzedrine tablets. He related story after story about the magic of the "little jewels," as he called them. You could pop a couple of them and drive for two days and three nights to get to the next gig anywhere in North America. This was long before the advent of the sleek highway buses used by most of the stars today. Back then, much of the traveling was done in cars and station wagons with equipment trailers in tow. There was no place to sleep and no time to check into a motel. So you popped bennies, took turns driving, and never stopped until you got to your next performance.

The same guitar player was tall, dark, handsome, a hopeless drunk and a ladies' man. He related even more stories about the magic of making love all night with the help of the little bennies. Then came the clincher. According to my guitar pickin' friend, every artist or hot guitar player you could name ate these "little jewels" like popcorn. Talent, practice, and musical expertise (he suggested) all took a back seat to the "far out" playing of the guy who was hopped up on bennies.

The rest of the band was amazingly straight when it came to drugs, but at every gig they were falling down drunk. The guitar player constantly offered the magic white pills to me. The more I refused, the more stories he related. By the end of the first week, I couldn't hold out any longer. I accepted the pills which he slipped me before the show or between shows. However, I would slide into the washroom, drop them into my jeans pocket, and return to the bandstand. He'd give me a wink and I would nod my head and that seemed to satisfy him. By the end of our gig, I had a dozen or so saved up, and on my way back home to Bentley, I wound down the car window, dug them out of my pocket, and fired them out into the night. I was dumb, but I wasn't stupid.

A few years later, about the time my marriage was falling apart, I discovered a bottle of Benzedrine tablets in an emergency first aid kit which my parents had kept tucked away on the top shelf of the pantry in the kitchen of our old farmhouse. I was pawing through the little blue tin box, looking for a band-aid, and there they were . . . those same little jewels, and not one or two tablets, but a whole damned bottle of them. Impulsively I stuck the bottle into my pocket, closed the blue tin, and replaced it on the top shelf.

I carried them around for a long time, but never sampled them until much later. As my marriage deteriorated, my drinking increased and my emotions took on a rawness that I couldn't seem to handle. I turned to popping the little white pills, thinking they would distance me from the problems in my life. At first I only took one or two every few days. They seemed to ease my emotional turmoil. But when I mixed them with the considerable amounts of booze I was consuming, reality began to slip away. At the time, I don't think I had any idea what was harmful to me and neither did those around me.

Over the years, I spun through every kind of prescription drug known to man: Librium, Valium, Elovil, Seconal, Surmontil, Halcyon, Ativan, and more, usually held down with Bacardi and 7-Up. It was years later when I discovered marijuana, hashish, and cocaine. It wasn't long until I became a heavy, heavy marijuana user. But I never thought that I used much cocaine, and in comparison to the marijuana use, the "little white powder" seemed minimal.

On any given night, during this era, I might smoke a half-dozen joints, down a dozen Bacardis, shoot back six or seven shots of Jose Cuervo or Tequila Sauza, do a line or two of coke, and take a couple of sleeping pills at bedtime — most of the time not caring much if I ever woke up again.

But as I said, in my mind, I never did much coke, except for that first time in a tiny slum bar in Alberta, and the time in Toronto at the Country Music Awards, or the time at a Texas rodeo when we did $1200-worth in one night. And the time in the parking lot behind the club. And the time just before I hit the stage at one of the world's largest country music festivals. And the time in Portland, Oregon, at the Pacific Northwest Headquarters of a group of political activists. And the time in Hamburg, West Germany, at the "Home of the Stained Glass Fish." And the time the promoter sent a load of the white stuff to my hotel room with a note thanking me for "a helluva show." When we checked out of the hotel in the morning, the glass top of the coffee table looked like the lone survivor of an explosion in a flour mill. And the time, and the time, and the time . . .

Music, music, music. It is one of the most beautiful and creative God-given talents known to man. But you are never quite sure if it is a blessing or a curse. Mix it with drugs (and the frequently appalling working conditions provided by the people who pay you to play it), and you have some small idea of what much of my life has been all about.

My struggle back to sanity and reality is much too painful to recall. I have no idea how I survived the personal hell that I put myself through, with the mixture of God-given creativity and total devastation of my mind, spirit, soul, and emotional system. I loved too much, laughed too much, cried too much and, every day, I tried to accept and/or reject thousands of different thoughts, feelings, and emotions that went spinning through my mind at a million miles per hour. I tried praying, meditating, reading every kind of book on mind control, keeping busy, doing everything, doing nothing, but nothing seemed to make any difference.

Then, one night, I thought I saw a light at the end of the hall and, for the following minutes, hours, days, weeks, and months, I fought the battle of my life. Once again I see the sun, feel the rain, smell the flowers, and sing my songs. The war is over.

Filming the video for *Jesus It's Me Again*, accompanied by (left to right) Jennifer Johnston, Patricia Conroy, Michelle Wright, Lisa Brokop, Tracey Prescott, Stephanie Beaumont.

The Stories Behind the Songs

JESUS IT'S ME AGAIN

For years, my mother was the organist at the Bentley United Church, and she would rehearse and play the old church music at home. During the seven years our band had a Saturday night radio show on CKRD in Red Deer, Alberta, we always included our gospel song of the week. Songs like *What A Friend We Have In Jesus, Amazing Grace, Farther Along,* and *Old Time Religion* were among the most requested.

I was exposed to gospel music from the very beginning, and although I never considered myself a deeply religious person, the feeling and the spirit was always there. The most wretched times in my life have been when I lost touch with that spirit. On my SOLDIER OF FORTUNE album, which was released in 1974, there is a song called *Mother, Love and Country,* with these lines: "I am not a Christian soldier, / just a plain, God-fearing man."

In Shirley MacLaine's book *Going Within,* she says, "Prayer is speaking to God. Meditation is listening to God." As a child, I went to Sunday School and Children's Church. We recited the Lord's Prayer every morning in school at the beginning of class. But at that early age, I don't think I really understood much about it. My favorite prayer was the Twenty-Third Psalm. However, I usually heard it only at funerals and I found funerals extremely difficult.

My mother's and father's funerals were hard enough on me. They both died of cancer. But after the months of suffering they each went through, I learned what the phrase "laid to rest" really meant.

When my niece lost a son only a few months old, the funeral was held at the tiny Lutheran Church in the Sunset Hills, about ten miles west of Bentley. I went with my brother's wife to lend her support. She was the grandmother of the infant. Some of the local children stood at the altar behind the little rosewood casket. With flowers all around and the afternoon sunlight streaming in through the stained glass windows, they sang *Jesus Loves The Little Children.* I fell apart, and my sister-in-law, whom I was there to support, ended up having to guide me through the rest of the ceremony and the graveside service. Those same feelings sweep over me whenever I perform *Jesus It's Me Again*, and I know it always touches a large percentage of the audience.

The opening lines of the song came as a silent prayer which I used to help myself through tough times. At first I didn't realize it was the birth of a song. To me, it was just a prayer, with no hint of music or melody. Then, one stormy spring day, I was sitting on the edge of the bed, with my guitar in hand, in a rundown hotel room. The lines came to me and I began singing them. When I came to the end of the lines that had been in my mind for years, I just kept singing. I don't know where the words came from; they just flowed. The words were there, the music was there, and the song was complete. I sat with tears welling up in my eyes, singing the song over and over again. Each time, I marveled at the way the song had come to me and the instant perfection and beauty of the words and music.

JESUS IT'S ME AGAIN

LATELY, LORD, I ALMOST FEEL LIKE DYIN'
I WAKE UP LIKE A CHILD ALONE AT NIGHT
SOMETIMES, LORD, I JUST CAN'T KEEP FROM CRYIN'
AND I CAN'T FIND THE STRENGTH TO CARRY ON

(CHORUS)
JESUS, IT'S ME AGAIN
DOWN ON MY KNEES, AGAIN
ASKING YOU PLEASE AGAIN
REACH OUT YOUR HAND

JESUS, IT'S ME AGAIN
DOWN ON MY KNEES, AGAIN
BEGGING YOU PLEASE AGAIN
REACH OUT YOUR HAND

FROM TIME TO TIME, I'VE TRIED TO FIND A REASON
AND I'VE TALKED TO YOU A TIME OR TWO BEFORE
BUT THIS TIME, LORD, IT'S MORE THAN I CAN HANDLE
AND I KNOW I JUST CAN'T TAKE IT ANYMORE

(CHORUS)
JESUS, IT'S ME AGAIN
DOWN ON MY KNEES, AGAIN
ASKING YOU PLEASE AGAIN
REACH OUT YOUR HAND

JESUS, IT'S ME AGAIN
DOWN ON MY KNEES, AGAIN
BEGGING YOU PLEASE AGAIN
REACH OUT YOUR HAND

© Sparwood Music

"Prayer is speaking to God." Writing this song was listening to God. In 1984, in Halifax, Nova Scotia, the song received the award for Song of the Year in Canada, and it still remains one of my most requested songs to this day.

(Above) *Receiving a Big Country Award, Regina, 1979 with Terry Carisse and Tenderfoot on stage.*

(Left) *Dick Damron holding the Canadian Country Music Association Picker Award for Entertainer of the Year, with Charlie Pride and former CCMA president Ma Henning.*

(Top) *Dick Damron on the long-running Family Brown TV show with Tracey, Papa Joe, Barry and Lawanda, in the early 1980s.*

(Left) *Dick playing his trusty five-string banjo, always a highlight of his stage show in Europe and Vegas.*

Dick with longtime CBC Broadcaster Laurie Mills at the Dick Damron Country Music Festival in the Medicine Hills, 1976.

CHAPTER EIGHT

Mexico

TEQUILA CHARLIE'S

SATURDAY NIGHT AND THE MUSIC IS LOUD
AND IT LOOKS JUST LIKE THE SAME OLD CROWD
THINGS ARE ROCKIN' AT TEQUILA CHARLIE'S TONIGHT
THE SENORITAS ARE LOOKING FINE
TEQUILA'S FLOWING JUST LIKE WINE
THINGS ARE ROCKIN' AT TEQUILA CHARLIE'S TONIGHT

(CHORUS)
ONE MORE MARGARITA
A LITTLE MORE SALT AND LIME
JOSE CUERVO, YOU'RE A FRIEND OF MINE
OLD CHARLIE'S LOCKIN' UP THE DOOR
NO ONE LEAVES 'TIL THREE OR FOUR
THINGS ARE ROCKIN' AT TEQUILA CHARLIE'S TONIGHT

© Sparwood Music

Grande Torino

The shiny, two-tone Grande Torino hardtop drove like a dream, much better than my 1929 Chrysler with no windshield and an electric fuel pump which died, forcing me to strap a gas can on top of the hood and run a rubber hose down to the carburetor to keep it running. I once had a '36 Chevy whose steering was so bad that, in order to save my life, I had to give up driving on the highway and drive around in the local farmers' fields.

I owned a 1939 GMC pickup that ran like a charm until one stormy winter night when I hit a patch of black ice, slid into a snowbank, and flipped it down the hill and onto its roof. I had two 1940 Dodge cars, one to drive, and one to use for spare parts. Unfortunately, you could not tell them apart. They both belonged in the junk yard. I had a 1949 Chevy two-door, but it couldn't stand up to being driven down sidewalks and across railroad tracks and smashing into telephone poles in the back alleys of every oilfield boomtown in western Canada. One day it just rolled over and died.

I progressed on to station wagons. They were handy for hauling around guitars, fiddles, banjos, and sound equipment. The first one was a little lemon-yellow 1957 Ford Ranch Wagon, a great little car that took me over 130,000 miles and was anything but a lemon. Next came a two-tone Country Squire wagon, loaded with everything known to man. This one should have been yellow because it was the biggest lemon I had ever owned. I replaced transmissions, starters, alternators, and fuel pumps. Every time we took a road trip to a gig, we walked home. I traded it in on the shiny, new Grande Torino, and headed to Mexico for my first real vacation. I was 40 years old and I needed a day off.

I drove the luxurious Grande Torino down through southern Alberta, across the U.S. border at Sweetgrass, Montana, and on down to Idaho, Utah, Nevada, and Arizona with another border crossing at *Nogales*, and into Mexico for the first time. Little did I know that I would soon be living almost a quarter of my time in this country, and write 90 per cent of my music on the west coast of Mexico.

Mexico has become a second home to me. After one winter in

Guaymas and San Carlos Bay, I discovered that, in order to soak up the sun and really enjoy the Pacific Coast, I needed to drop below the Tropic of Cancer. Mazatlan was my next stop, and although I have since traveled to Puerto Vallarta, Los Cabos on the tip of the Baja, Guadalajara, Paracho, Copala, and Villa Blanco up in the Sierra Madres, Mazatlan has become my haven and my respite from the cold Canadian winters. About a thousand miles south of the California border on the northwest coast of Mexico, Mazatlan, in the state of Sinaloa, basks in the south Pacific sun.

When I first hit Mazatlan in 1976, the tourism "thing" had just begun, so it was pretty relaxed. As the years drifted by, I moved up the north beach along the Cameron Sabalos to escape the wrath of money-hungry developers. Witch Beach, up at Cerritos, as far north as the Sabalo runs, has become a hang-out of mine. The Pacific Ocean crashes against the rocks, and a half-dozen Mexican dogs lie sleeping in the shade on the steps of the Palapa that serves as a bar and restaurant.

Miguel always has time to stop and chat. He never seems to tire of correcting my broken Spanish. He tries to say "Peter Piper picked a peck of pickled peppers" while I struggle with *"Parangaricutiri Micuaro."* He laughs and shuffles off to serve Carta Blanca and Tecate to a few people who straggle in from the beach. This may not be your idea of heaven, but it's a long way from hell.

When I grow restless in Mazatlan, I can make my way out of the city onto the intercontinental highway, take the cutoff to Durango through the Mexican countryside, and travel up into the Sierra Madres. Daniel's Restaurant in the tiny, ancient village of Copala claims to have the best Mexican food in the world, and I would never argue against that. Pigs and chickens run loose in the dusty streets and children either try to sell you a five-peso ride on an aging burro or sell small chunks of ore from the surrounding silver mines. The sound of El Solito's harp cuts through the quiet of the afternoon, and a soft warm breeze wafts the scent of the bougainvillaea through the tiny village. Meanwhile, palefaced politicians, account executives, brokers and high-pressure salesmen in the cities of our nations refer to these people as "the less fortunate."

177

Winter Haven

I had never really dealt with life as a personal property and had never realized that there was life outside of my own little music world. The only luxury I had allowed myself away from the music biz were my winters spent in Mexico. That served two great functions in my life: the healing and recharging process, giving me the chance to write my music. One obvious song is *Tequila Charlie's*, written for the little Mazatlan *cantina* where I spent many nights jamming with "the bluesman," Genaro Palacios.

HE AIN'T FROM CHICAGO
OR NEW ORLEANS
BUT HE PLAYS THE BLUES
AND HE PLAYS 'EM MEAN.
HE'S THE BLUES MAN.

Then there was *Hotel Mexico* and many of the guitar instrumentals that appear on the MIRAGE CD: *Spanish Dancer, Carnival in Mazatlan, Flying to the Sun*, and *Fiesta Mexicana*. Some of the country songs written in Mexico include *The Legend and the Legacy, Mid-Nite Cowboy Blues, Cinderella and the Gingerbread Man*, and *There Ain't No Love Around*.

I wrote *I Stopped Believing In You* after taking in a traveling circus on its closing night. As I left the circus, the crew was already in the process of tearing out the bleachers and lowering the gigantic tents that were battered and torn from years and years of hosting thousands of circus performances all over Mexico, Guatemala, Nicaragua and South-Central America.

I FEEL LIKE A KID
ON THE DAY THAT THE CIRCUS LEFT TOWN.
LIKE AN OLD-TIME CONDUCTOR
THE DAY THAT THE RAILROAD
CLOSED DOWN.

Mexico, with all it has grown to mean to me, has become some kind of winter haven. I walk the beautiful sandy beaches almost every

day. It is simple. North to Cerritos where I can find almost total soli-
tude, or south to the tourist hotels, the clamor of Playa Mazatlan,
the luxury of the El Cid and Pueblo Bonita, the dozens of tacky
Mexican t-shirt and turtle-oil shops tucked away in Zona Dorado.
I search for that delicate balance between resting and writing, never
quite finding the perfect combination, but coming close, real close.
All you have to do is listen to the music — it's all here.

Carnival in Mazatlan

Genaro Palacios becomes an instant amigo and we play at Tequila
Charlie's and at the opening of Maz Agua, Mazatlan's only water
park. The high concrete water slide with an incredible angle of
descent, a slight trickle of water and a big red circle emblazoned on
the top is instantly tagged "Kamikaze." And we play a parade at the
Carnival.

The Mazatlan carnival is the second largest in all of Mexico,
and the whole week of fireworks, fiestas, and drunkenness at the
Malycon along the sea wall is little more than organized chaos.
Thousands upon thousands of people from all over Canada, the
United States, Mexico, and Central America converge on this one
small area of Mazatlan.

The power source on our parade float is intermittent and not
properly grounded. I lean in to blow a blues solo and, when the
metal casing of the harp touches the microphone, a jolt of *electricos*
shoots through me, almost knocking me on my butt. I try standing
on a piece of cardboard. Same result. I try removing my bandana
and wrapping it around the harp. Another jolt. Then the parade
grinds to a halt. We sit for over two hours while police, military, and
parade officials try to figure out a way to get one of the huge floats
around a narrow street corner where it is lodged.

The crowd becomes impatient, then irate, pelting us with everything they could get their hands on. The usual confetti-filled eggs,
huge Mexican firecrackers, cherry bombs, aluminum beer cans, and
every once in a while a beer bottle or a still half-full bottle of
Tequila, Mezcal, Aguardiente de Canos, or Rizea (a Mexican home-
brew that makes the strongest Tequila taste like soda pop). Finally,
the ultimate insult. A bulging used pamper lands at our feet in the

middle of the float. And there is no place to run. The throngs of people jam the parade route and many of them are trying to climb on the float to keep from being crushed. It is pitch dark and almost midnight by the time they finally dismantle the huge float so it can pass through the street.

Booze Cruise

That was my last Carnival parade, needless to say. Another winter, we played the famous "Mexican Booze Cruise" every Sunday night. An aging relic of a boat known as *La Reyna Isabel* left the harbor at sundown and skirted Las Tres Islas off the Pacific coast of Mazatlan. The "old girl" was far from being sea-worthy, but some-how the drunken crew managed to keep her afloat in all kinds of weather. The American woman who owned and operated the Booze Cruise would never cancel because of bad weather. Money and greed were the controlling factors. Along with your $10-ride, you got all you could eat and all you could drink. The food was greasy fried-chicken and week-old tortillas. The booze was rum punch and margaritas mixed in huge wash-tubs. You just dipped in your plastic go-cups anytime you wanted a refill.

We often witnessed the fully-accredited mixologists preparing the booze while we were setting up the band. Gallon jugs of cheap tequi-la and even cheaper ron blanco were lightly splashed with cheap orange juice and lime juice. A couple of small bags of salt were tossed into the Margarita tub. When the old *La Reyna Isabel* left the harbor with 40 or 50 people jammed onto a deck that might comfortably hold 15 or 20 and headed out to sea, we cranked up the band and the crowd hit the tubs to make sure they got their ten-bucks-worth.

I played bass, Genaro Palacios played harp and guitar, and Victor Robles (who I dubbed RCA Victor) tried to play drums and keep his cymbals and snare from crashing onto the deck as we rolled and heaved through the heavy seas. I braced my back against the bass amp to keep it from falling over and tried to hold one foot on the mike stand to keep it steady. In country circles they used to sing *I Don't Think Hank Done It This Way*. Somehow, my vision was more of "Jimmy Buffett on acid" or "The Voyage Of The Damned."

Most of the "Damned" spent the night being seasick and recycling the wild concoction of booze back into the Pacific.

I don't ever recall seeing a life jacket or a raft of any kind. When we arrived back at the docks, I swore I would never do it again . . . until the next Sunday. The final blow was the night RCA Victor got in a brawl with a loud-mouthed American tourist. When we docked, the Federales whisked him off to jail. Two hours later, he was back playing drums with us at Tequila Charlie's. The Mexican Law Enforcement officers had fined him a few pesos (about $12 U.S.). He then caught a bus back to the Zona Dorado, and was only a few minutes late for the gig.

After the "Parade" and the "Booze Cruise", my other Mexican bookings paled by comparison. Over the years, I played Mr. Foxes with my old pals Denny Eddy and Lou Paul. I played at the Playa Bruja up on Cerritos north beach with Tom Beatty, Lance Jackson, Brent McAthey, and Laura Vinson. Through my many winter stays, I have played at La Mision, The Night Out, Tequila Sunrise, The Joint, Le Gourmet, a couple of high society gigs at El Cid golf course and a few low budget cantinas. None of these gigs paid much in the way of cold hard pesos, but the barter system is alive and well and in a constant holding pattern somewhere over the Pacific Coast of Mexico.

Mexican Security

For some reason or other, Mexicans always have their radios turned up twice as loud as the speakers will handle and they never bother to fine-tune them on a station. That loud distorted sound can be heard coming from houses, motels, hotels, bars, and restaurants all over the country.

A Mexican friend once told me of a great idea for security. You simply leave your radio cranked to the max and tuned off the station. Would-be thieves will think there are Mexican people living in your hotel room and will pass on by in their search for rich tourists.

What a great idea! The next night when I went out, I set my radio up with that "Mexican sound" and left it blaring in my hotel room. When I returned a few hours later, my radio was gone.

Guitar Town

The first time I visited Mexico, I became fascinated with the sound of their hand-crafted Spanish guitars. I had been captivated with the big, bold sound of the steel-string acoustic guitars played by country artists, the electric guitars of Roy Clark, Chet Atkins and Jerry Reed, and the rockabilly sounds of Carl Perkins and Scotty Moore. But this was different.

The smaller nylon-string guitars had a softer, warmer, gentle feminine sound and I knew I had to have one in order to pick up on that style and sound. I learned that the best guitars in Mexico were built in Paracho, Michoacan. Two or three dozen guitar makers lived in this tiny village, a few hundred kilometres back in the countryside from Guadalajara. I began to make plans to take the journey to this magical "guitar town" and to buy the best guitar I could lay my hands on.

Lou Paul, his wife Jan, and I poured over a handful of Mexican maps until we discovered Paracho, a tiny speck in the state of Michoacan. We took a Mexicana Airlines flight to Guadalajara and stayed over night at the aging Calinda Roma Hotel. The next morning, we rented a car and drove the narrow, winding roads to Paracho. We arrived in the early afternoon and began a search for the "great guitar."

Both sides of the single main street were lined with guitar shops. We were like kids in a candy store. Little old ladies sat on the sidewalk polishing the newly-made instruments. Young children worked with their fathers sanding guitar necks, filing the head stocks and learning their father's trade.

We went up one side of the street and down the other, checking almost every guitar in every shop and listening to the guitar makers with sawdust and glue still clinging to their hands as they demonstrated the guitars and explained each guitar in detail. We understood very little Spanish, but one could sense the great pride they took in their craft. I settled on my choice, Lou picked a guitar which he liked, and just as we were about to leave, I made a quick trip back and bought the mate to my first choice. We loaded up our guitars and headed back to Guadalajara. The next morning we flew back to Mazatlan.

When I arrived at The Paraiso, I couldn't wait to get the guitar out of its case. I sat down on the bed, and in a half hour I had written an instrumental guitar tune. I called it Paracho, Michoacan. A few years later, when I recorded the tune in Nashville, the title got changed to something a little more American — *Flying To The Sun* — which is on my MIRAGE CD. The tune was recorded with that same guitar. The Nashville guitar players on the session drooled over it. Greg Galbraith, a long-time session musician who has played on many of my records, remarked, "If it ever has pups, I want the pick of the litter!"

I still have that guitar today and I am as proud of it as the man who built it. It is more than just a piece of Mexican *Madera*; it is a living, breathing, musical instrument that echoes the spirit of my soul.

Each year around the end of March, I notice the days begin to lengthen and the glorious Mexican afternoons stretch themselves into the early evening. By this time I am beginning to feel at one with the life, the people, and the easy pace of their existence on the far west coast of Mexico. But I am also beginning to feel the urgency of my music career and the call to arms.

My first step will be the long journey from Mazatlan to Puerto Vallarta, to Monterey, to Houston, and on to Nashville. The hard part is always saying good-bye again to my Mexican *compadres* and the laid-back, easy-living lifestyle of the past few months. The only thing that holds back the good-bye tears is the excitement of flying to Nashville and getting into the recording studio, where all the notes, words, tapes, and scribblings will be born into songs and music and records.

The Stories Behind the Songs

MASQUERADE

He was a stunt man from Los Angeles, he said. He had just done the international show at the Houston Astrodome. He made $50,000 per performance. No, he had not done the Calgary Stampede; they paid only $10,000 per performance. He never worked for less than $50,000. He had done every Hollywood movie you could name.

We all sat around on the sand on our beach blankets, under the blazing Mexican sun. A slight breeze drifted across the sparkling, blue Pacific Ocean. The scene was perfect and everyone listened in awe to the stunt man. The stories continued on into the afternoon. Everyone was convinced this guy was hot stuff.

Then it happened. An old friend from Ponoka, Alberta, a small community a few miles from where I was born and raised, came strolling along the beach. He stopped by to chat. After brief hellos, he turned directly to the stunt man and said, "How are you doing, Joe? Did you get the cement all poured at the silo before you left up there? Damn, I thought you were going to freeze to death trying to pour cement all winter!"

His masquerade was over, but my song had just been born. I slipped away from the tiny knot of people on the beach and made my way along the water's edge, towards my *hacienda*.

"Those cheap sunglasses are a clever disguise, / They can't see your soul if they can't see your eyes." The words came in a rush. I had to get them down. I pushed open the door to my humble abode, picked up my guitar, snapped on my tape recorder, and sang the first and second verses non-stop. Within an hour, the rest of the song took form.

MASQUERADE

THOSE CHEAP SUNGLASSES
ARE A CLEVER DISGUISE
THEY CAN'T SEE YOUR SOUL
IF THEY CAN'T SEE YOUR EYES

WHAT A MASQUERADE
WHAT A MASQUERADE
THEY CAN'T SEE YOUR SOUL
IF THEY CAN'T SEE YOUR EYES
WHAT A MASQUERADE
WHAT A CLEVER DISGUISE
WHAT A MASQUERADE

YOUR FUNNY WAY OF TALKING IS A PERFECT DISGUISE
IF THEY CAN'T HEAR YOUR VOICE
THEY CAN'T HEAR YOUR LIES
WHAT A MASQUERADE
WHAT A MASQUERADE
IF THEY CAN'T HEAR YOUR VOICE
THEY CAN'T HEAR YOUR LIES
WHAT A CHEAP CHARADE
WHAT A CLEVER DISGUISE
WHAT A MASQUERADE

(CHORUS)
YOUR IDENTITY IS A MYSTERY
YOU KNOW YOUR SECRET IS SAFE WITH ME
I WON'T BLOW YOUR COVER, IF YOU DON'T
BLOW MINE

© Sparwood Music

A few nights later, at a beach party, I sang the song to many of the same people who had spent the afternoon with the stunt man. When I struck the last chord on my little hand-made Mexican guitar and sang the last line of *Masquerade*, everybody chanted "*Otro! Otro! Otro!*" (Spanish-Mexican slang used in entertainment circles as an enthusiastic request for an encore.) *Masquerade* was a hit song in their sun-drenched tequila-soaked minds. And I was a happy song-writer. To hell with record companies and royalties.

(Top) *Damron headlined the 1985 Easter Seal Western Festival in Sacramento, California.*

(Right) *The brochure for the Legend and the Legacy tour.*

186

(Top) *Hotel Mexico, the inspiration for one of Damron's 1980s singles.*

(Middle Left and Right) *Dick and Lou Paul in search of the great guitar, Paracho, 1989.*

(Right) *Brent McAthey with Dick outside his winter headquarters in the Hotel Pato Blanco, Mazatlan, 1995.*

CHAPTER NINE

Total Departure

TOTAL DEPARTURE

I'VE BEEN SO CLOSE TO HELL
I COULD ALMOST FEEL THE BURNING;
I REACHED OUT TO HEAVEN
AND ALMOST TOUCHED THE SKY.
BUT SOMEWHERE IN BETWEEN
THERE'S A PLACE THAT I SURVIVE IN
AND I'VE BEEN LIVING THERE
A LONG, LONG TIME.

© *Sparwood Music*

4:45 a.m., Wed. June 3rd, 1992

I've been lying awake for hours. Everything in the world running through my brain. Words, music, songs, stories, and miles and miles of highway between Bentley, Alberta and Las Vegas, Nevada. My daughter Barbara and I will be driving to Vegas next week, and I have this old habit that formed in the years when I lived on the road. When I have hundreds or thousands of miles ahead of me and I need to sleep the most, I lie awake tracing every mile of the journey over and over in my mind. It's exhausting. I hate it, but up until this day it is a habit I have not been able to break.

I snap on the bed lamp and, as my eyes adjust to the light, I see the Willie Nelson autobiography among a small stack of books on my night table. Shakti Gawain's *Reflections in the Light*, a worn copy of Oral Robert's *Daily Blessing* that spanned October 1st to December 31, 1984, and had traveled Europe and the United Kingdom with me on my '84 tour, *Citizen Hughes*, John O'Hara's *Sweet and Sour*, June Carter Cash's autobiography, Thoreau's *Writer's Journal*, *Behold A Pale Horse*, *It Isn't Always Easy*, and Tom T. Hall's *Story Teller*.

I've read all of these books and suddenly just looking at them, I get this gigantic rush of mind-overload. Everything in every single one of these books is trying to register someplace in my night-weary brain.

I pick up *Willie* and begin to read, hoping that focusing in on it will relieve the spinning action of the other half-dozen volumes. It works. I read a chapter or two. I can hear the wind and the raindrops on my bedroom window. I get up and go to the back door. I lay *Willie* down on the counter, open the inside door and snap on the yard light. I stare out into the morning rain and the greyness of the coming dawn. The grass is soaked, the tall green poplars are swaying in the wind, the rainwater is splashing on the doorstop.

I'm lost for a moment, captivated by the magic of it all. Then I see the *Willie* book laying out there in the rain. Just as I am about to open the storm door to retrieve the book, I realize it is a perfect mirror image, through the rain on the window. I close the door and go back to bed. It's six o'clock. God I'm tired. I need some sleep. I've been spending too much time alone. Good night Willie, wherever you are.

PIECES OF LIFE
I SEE THEM FLASHING BEFORE ME
HEART LIKE A WHEEL
SPINNING MY LIFE IN A SONG
FOLLOW THE WIND
FROM HELL TO THE EDGE OF FOREVER
PIECES OF LIFE
PIECES OF LIFE

Vegas, December 6th, 1995

I'm awake at 5:00 a.m. and halfway out the door when my wake-up call comes. I catch a cab to McCarran Field and check in at Delta Airlines for L.A. and on to Mazatlan. We board at 7:40 a.m. for the 8:00 a.m. flight. Only minutes after settling into my window seat for the short flight to California, the captain's voice fills the cabin: "*Attencion* K-Mart Shoppers . . ." No, no, no. It was even more predictable than that. "Due to conditions at L.A.X., this flight will now be leaving Las Vegas at 9:30 a.m."

I sit back in my seat with a thump. Oh well, an hour and a half to sit. The phrase "Leaving Las Vegas" grows in my mind like a mushroom. Maybe that's what I was really doing this time. My love affair with the slot machines and the roulette wheels and 99¢ breakfasts is over. Could the never-ending battle with Immigration and the losing battle with the I.R.S. all be behind me?

December 8th, 1995

Home at last. What a mixed bag of feelings and thoughts. It seems as if I just made it over the border in time. Escaping for a few months to try to get a grip on my totally unrelenting and disorganized life. How big? How small? Taxes? Video? CD? Bookings?

Old habits die hard — or do they die at all? It seems they become harder and harder to manage. It sucks up my creativity and screws up my peace of mind. In the next few weeks, I will make some major decisions. They will come slowly and surely, without agony and defeat. Should I make a list and check each item off as they surface? I think not. I think one major resolution will come to cover it all. That would make it all so easy. I will wait and see.

December 18, 1995

I'm back in my winter headquarters at the Hotel Pato Blanco in Mazatlan, Sinaloa, Mexico. I have been here 12-days-and-counting since my departure from Las Vegas. I have unpacked my suitcases and the boxes that I store here from year to year. After a day or two spent eating meals in restaurants, I caught the Sabalo-Cocos bus down to the Gigante market to lay in some supplies of bread and milk and beans and fruit. It was my first exercise in speaking Spanish again, trying to remember all the right names for things: bread is *pan*, milk is *leche*, beans are *frijoles*, rum is *ron*, but the giant bottle of Tequila is still *Tequila*.

My fifth-floor apartment looks a little desolate. I throw open every window. The late afternoon sunshine and the breeze from the Pacific Ocean fill my space to overflowing. I start feeling a little better. I have learned, from years of coming and going, that I can't rush it. At sundown, I light a candle and some incense. Some of the old feelings respond and I drift off to the sounds of waves crashing on the rocks just below my window. As darkness falls, the candle becomes my only source of light, and I stare at the warm, glowing flame for a few minutes, put on an incredible guitar tape, Tony Rice and John Carlini's *River Suite*, and drift away into the warm mix of light, sounds, and smells.

I see myself 20 years younger, staying at hotels such as La Palapa and El Pescador for a few short weeks. As my love affair with Mexico intensifies, I begin staying for longer periods of time. I move to the Buganvillia, Ibis Apartmentos, La Misíon and then discover The Paraiso, where I stay for a few months at a time for the next seven years. My trusty blues harp is always tucked away, like a gambler's derringer, and I have many a shoot-out with the local bands.

Back in March, 1992, Denny Eddy and I performed a benefit concert at the Ciudad de Los Ninos, Mazatlan's facility for homeless children. This orphanage was old and crumbling and was located three miles north of the city limits on the International Highway.

There were 73 boys and girls from ages two to fifteen under the care of the Gray Nuns. We set up our equipment on what was originally designed to be a basketball court. It had never been completed. The older boys dragged a dozen-or-so big, brown wooden benches out of the buildings and formed a semi-circle around our location. We played and sang to the enthusiastic audience throughout the scorching-hot Mexican afternoon.

When we were packing up to leave for our short drive back to the Hotel Pato Blanco, someone in our party remarked how clean and well-nourished the *ninos* appeared to be. They didn't look to be suffering.

"The scars are on the inside," one of the nuns replied, quietly.

Not Etched In Stone

Just outside of Ottawa, Ontario, in the rolling wooded countryside, a great little country music festival called the "Ompah Stomp" is held every year on the Labor Day long weekend. I have played the event a couple of times.

In 1989, I was on the show along with Bobby Bare, Terry Carisse, Marie Bottrell, and a host of other Canadian country artists. I flew in to do the show with only my guitar and my trusty blues harp. Blue Highway was booked to back me. I had sent a tape to Jon Park Wheeler, the guitar player with the band. He was to write the chord charts for the band and have a brief rehearsal.

I hit the stage late in the afternoon. The crowd was into it. Over the years and, especially back in the late 1970s and early 1980s, I had played the Ottawa area a lot. CKBY Radio has always played my music and I had appeared numerous times on the now defunct Family Brown tv show. It was like old-home week and I recognized dozens of familiar faces in the front area of the vast crowd. Artists and musicians from the other bands crowded the wings and the backstage area.

The crowd danced and screamed and cheered; the music soared out over their heads and into the surrounding hills. The magic feeling, which an entertainer gets when he knows everything is right, overwhelmed me. The crowd, the sound, the afternoon, and the music all came together. The band was magnificent. Sam Henry was on drums, feeling the old magic that we had generated years ago with Ralph Carlson and Country Mile. Al Bragg played steel and keyboards, John Ryan laid down a rock-solid bass line, and Jon Park Wheeler created some incredible solos over the charts he had written.

The icing on the cake was *There Ain't No Love Around*, a minor-mode song that I had written in Mexico years before this and which I still perform on stage today. I started the song cold, just me and the acoustic guitar, with some light finger-style picking.

THERE AIN'T NO LOVE AROUND.
JUST THE AGE-OLD BASIC DESIRE
LOVE AIN'T NECESSARY ANYMORE.
THERE AIN'T NO LOVE AROUND.
DON'T YOU THINK IT'S KIND OF SAD
WE DON'T LOVE EACH OTHER ANYMORE.

— *There Ain't No Love Around* © Sparwood Music

The chorus built to a half-time rock feel and I could feel the energy building. The instrumental solo flew into a wide open, balls-to-the-wall "A-Minor" jam. The freedom, the intensity, the desire all became one. I knew it, the band knew it, and the crowd loved it. We had lift-off. This was not just music, this was not just another afternoon at the Ompah Stomp — this was an *experience*.

I eased the band back and slid the vocal into the last chorus. We blasted back into the "A-Minor" solo. We were right back out there, flying off into the ozone. We took it all the way, and, at the end, there was nothing left but my finger-style acoustic guitar with a long, rolling new-age Minor repeating over and over and drifting endlessly into the early evening. I closed the show with *One Night Stand*, introduced all the band members, and pushed my way backstage.

A few minutes later I saw Jon's chart for *There Ain't No Love Around*. There was a note at the bottom: "Damron's charts are not etched in stone. 72 bars more or less. Good luck."

This says more about my life and my music than anything ever written. Thanks, Jon, for knowing and understanding. Not too many people have seen it through your eyes.

Nashville Revisited

Long before TNN or CMT or Opryland or country music videos, south of Chicago, north of Atlanta, and somewhere close to the heart of Tennessee, Nashville hugged the Cumberland River, huddled in the wooded, rolling Tennessee Hills and sheltered the childlike innocence of country music.

I went to Nashville in 1961 and returned again and again, in '63, '65, '69 . . . all through the 1970s and '80s I went back to record and attend music business functions. It was a dream-come-true relationship. But it took me until the '90s to realize how much we had both changed. I used to hang out at Tootsie's Orchid Lounge, The Wagon Wheel, T.J.'s, and Deeman's Den. I would go backstage at the old Ryman Auditorium and hear Johnny Cash, Hank Snow, Hawkshaw Hawkins, Jean Shepherd, Marty Robbins, Roy Acuff, and many others. And when the last song was sung, and the Opry fell silent for another week, the artists and the pickers and grinners loaded up and headed back out on the road to cover the great expanse of North America with their music. From Florida to Canada and from coast to coast, they played everything from school houses in Kentucky to Detroit's Cobo Hall (the home of some of the early country music "package shows").

I would go down the alley and across the street to Ernest Tubb's Record Shop and the Midnight Jamboree, and when that was over, I would go next door to Linebaugh's Restaurant to dine on a bowl of dinner soup, loaded with soda crackers and Heinz Ketchup. Coffee was 25¢ a cup and charging for refills was unheard of in those days. I sat in a booth by the window, watching the derelicts, late-night country fans and Opry leftovers shuffle by, and drank coffee 'til the sun came up.

Sometimes, I recognized some of the pickers from various bands. Once in a while Tompall Glaser or Marty Robbins or some songwriter would come in for a coffee or to play the pinball machine. The Jukebox went nonstop, cranking out Hank Williams, Patsy Cline, Hawkshaw Hawkins, Ferlin Husky, and George Jones tunes. It was like I had died and gone to Hillbilly Heaven, even though I was lonesome, tired, depressed, and didn't know a soul. Sitting there people-watching and drinkin' coffee sure as hell beat being alone back in my room at the James Robertson. Once in a while, one of the local drunks would come by my table and hit me up for a quarter for a coffee. I shrugged my shoulders and held up my empty palms and they moved off to other prospects. Sometimes, I would overhear a conversation at another table about somebody's wife or somebody's truck or somebody drinkin' whiskey. I'd grab a napkin and write down, "My wife ran off with a truck drivin' man and I'm sittin' here drinkin' whiskey . . ." After a few minutes, the great creative rush would subside and I would crumple up the potential hit song and drop it on the floor under the table.

In Nashville (the city of winner, losers, and gross injustices), for every artist who rises to the top of the heap, there are dozens who come to Music City, U.S.A. only to have their hopes and dreams shattered by people who know every trick in the trade. Some very talented people never get heard because they don't know the right people or don't have the money to "cross the palms," "grease the wheels," or "pay the shot."

Nashville's Exit Inn, a music club that seems to be opened and closed on a regular basis, is located in Ellison Place, only a short cab ride from the Hall of Fame Motor Inn, where I usually stay now when I am in town recording.

It was "Ladies Night" at the Exit Inn. I found my way in the back door (the front door off the sidewalk is always closed; therefore one enters through the back exit. Get it? The Exit Inn!). The place was small, dark, dirty and stuffy and was about three-quarters full. I grabbed a chair up front. The stage was loaded with some of Nashville's finest pickers. Some I had worked with, others I either recognized or heard someone in the crowd drop a name or two as they took the stage. "What a band," I thought. "This is going to be great."

The band did a couple of tunes and then I realized "Ladies Night" at the Exit Inn had nothing to do with free drinks, cover charges, or male strippers, as it does in many Canadian bars. In the next few hours, I heard four of the greatest female singers I had ever heard anywhere, on or off records, radio, or tv. It was a showcase of gals from all over the country — Detroit, Florida, Texas, and California — all in Nashville trying to get that big break.

I found out later that night that, after weeks, months and years in town, some were getting close. One was singing demo sessions for a publishing company. Another was working as a secretary in a record company. The third singer was staying with a friend. And last, but certainly not least, was a cute little dark-eyed gal who sang her ass off. But as they say in the biz, she couldn't get arrested. She was leaving to go back home to Texas the next day.

I recently saw an article in a Music City publication that described a great female singer who had hung around for a long time trying to get a record deal as "a rebel in a rubber stamp town." They say you gotta be different, original, etc. But if you don't fit neatly into the scheme, or have the big bucks behind you or know somebody, it's a long hard trail to oblivion or at least to singing on the weekends in a Knife-and-Gun club back in east Texas where they all keep telling you that you should be in Nashville.

The next morning I was sitting in my producer's office in the United Artists Tower. I was thinking of the Texas gal waiting in the airport for her flight home. I was still hearing her voice, which sounded like Patsy Cline, Linda Ronstadt, and Kim Carnes all rolled into one . . . when, suddenly, I heard some of the worst wailing ever to come from the throat of a female of any species. This tape was being played over and over. It was out of tune, out of meter — Number 1 on the top of the Top Ten list of the worst songs I ever heard in my life. Joe Bob Barnhill and I just sat and looked at each other as this musical torture emanated from the back office. When the man responsible for playing the tape emerged from the back room, I recognized a well-known record producer.

Joe Bob said, "What are you doin' with *that* stuff, man?"

"I'm getting ready to record her in the morning," the producer replied.

"Jesus Christ, man, she can't sing!"

"I know," the producer said, "but her husband owns a chain of hotels in Florida."

Another cool, rainy afternoon in Nashville I had some time to kill between sessions. I left my room at the Hall of Fame Motor Inn, crossed the street, and walked up the hill to the Four Corners. There were a half-dozen little shops and bars in the area. I picked one with a Coors beer sign and a faded Confederate flag hanging in the window. I pushed open the sagging door and was greeted by the smell of stale beer and cigarette smoke. A lone man sat behind the counter. He nodded but said nothing.

The shop was dirty and dusty and contained Nashville ashtrays, Nashville playing cards, Nashville beer can covers. Goo-Goo Clusters, Hank Jr. ball caps, Xerox copies of Elvis' will, shopworn tee-shirts, and other gifts and souvenirs equally as valuable.

There was a guitar hanging on the back wall. I stopped to examine it. When it was brand new, it may have been a $20.00 guitar. It was cracked and old, the neck was twisted, the bridge had lifted until the four remaining strings were a good two inches off the finger board.

The man behind the counter saw me eyeing the guitar and spoke for the first time, "You know who used to own that guitar, boy?" He paused for emphasis, "Waylon Jennings!"

"Oh, really?" I said quietly as I made my way to the door, out of the shop, and into the rain. I went next door in search of more Nashville treasures.

The walls in Tootsie's Orchid Lounge on Nashville's Lower Broad are plastered with faded old 8"x10" black-and-white photos, dog-eared album jackets, 45 r.p.m. records, beer signs, and postcards from around the world. Thousands of signatures, autographs, and stickers cover almost every available inch of the bar, run along the hallway and spill into the back room. Among the grime and graffiti, a small piece of brown paper is tacked up inside the door. It reads, "Times are rough and things are hard. Here's your fuckin' Christmas card."

Yet another time I was sitting in Joe Bob Barnhill's office in the Faron Young Building. Joe Bob and I were working on material for an upcoming session. A well-dressed man in his late thirties entered the office. I don't remember his name, but he was from Dallas, Texas, and he carried a shiny, new leather attache case. He began telling us about all the songs he had written for everyone from Willie Nelson to Kenny Rogers. He talked of hit songs, million-sellers, and contracts for hundreds of thousands of dollars. As he talked, he fondled the briefcase. Undoubtedly, it contained more hit songs, more million-sellers, and thousands of dollars worth of contracts. After he had laid it on thicker and heavier than even a mere mortal in Nashville could be expected to bear, he got up to leave.

As he reached the door, Joe Bob nodded toward the case and calmly said, "Careful you don't spill your coffee on your sandwiches."

The Worst Songs

Brian Sklar, Prince Albert, Saskatchewan's own "Captain Canada," was driving us from Prince Albert to the Saskatoon Airport at 5:00 in the morning on a bitter, cold November day. Billy Joe Shaver, Doyle Holly, who had worked with Buck Owens for years, and I had been guests on the *Number One West* tv show. We had taped it live at the Prince Albert Penitentiary.

To pass the time away during the drive, we were all sharing music biz stories. After a while, the talk turned to songwriting and songs. Shaver had written some big hits for artists like Waylon and Willie. Doyle Holly, when he wasn't on the road with Owen's band, worked in Buck's publishing company, listening to songs sent in from all over the world. Holly began listing some of the worst songs he'd ever heard. I tossed in, "I Just Got Over You And Now I'm Under Him," as a potential hit song for a female artist.

Sklar, who was staring into the blinding snow and trying to hold the stationwagon on the ice-bound Saskatchewan highway, commented, "Someone should do an album of all the worst songs."

Billy Joe's voice came from the darkness of the back seat in a slow Texas drawl, "I think Doyle already done that."

Critics

I have received the highest praise and the deepest cuts from music critics all over the world. The closer to home, the deeper the cut. When you and your music are distanced from the closeness of the home country critic, there is nothing to judge you by except the sound of your music and the performance you give. "Familiarity breeds contempt." It's hard to overcome preconceived notions and personal vendettas.

When my LOST IN THE MUSIC album was released in Canada, I was told by an Ontario based-critic that the album was so weak that he did not want to embarrass me by reviewing it. A few months later, when the same album was released in the United Kingdom, it was the "pick of the month," over albums by Dolly Parton, Willie Nelson, Asleep at the Wheel and about ten others. When I did a show with a number of American artists in a large city with two daily newspapers, one paper reported, "Damron far outclassed his American counterparts." The other paper said, "Unfortunately, Damron should not have been on the show at all." I guess it's in the ears of the beholder.

When James Muretich of the *Calgary Herald* called to do an interview, I was on the road. My girlfriend answered the phone. When Muretich asked for me, she replied, "I don't know where the fuck he is. I'm just trying to get some sleep around here." His story in the *Herald* began: "Dick Damron has a very unusual answering service." Two or three years later, the same James, when reviewing the Juno nominations, wrote: "I can't see how Damron was nominated as he hasn't done anything all year." I don't often respond to critics, but at that time I had just returned from 28 one-nighters in five different countries, as well as a string of dates in the U.S. that took me from Nashville to Indiana, Colorado, and Oregon. I had a new album released and had busted my ass all year in Canada. I phoned him up, told him what I had been doing and, without giving him a chance to reply, I quickly added, "I don't know how long you've been unconscious, but if you ever wake up, the fucking shock will kill you."

When Gordon Lightfoot toured the west a few years back, an Edmonton critic wrote a scathing review, totally "raping" his songs, his music, his performance, and his guitar-playing. When the critic was asked how he could do that to someone of Lightfoot's status, he replied, "Man, it made me feel just like I was pissing on a monument." Sad, sad, sad.

Another time, when I was appearing at a huge international country music festival, my road manager saw the critic arrive about a half-hour after I had opened the show. He could not possibly have caught my part of the show, but he covered his ass by writing: "Damron turned in his usual high-energy performance." At yet another gigantic festival, with some top names in country music on the bill, the reviewer said, "The real star of the show was Canadian Dick Damron, who all but totally ran off with the show." He spent the rest of the column defiling my singing, my songwriting, and my guitar-playing. I didn't understand.

One of my all-time favorites is still: "Damron amused, rather than entertained, the huge audience." In a Las Vegas review, with everybody from Bill Cosby to George Strait in town, the story ended: "Dick Damron's show was one of the most worthwhile evenings on the Strip." Maybe he got free drinks? Or got lucky after the show?

Another critic wrote, "Damron, who should be internationally famous but somehow isn't, turned in a high-energy show spiced with lyrical genius." The next time I played the same city, he shit all over me. A British record reviewer, not aware that my SOLDIER OF FORTUNE album was cut in Nashville with all the top Nashville session men, compared the "Canadian" album unfavorably with what would have been available to me if I had ventured south of the border. Only three of my 27 albums have not been recorded in Nashville. When my tenth album was released, a knowledgeable country music expert wrote, "It is only Damron's second album in over 20 years in the business and justifiably so, as it generates the life force of a store-bought mannequin."

A British journalist reviewed my SOLDIER OF FORTUNE album saying my lyrics were "Kristoffersonish." Later, at the Wembley Festival, this critic told me the line "He's still got the devil to pay" was a direct steal from Kris Kristofferson.

"How old is Kris?" I asked, knowing he was around 30. The journalist looked at me, wondering what the hell I meant. So I told him my grandmother was 80 years old when she died, and when I was five years old, she used to tell me that if I got into trouble "there'd be the devil to pay."

The first trap a songwriter falls into is writing for critics or publishers or producers and not for people. But, unfortunately, a writer/artist must get through publishers, producers, and music directors to get to the people. You must get through the publisher and the producer in order to make a record. The record has to get by the music director to get to the listener. A British trade magazine recently stated: "The music director syndrome is the most blatant form of censorship in the world today." The music director decides what thousands, sometimes millions of people will be allowed to hear on radio.

Norman Mailer once defined critics as "eunuchs at a gang bang." Letting them get to you can only lead to mediocrity. As western romance author Louis L'Amour once advised, "A writer should write for people, not critics or other writers."

When I came back from doing the 1978 International Wembley Festival in London, England, with Barbara Fairchild, Carroll Baker, Don Everly, Carl Smith, Freddie Hart, Jody Miller, Don Williams, Skeeter Davis, Ronnie Milsap, Marty Robbins, Dave and Sugar, Carl Perkins, Donna Fargo, Ronnie Prophet, Tompall Glaser, Larry Gatlin, Dottie West, Kenny Rogers, Moe Bandy, Merle Haggard, and another dozen or so British and Irish country artists — definitely one of the largest country music festivals in the world at that time — a Red Deer, Alberta, country DJ announced that I had just returned from doing a small show in northern Alberta. There is a "Wembley" in northern Alberta. Same name, different show.

Don't get me wrong, critics, journalists, and reviewers are not all bad, but they don't like to be manipulated. When I did the International Show in Nashville to mark the 47th Anniversary of the Grand Ol' Opry, the place was swarming with artists, agents, managers, press agents, and record company promo people, all vying for the big press opportunity. I had flown to Toronto, caught a ride with steel guitarist Al Brisco to London, Ontario, and then hitched a ride with Joe and Marilynn Caswell on down to Nashville and was just "hangin' out" and lying low. As I left the show, wearing my ragged jeans and jean jacket and a leather headband holding back my shoulder-length hair, a lady with a barrage of camera equipment snapped away at me. The next morning, the picture appeared on the front page of the entertainment section of *The Nashville Tennessean*. The caption read, "Picker Peter Damron in Town for Country Bash." I don't know where they got the name Peter, but they spelled Damron right and all the music people knew who it was. One of the big-name artists, obviously pissed off because it wasn't his picture, approached me and told me I was being disrespectful to country music — dressing like that.

Like I said, the press is not all that bad. When I brought home the award for Male Vocalist of the Year in 1983, the live-in lady of my life said, "I don't know where you're gonna put that damned thing. This place already looks like a shrine to Dick Damron."

One year, at the Wembley Festival, it was late in the afternoon and I was the last one to rehearse. I was scheduled to open the show and only had about an hour to go back to my hotel, shower, change, and return to open the show. As I made my way down the backstage stairs, a pretty young lady flashed her press pass and asked if we could do an interview. I told her about my schedule and she asked if she could come along to the hotel and do the interview while I got ready for my show. We talked in the cab and she made notes. When we got to the hotel, I hit the shower. In a few minutes, I was out of the shower and back in the room, wrapped in a towel with another towel over my head. The young lady from the press had dug out the pillows and was stretched out on the bed. The buttons on her blouse were open down far enough to show that she had removed her bra. Her faded denim skirt was hiked up above her knees, exposing her sleek, slim legs almost to the thighs. She was ready to do the interview.

"Jesus Christ," I said. "I've only got five minutes." I dropped the towels and slid down beside her. Five minutes later, or maybe only four-and-a-half, I was pulling on my clothes, grabbing my guitar, phoning for a cab, and running for the door. She was lying across the bed, puffing on her after-the-fact cigarette.

"I'm sorry we didn't have more time," I said.

"Oh, it was lovely," she moaned, as I pulled the door closed and ran for the elevator.

Like I said, the press isn't all bad.

I never did see the interview and I can't remember what magazine she said she wrote for. I think it was in Scotland, because she was Scottish. Do they have a country music publication in Scotland or just backstage ladies?

Perhaps a Toronto-based country music journalist nailed it right on the head when he wrote: "Damron made it on his own, just when making it on your own lost all meaning and importance in the music business."

The Saddest Part of All

The saddest part of all is that Canada is a country full of people following the American Dream. Canadians have no dream of their own. Canadians don't blaze trails or seek out unchartered courses in search of their own reality. Canadians settle for the easy way out. To be second best is second nature. They shoulder their load of self-imposed inhibitions and carry them into infinity.

Being Number 1 in Canada means nothing; being Number 99 on the American "Top 100" means everything. Canadians cry about the unfairness and apologize for their lack of success. Canadian music moguls are quick to remind us that the music business is now 10 percent music and 90 percent business, and that the money comes from grants and governments and financial backers, not from playing music and selling records. Somehow, Canadians are content to be second best in the 10 percent that is left. Can anyone out there sing *Oh Canada* all the way through without stopping?

Snakes And Ladders

One long weekend in August 1994, I played three different events in three days in two different provinces. I drove about 800 miles and got about 10 hours sleep on this whole mini-tour. For this, I received half the agreed fee for one gig, a bad cheque for playing the music festival, and nothing for the other show. It must be some kind of record, because in the previous 35 years in the business, there were only four or five times that I had got screwed by the fickle finger of some agent, manager, promoter, or club owner. Maybe it was a sign of the times?

"Trust me" means "watch your ass," and "I'll get back to you on this . . ." means "you'll never hear from me again".

The late Bobby Darin once said, "I want a manager who can draw blood." You just have to be careful that it's not your blood that they are drawing. There is a great story about a manager who knew his artist was terminally ill. No one else knew he only had a few weeks to live. The manager flies into Vegas and books 35 weeks over a four-year period at $75,000 a week. A few months later the artist dies "suddenly" and Mr. Manager sues the artist's estate for "loss of income."

In Canadian country music circles you don't have to lay awake at night worrying about $75,000-a-week gigs, but there is always some strange theory of relativity that fits into the scheme of things. In my early days of playing country dances, sports days, fairs and events sponsored by Car Clubs, Legions, Elks Clubs, etc., things were pretty simple. And the more simple and straight-forward the deal — the better. There weren't too many screw-ups. However, when you're young and ambitious, there are always a few folks ready to sock-it-to-you.

In 1982, when I was on tour in Holland, someone showed up with a brand new European bootleg album called THE ROCK HOUSE featuring two of my tunes, *Gonna Have A Party* and *Rockin' Baby*. The scratchy quality of the reproduction made it pretty plain that the tracks had been lifted from the 45's and not taken from a studio-quality master. Although the correct publishing information was used on the label copy and the sparse liner notes, I had no illusions of ever seeing a royalty cheque. Still, I felt a certain rush of pride at having what I thought was my first bootleg record release in Europe.

I learned later from the late Graham Rowe, who was a DJ on pirate radio ship *Radio Caroline*, that my early music was no stranger to the off-coast broadcast station. And as the years passed and my European tours expanded, many other discs and tapes began to surface. When I did an interview with a DJ from Radio "Eta Piraten," he constantly corrected me on my off-handed answers to questions about records and release dates. I soon found out that he knew far more about my early records than I did. More pride!

A few years later, however, I began to resent some of the 20-year-old deals that came to light. One of these included an outright trade of 500 Dick Damron SOLDIER OF FORTUNE albums to a Norwegian music entrepreneur for an aged Box Car Willie master. Another featured an underground record pressing plant that turned out thousands of Dick Damron albums which cost about 90¢ a piece to manufacture, sold for $17 U.S. in a number of European countries, and were such poor quality that most of them were returned to record stores (who were stuck with them).

After this blitzkrieg, it was not at all uncommon for fans to turn up at concerts with some of these records. Strangely enough, most people wanted them signed, telling me how bad the pressings were, but refusing refunds and refusing to give up their "treasured piece of shit." I apologized 'til I was blue in the face. When I visited a record store in Rotterdam, I came face-to-face with the owner who had been a long-time supporter and now was cold as ice. He showed me a stack of the sub-standard albums with no shrinkwrap and no inner sleeve. Then he stuck one on his store turntable. It snapped, crackled, and popped like a bowl of Rice Krispies and wobbled like a dime-store frisbee.

I did everything to try to appease the manager, including exchanging a handful of concert tickets. He never showed up at the concert and I never saw him again.

About this time, I began to get a glimpse of reality. The excitement of playing the gigantic Wembley International Country Music Festival (with artists like Merle Haggard, Kenny Rogers, Dolly Parton and Marty Robbins) to thousands of dedicated country fans began to fade. The kick of playing "Far Away Places With Strange Sounding Names," to quote an old song, didn't kick me any more.

I had my memory banks overloaded with sights and sounds and images and languages, not to mention Customs and Immigration and Taxes and Taxes and Taxes. I realized that my dad's early philosophy about degrees of honesty did not fit this situation at all. If you paid every tax, commission, fee, and due that was leveled at you, there was no way you could break even. Hell, people do it all the time now. Just get those government grants, book a few gigs and spend the rest of the so-called tour holidaying in Switzerland. So, instead of whining and bitching and sniveling, I did one last "Tour From Hell" and caught an all-night flight back to Canada.

No more sleeping in the back of the van amongst the record boxes with Gordon Davies' girl friend's old wet dog. No more going for five days without a shower or a hotel room or a moment's peace! No more wondering if-and-when or how much you were gonna get paid. No more driving on the left-hand side of the road through some quaint little Welsh village in the fog at 90 miles an hour at four o'clock in the morning.

But I do love the great country music fans in the U.K. and on the continent, and I thank all the pickers and soundmen and DJs. And I'm thankful for the great friendships I made with Stewart Barnes, Jeannie Denver, Leen and Coby van der Vent, Sid and Glenys Bowell, Roger Humphries, The Wheelers, John Freeman, Sue Jackson, Mike Storey, Bob Powell and, hell why not, "The Old

Sheepherding Mutton-Buster" Gordon Davies, and every agent, manager, or promoter who drew blood! God Save The Queen.

Friends . . .

Songwriters tend to repeat themselves when they think nobody's listening. Ropers, dopers, users, boozers, and starstruck friends, individually or one at a time, make a helluva captive audience for a frustrated writer when he is going through a dry spell. Just to hear a gasp, or a "right on!" from someone in the room when you run a string of chords together that never seemed to fit before, or sing a lyric (that you've had kicking around in your head for weeks), is like a mild form of foreplay to a quote-unquote "songwriter."

You know that song is a piece of crap. You've tried to get rid of it, but it keeps coming back like a bad dream, and then someone hears it with a different ear. At 4:00 in the morning when you're alone in that hotel room, you sneak the guitar out of the case, sit down among the ruins of a night of party-goers and the "piece of crap" suddenly rewrites itself into one of the best little country songs you've ever written. Two years later, some reviewer discovers the song on your new album and calls it "absolute lyrical genius." The phone rings, you pick it up. It's an old friend calling from half-way around the world. He just got your new album: "It's great! The best thing you've ever done, but that one song on there, is a real piece of crap, man . . ." A full circle of friends keeps you humble.

Somewhere, there must be a common denominator between the wildest and craziest people on the planet and the kindest, gentlest folks I know. I have never quite figured out what has brought us together or what it is that keeps us all orbiting in some strange and mystical holding pattern.

When my brother, Howard, was killed in that tragic helicopter crash a few years ago, I was torn between sitting at home alone and going crazy with my grief, or fulfilling my booking at the Country Roads Saloon in Calgary (and having to face hundreds of people every night). Past experience told me I had to keep going, to keep from being overcome by it all. Denny Eddy showed up out of the blue and spent the entire week with me.

Paul Letkiman (a frustrated blues player, writer, and part-time mental patient) followed me around the western Canadian bar circuit, showing up at the strangest times and places. Sometimes, he was already checked into the room across the hall when I arrived, and there would be a note under my door saying, "Dick, I'm here!"

One night in Medicine Hat, Alberta, when the Silver Buckle was almost pulled to its last notch, the crowd was about as belligerent and unmusical as the dregs of humanity can be. After the gig, I returned to my room. I was angry and depressed over the ugliness of the night. At about 3:00 a.m., I was sitting on the edge of the bed in the luxurious star suite, carefully disguised as a scum-bag hotel room, when a note slid under my door. It read: "Dick Damron's songs are like candles in the hands of fools" — Paul.

Tom Beatty, a 1960s wandering minstrel, shows up at my place on a beautiful autumn afternoon, just stopping in to say hello on his way back to the British Columbia coast, to escape the onslaught of another frigid Alberta winter. He ends up staying for five days. He drinks my booze, tops a towering pine tree in my yard, sings *I'm Heading For The Hills, Lenore* 15 or 20 times and helps me paint my house. On the sixth day, he pulls out of the yard in his battered old blue station wagon with a brand new "Dick Damron Country" sticker proudly-displayed on his rear bumper. I won't hear from him again for weeks, months or years. Then, a collect call will come in the middle of the night from God-knows-where. It will be Tom.

The late and great fiddler, Al Cherney, used to drop in once in a while when he was in the West and I wasn't on the road. One day, he picked up my old road-weary fiddle and began to play. I grabbed my guitar and joined in. After a few familiar tunes like *Faded Love* and *Old Joe Clark*, he kicked off into an up-tempo Ukrainian Kolomeyka. It was in a minor mode and the chords flew by a mile a minute. I was totally unfamiliar with the tempo and chord changes. When I was just about ready to give up, he slowed the tempo and, playing very softly, he glanced at me over his shoulder. "What's the matter, man? Am I standing in your light?"

Dennis T. Olson is a bonafide crazy man. He showed up one Christmas Eve in Mexico, dancing backwards, bouncing off the walls, and singing self-penned gospel songs. After a few days and nights of fighting for self-preservation, I had to throw his guitar in the swimming pool to finally get his attention.

Lance Jackson could show up at any minute in Bentley, Mazatlan, or Nashville. He might not have any clothes or money, but he will have his trusty guitar with him, if he hasn't pawned it, and he can stay three hours or three weeks.

Terry Cousineau is on my "squawk box" (answering machine) a couple of times a year from Nashville or Branson, Missouri. Still writing songs and *Dancing In The Devil's Doorway.*

"Newfie" Roy Payne and I were once known in our Toronto Days as "the" illegitimate sons of the Mystic Mothers of Nashville. I am an "Honorary Newfie" as well as an "Honorary Texan." Call me, so I can change my ticket, Roy.

One of the best weeks, I ever spent, was three hours on the bus with Ronnie Hawkins at the 1995 "Ivan Daines Picknic."

I wish Dean Preston would win that $150 million-Ewoks lawsuit against George Lucas so he could pay me back, and I could buy the Hotel Pato Blanco on the Pacific Coast in Mexico.

One time C-Weed thanked me for being a native and not trying to teach him the white man's ways. "I hear you have a club in Winnipeg, Why Don't You Book Me? I need the money (serious money) and you need the experience."

I gotta go to Ottawa someday and have a long visit at the airport with Ralph Carlson.

George Hamilton IV gives me hope. Father Hefferman gives me faith. Jake Peters is in my will. Laurie Mills is playing my music. Sammy Taylor is my illegitimate son. Dennis Charney is a good ol' boy. Gordon Davies is getting married again. Elmer Tippe is playing *Faded Love.* "Fiddler" is on the roof and off the wall. Joe Bob Barnhill is alive and well in Nashville. Brent McAthey's *Waitin' For The Sun.* "Scoot" Irwin's on the phone. I'm playing Ivan Daines Picknic on my 100th Birthday, Las Vegas in the year 2,000. My next record will be a Fifties country rock instrumental, easy-listening, porno, new age, laid-back, hard-driving, Gospel, new country album — and nobody will play it.

Heroes . . .

In the immortal words of Willie Nelson: "My heroes have always been cowboys." When I was a kid, my heroes were silver screen singing cowboys like Roy Rogers, Red Ryder, and Gene Autry. As I grew into the rodeo circuit, the names changed to Casey Tibbs, Jim Shoulders, Buddy Heaton, and the Lindermans.

As time went by, the names of my heroes changed and evolved to include Willie Nelson. He has been one of my heroes since way back when the elderly lady clerk in a Calgary record store was convinced I must mean Nelson Eddy when I asked if she had any Willie Nelson records, as that was the only "Nelson" she could find in her aging record directory. The first Willie Nelson album I finally got my hands on was his first Liberty release. I listened to it a thousand times and read the liner notes every time I listened to it. I was hooked, and I still am. As a sign in the Willie Nelson General Stores says, "Man never fails, he only quits trying."

Then, the list of cowboy heroes got real strange, and now includes Ray Charles, Howard Hughes, and Ernest Hemingway. Willie, Ray, Howard, and Ernest. If there is a common denominator, I have not found it — and I won't even try to explain it. I have read almost everything written by or about these four men. They stand alone. Just try to add a fifth name that fits. Richard Nixon? No. Pat Boone? No. Johnny Cash? No. Elvis Presley? No. There is a difference.

Will the Circle Be Unbroken

The last day of August lays softly in the late morning sun. It clings to an unsure end of the summer of 1992. The early frost has turned the countryside to a bright shimmering yellow, dotted here and there with green and gold stands of timber. It could very well be the last day of summer or the first day of autumn. In my heart, it is already the beginning of a long, cold winter.

Far from the peaceful surroundings of the family roots, deeply planted in the glorious farming mecca of the Blindman Valley in central Alberta, the screaming echo of a deadly whirling helicopter crash in the far northern reaches of Canada's Northwest Territories has taken my brother away forever. Not just away from me, but away from my brother Bob, and my sister Lorna. Not just away from me, but away from the high times in Las Vegas casinos and away from the Mexican winters we shared. Away from the train ride from Nogales to the heart of Mexico, and away from the bus ride, winding through the mountains and down the west coast to the tiny fishing village of La Punita.

His guitar is silenced forever, from the small town dance halls of the Fifties to the scum-bag bars of the Sixties. He traveled with me to Nashville by train in 1963 and again in 1965 when we drove the thousands of miles to Nashville and back. The guitar has fallen silent and will never ring again by the pool in the courtyard of the Paraiso Mazatlan. There is one less number in the old winter club with Duke and Brian and Marcella, and Peter and Francis and Denny and Bev and Gayle and Elaine and Lou and Jan.

Back in the north he will never again answer Robert W. Service's *Call Of The Yukon*. He won't walk the streets of Atlin or Whitehorse or Dawson City or fly the skies over British Columbia, Yukon, or the Northwest Territories. He will no longer skirt the cold northern lakes or skim the treetops with fixed wing or chopper, or fly that battered old DC-3 overloaded with mining equipment out of some hidden valley. Gone are the days of the gold and silver mines; gone are the days of Dawson Eldorado.

On this last day of August, I remember 40-some-odd years ago, on a cold rainy night in June, when we drove through the mud and rain to see you for the first time, Howard. The nurse held you up to the window, all red and wrinkled and only a few hours old.

Now I remember your beautiful Lori and a December wedding in Florida, and I remember our last family Christmas and your tiny infant son, Luke. The first time I saw the little man and the last we saw you alive. We love you, and we miss you.

Flying off into the wind like some lonely lost soul seems to be the vision I hold for myself. Once in a while, usually when I am a million miles from nowhere and strung out on the road, I envision myself sitting quietly in front of a fireplace, with a good cup of strongly-brewed coffee, working quietly on the Great American Novel.

To rise in the morning without pulling on my boots. No plane to catch, no miles to make. Then I think, "Jesus Christ, I'm only in my fifties!" There are a lot of good years out there and a lot more miles to make and songs to be sung. And when I do venture out there, the spotlight, although it doesn't shine right through me like it did in the days of *A Thousand Songs Of Glory*, is still warm and inviting and it spills its magic on an old road-weary warrior, who feels a little guilty at the thought of not having as much to give as he did back then.

It's too late to die young and leave the crowd screaming for more. Janis Joplin knew, when she said, "Don't compromise yourself, baby, you're all you've got."

Is it really such a sin to grow old gracefully? Or is that merely some strange illusion? Is it the truth, the God's honest truth, that when the day of departure finally arrives, I must leave this world kicking and screaming, exactly as I entered it? What other answer can there be? If I don't complete the circle, the soul will never rest.

Perhaps this is what my mother meant back in 1977 when she sent me a small book entitled *Quiet Times: Discovering the Beauty and Meaning of Moments to Ourselves in the Midst of a Busy World*. At the time, others suspected that I was totally possessed and consumed by what was taking place in my country music world. She wrote inside the front cover: "Dickie Damron, September 1977, Best Wishes for another successful year."

In January 1992, I discovered the little book while I was looking for some reading material to take to Mexico. It took me 15 years to get the message: "Be successful, but take some quiet time to discover the beauty and meaning of life."

One clear, cold November morning in 1994 I had woke up early and lay awake in bed reviewing my childhood, bit by bit, tiny piece by tiny piece. I am not certain why my mind was swept away by this train of thought — it certainly did not spring from my dreams of the past night. Or did it?

I had just opened my eyes from a bizarre dream in which my brother, Bob, and I were removing a large rock from within my stomach with our bare hands. I had located it on the right side of my lower abdomen and had managed to move it to a position just above my navel and under my rib cage. I could see the rock clearly through the thin skin and I moved it into the center of my belly. Bob reached down with both hands and assisted me in removing the rock from my body. There was no blood or flesh present, only a light dry papery film that we brushed away. Once the rock was removed, I was whole again. This dream, I supposed, was prompted by the recurring stomach pains for which I was currently undergoing medical tests.

My mind quickly fell from my dream experience into a deep examination of my early childhood. I could see my grandmother clearly. She was standing on the back porch of the "house in town," as we had always called the house that my granddad had built in Bentley after they moved in from the family farm. It was 1939 and I was five-years-old.

My grandmother (Martha Imogene Trobough Damron) was a tiny, frail, little wisp of a woman who had somehow survived the long move from Omaha, Nebraska to the wilds of Alberta, shortly after the turn of the century. She had given birth to three sons: my father, my uncle Bud, and my uncle Joe. Joe was her first born and was killed in a freak car accident near Gull Lake when he was 20 years old.

From the time I was old enough to understand this tragedy in her life, I felt a certain undefined sadness and sorrow about her, which I am sure she carried with her to the grave. I always remembered her as being tired and frail. She contributed to my childhood wisdom by telling me: "Little boys should be seen and not heard." And, if I did anything wrong, she always admonished me: "There would be the devil to pay." She always responded to any kind of "thank you" or compliment by saying, "Don't mention it." This response always confused me because I received many a licking from my dad if I did not say, "please" and "thank you" or "excuse me" for almost anything I did in the presence of my parents or grandparents. Anything small, animal, vegetable, or mineral was referred to as "no bigger than a minute."

And I remember well, when I was not much more than a child, when the neighbors lost a baby who was only a few months old from a crib death. When I told my grandmother about the death, I quickly added the fact that they had five other children. She placed her hand gently on the top of my head and said softly, "They are all precious in the eyes of God." I have never forgotten that moment or that lesson on the value of life.

My grandmother bought me my first guitar. It was a "Music

Master Deluxe" that we ordered from a Sears catalogue. It was actually the second guitar in the house but this one was all mine. Grandma bought it for me as a gift, on the condition that I learn to play the piano. The guitar arrived after my second piano lesson and I never touched the piano again. I always felt guilty about that. I kind of got the guitar by default. But who could expect me to lay down that beautiful, shiny new guitar long enough to sit up at the piano and learn to play boring scales. Besides, at that time, I thought only girls and sissies played the piano, and I was trying so hard to be a little man.

Grandma died when I was in my early twenties. It was the first death in our family, that I can remember, and it was not easy. A few years ago, some family photos surfaced. There was one of my grandma and granddad's wedding in Omaha and another of her with her three young sons. In the photo, she looks absolutely gorgeous, not unlike my daughter today. This new image of her has replaced the sad, frail woman whom I remembered as a child. It's all about time.

Transit

Day of Waiting. Today, I taste the sweetness and the sadness of returning from my winter home on the sunswept shores of Mexico to Bentley, the center of my own tiny universe.

God help me to arrive whole and spiritually intact. No taxi or airline or man-made transport can move a spirit. Only the body travels with heavy and awkward feelings of distress. The spirit and soul travel a different path and a different road. So, I try desperately to sit quietly and await their arrival. Without spirit and soul, I am an empty shell. When will they arrive? When will I feel whole again? Each and every year, with age and experience weighing heavily in my heart, I make myself unfulfilled promises of an easier time of re-entry. This is a day of waiting. Please God, I ask no special favors. I ask only the strength and patience to handle the lonely desperation I feel today.

Looking west from the fourth floor window of my hotel room, the Pacific Ocean lies a scant 50 feet away and sinks into the distant horizon as far as I can see. The moon rides low and bright in the 5:00 a.m. sky, and spatters its light over the sea. Less than 24 hours from being full, the moon highlights the breakers as they crash against the sand. The energy is intense and I am grateful for the fountain of power that is there for me to draw from.

It is the morning of Monday, February 17, 1992. I am 35 days from my 58th birthday, and I am wondering why I have never learned to draw from the unending sources of energy and power. Earth, sea, sky, moon — and the *estrellas* (the beautiful Spanish word meaning "stars").

I will learn. I will learn. I will learn.

January 4th, 1996

I have been in Mexico for almost a month now. It's a bright, shiny Mazatlan morning, and I am coasting along, waiting for the Great Spirit to move me into writing another chapter for my book. I feel the power building and must let it take its natural course.

"Fly Freedom Fly." Stories and songs spring forth and focus on the guitar music, the singing, the writing of words and music and the celebration of people! Amen.

Vanishing Point

My lifetime love affair with words and music has taken me from the heart of the Blindman Valley — where my father and his father before him lived and grew and always remained close to the earth — to the far-flung corners of the world.

Music became my mistress, and words my only means of salvation in a world that I knew so little about. Yet, somehow, I found the strength and courage to do what I must do — in order to survive the loneliness, sadness, and despair — to fly to the edge of creation and see the beauty and taste the sweetness that flashed before me at the speed of light.

I have known the absolute joy of creativity when words and music came together like a gift from God, and spun their way out of the night into my little world, allowing them to be captured on some small scrap of paper or recording device, later to emerge full-blown into a song that I carried in my heart. A song that would reach out and touch people by the handfuls in tiny bars and clubs and pubs. And touch people by the thousands on radio, television, records, and at some of the largest music festivals in the world.

I found that music was my ticket to anywhere I wanted to go. And, wherever it led me, I would follow, sometimes joyously flying, sailing, soaring to the heights of total euphoria, and, other times, screaming, kicking, crying, and denying my very existence, never knowing how to control the highs or lows that I would experience. I honestly believe that there was never any real attempt on my part to set any limits on the upward flights or the downward spirals I was destined to ride out on my so-called journey through this thing called life. No matter what I thought or felt or experienced, when God took me by the hand and led me through the shadows and the darkness and desperate days of my life, or when I fought my demons alone and was lost and totally god-forsaken, somehow, subconsciously, I knew I must do it all. It had little to do with Number 1 records and the awards and charts, or managers, agents, critics and record executives. It had everything to do with life and life itself and always has and always will. From here to infinity. From the moment of my conception to the vanishing point when my ashes are blowing in the wind and my voice is silenced forever. I will not pass this way again.

WHAT GOOD IS YOUR LIFE IF YOU CAN'T HEAR THE MUSIC
WHAT GOOD IS MINE IF I CAN'T SING MY SONGS
I LIVE FOR THE DREAM, DIE FOR THE PLEASURE
AND I'VE TOLD IT ALL IN THE SOUL OF MY SONGS

DON'T PLEDGE ME LOVE, SHOW ME NO MERCY
DON'T BE AFRAID TO CAST THE FIRST STONE
THE TEARS IN MY EYES ARE MY LAST TASTE OF GRACE
AND THE VANISHING POINT IS LEADING ME ON

GOD KNOWS I'VE STOOD ON THE TOP OF THE MOUNTAIN
HE'S SEEN ME FALL TO THE VALLEY BELOW
FROM THE BITTERSWEET TASTE OF LIFE'S SHINING PLEASURE
TO THE VANISHING POINT IN LIFE'S EVENING GLOW

— *The Vanishing Point* © Sparwood Music

(Top) *Wilf Carter and friends on stage with Dick Damron and Ivan Daines at Ivan Daines' Cowboy Country Music Picknic, 1988.*

(Middle) *ATI Records CEO Scoot Irwin with Dick and George Hamilton IV at Ontario's Classic Country Music Reunion in Trenton, Ontario, 1996.*

(Bottom) *Dick and Joe Bob Barnhill in Nashville's Sound Control Studio working on Damron's TOUCH THE SKY gospel album.*

218

Dick Damron with Michelle Wright (top left). Dick at the Canadian Country Music Awards in 1996 with Lisa Brokop (top right), Terri Clark (bottom left), and Shania Twain (bottom right).

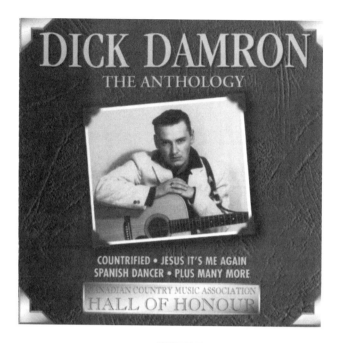

For years he was an RCA Records mainstay recording country music that was played from coast to coast. He also established a strong publishing library, with many Canadian performers having recorded his songs throughout the years.

Dick Damron's legacy and contribution to the Canadian country music industry is undeniable.

Remaining with RCA for more than 30 years is testament to his dedication to the label and conversely, RCA's respect for this shy country artist who retained a coveted position on the roster for many years.

Dick is still active today playing mostly throughout his home province of Alberta and still taking his yearly sojourns to Mexico and Las Vegas, and occasionally venturing down to Nashville, where for years, he has been doing his recording.

In Alberta, country people have a saying...If you don't know Dick, you don't know country!

Dick Damron was inducted into the Canadian Country Music Association's Hall Of Honour in 1994. Having lived in the province of Alberta for 30 years I can understand well why his fans there refer to him as "The Legend And The Legacy". This anthology is a tribute to his many talents as a country singer, writer, and picker. Enjoy!

— Tom Tompkins, President, Canadian Country Music Association

74321-30632-2

220

DISCOGRAPHY

SINGLES

45 RPM Singles:

Gonna Have A Party / Rockin' Baby, Laurel 45792 (1958).

That's What I Call Livin' / Julie, Quality 1213X (1960).

That's Life / Black Maria, Quality 1260X (1960).

Little Sandy / Nothing Else, Quality 1319X (1961).

The Same Old Thing Again / Times Like This, Quality 1374X (1961).

Double Trouble / Strangers Again, RCA Victor 47-8162 (1963).

Hello Heartaches / Pretty Moon, RCA Victor 57-3312 (1963).

Hitchhikin' / Stop Feeling Sorry For Yourself, RCA Victor 57-3330 (1964).

The Cumberland / The Night The Dice Grew Cold, RCA Can Int 57-3387 (1965). A-side by Nellie Smith, B-side by Leona Buttram.

The Hard Knocks In Life / A Thing Called Happiness, RCA Can Int 57-3388 (1965).

Countryfied / No One Knows It Better Than The Clown, Apex 77110 (1970).

Rise 'N' Shine / When Our Love Was Young, MCA 2011 (1971).

The Long Green Line / Jackson County (Dick Damron) Columbia C4-3043: *Golden Girls Sometimes (Paul Revere)* Columbia 4-45601 (1972). This item was mixed up with Paul Revere & The Raiders in the pressing plant. Some had wrong labels, some had Dick Damron on one side and Paul Revere on the other, etc.

Going Home To The Country / Walk A Country Mile, Columbia C4-3078 (1972).

The Prophet / All That I Was Living For, Columbia C4-4007 (1973).

Bittersweet Songs / Somewhere There's A Mountain, Columbia C4-4048 (1973).

The Cowboy And The Lady / I Remember Love, Broadland BR 2141X (1975).

Mother, Love and Country / Backstage Ladies, Marathon 45-1132 (1975).

On The Road / Half A Jug Of Wine, Marathon C-45-1143 (1975).

Good Ole Fashion Memories / same, Condor C-97124 (1976).

Waylon's T Shirt / North Country Blues, Condor C-97133 (1976).

Susan Flowers / You Can't Call It Country, Condor C-97144 (1977).

Susan Flowers / Waylon's T-Shirt, RPA 7621 U.S.A. (1977).

Charing Cross Cowboys / Alberta Skyline, Condor C-97156 (1977).

Silver And Shine / The Minstrel, RCA PB 50491 (1978).

Whiskey Jack / The Only Way To Say Goodbye, RCA PB-50428 (1978).

My Good Woman (And That Ain't Right) / California Friends, RCA PB-50471 (1978).

Silver And Shine / The Minstrel, RCA PB-50491 (1978).

The Ballad Of T.J.'s / Slightly Out Of Tune, RCA PB-50544 (1979).

High On You / It Ain't Easy Goin' Home, RCA PB-50518 (1979).

Dollars / All Night Country Party, RCA PB-50575 (1980).

If You Need Me Lord / Better Think It Over, RCA PB-50602 (1980).

Reunion / Sundown Lady, TMC 1001 (1981).

Mid-Nite Flytes / Sweet September, RCA PB-50624 (1981).

Honky Tonk Angels And Good Ole Boys / The Last Of The Rodeo Riders, RCA PB-50670 (1982).

I'm Not Ready For The Blues / Homegrown, RCA PB 50738 (1982).

Jesus It's Me Again / Rolling Stone, RCA PB 50713 (1982).

Good Old Timey Country Rock 'n Roll / The Same Old Songs, RCA PB 50694 (1982).

A Little More Country Music / Give It All We've Got, RCA PB-50761 (1984).

Don't Touch Him / Tequila Charlie's, RCA PB-50799 (1984).

Ridin' Shotgun / Cozy Inn, RCA PB50788 (1984). *Cozy Inn* by Harlan Howard.

Last Dance On A Saturday Night / Burnin' A Hole In My Heart, RCA PB-50811 (1985).

Rise Against The Wind / Falling In And Out Of Love, RCA PB-50833 (1985). Two duets with Ginny Mitchell & Dick Damron.

Rise Against The Wind / Lover RCA PB-50833 (1985). Recorded without duet.

Falling In And Out Of Love / Softer Than Satin RCA PB-50822 (1985). A-side is duet with Ginny Mitchell, B-side is Dick Damron.

Masquerade / We've Almost Got It All, RCA PB-50864 (1986).

1955 / Ain't No Love Around, RCA PB-50895 (1986).

Hotel Mexico / I'm Not Ready For The Blues, RCA PB-50913 (1987).

Here We Are Again, RCA JB-51015 (1987).

You'd Still Be Here Today, RCA JB50930 (1987).

Cinderella And The Gingerbread Man, RCA JB50964 (1987).

St. Mary's Angel, RCA JB50997 (1987).

The Legend And The Legacy, RCA (1989).

Ain't No Trains To Nashville, RCA JB-51046 (1989).

CD Compilation Singles:

Mid-nite Cowboy Blues — RCA LASSOES 'N SPURS, Vol. 3, Track 7, KCD1-7152.
Wild Horses — RCA LASSOES 'N SPURS, Vol. 9, Track 6, KCDP-7181.

Hold On Tight — BOOKSHOP GOLD AND NEW, Track 9, BSRD-827.

A Rose By The River — Bookshop Compilation.

Midnite Madness — ATI NEW GOLD, Vol. 1, Track 2 (1993).

Countryfied, High On You, One Night Stand, Susan Flowers, Jesus It's Me Again — (Updated versions circa 1990) ATI 4X4, Vol. 2, Tracks 13-17 (1993).

Free Love (vocal version), Sierra Madre Morning, You Don't Know The Lady, Phantom Of The 50's — ATI 4X4, Vol. 3, Tracks 5,6,7,8, ATICD 1012 (1994).

Countryfied — Quality CD1 COUNTRY NORTH, Track 13 (1993).

Jesus It's Me Again — Nordic Country Music Organization COUNTRYMIX FOR COUNTRY FREAKS, Track 15, NCMO CD9302 (1993).

Ballad Of T.J.'s — Westwood Records Int HONKY TONK JUKE BOX SPECIAL, Vol. 1, Track 8, WIR9602-D (1996).

Countryfied — READER'S DIGEST 20 ALL-TIME GREAT COUNTRY SONGS. Vinyl (no record number or exact title available).

Countryfied — K-Tel MY KIND OF COUNTRY, WC313.

The Cowboy and the Lady — COUNTRY'S BEST: THE BEST OF BROADLAND, VOL. 1 (includes Joyce Smith's version of Damron's *Wish The World A Little Love*), BR1930.

Last of the Rodeo Riders and *The Wilf Carter Song* — WORD FROM THE RANGE (A Canadian Cowboy Collection), Glenbow GAI-001, project production by Ray Warhurst (1997).

Lead sheet for "Countryfied"

225

ALBUMS

THE NASHVILLE SOUND OF
DICK DAMRON (1965) —
Holiday Records, Holiday 1001
(Side One: *Pretty Moon, Hitch
Hikin', Strangers Again, Stop
Feeling Sorry For Yourself, Hello
Heartaches.* Side Two: *Double
Trouble, Little Sandy, Times Like
This, The Same Old Thing Again,
Nothing Else*). Vinyl.

Recorded at Starday Studios,
Nashville, TN. Produced by
Tommy Hill. Personnel: Pete
Drake (steel), Tommy Hill (guitar), Jerry Shook (guitar), Hargus
Robbins (piano), Kelso Herston
(guitar), Junior Huskey (bass),
Willie Ackerman (drums). Two
sessions 1961, 1963.

CANADIANA: SOUVENIR ALBUM
1867-1967 — Holiday Records,
Holiday 1002 (Side One: *The
Canadian Pioneers, This Big
Land, Blood In The Morning Sun,
The Little Log Church, The
Golden Spike.* Side Two: *Canada's
Golden West, The Land Of David
Thompson, Cross Country, The
City Of Gold, The Ballad Of
Louis Riel.*) Vinyl.

Recorded at CFCW Camrose,
Alberta. Produced by Dick
Damron. Personnel: Dick Damron
(vocals, guitar), Dan Damron
(lead guitar), Jack Wensley (bass),
Pat Sugura (drums).

DICK DAMRON — Point Records
(Canada), Point 346 (Side One: *A
Whole Lot Different, Walk Out
Of My World, My Heart Doesn't
Sing, Sentimental Memories,
Reflections Of A Fool.* Side Two:
*Autumn In Her Eyes, The
Cumberland, The Night The Dice
Grew Cold, A Thing Called
Happiness, The Hard Knocks In
Life.*) Vinyl.

Recorded at Music City
Recorders, Nashville, TN.
Produced by Ray Griff. Personnel:
Kenny Butrey (drums), Henry
Strzelecki (bass), Curly Chalker
(steel), Pete Wade (guitar), Don
Light (keys), The Harden Trio
(background vocals).

Recorded at Bradley Studios,
Nashville, TN. Produced by Gary
Walker. Personnel: Jerry Reed
(guitar), Jerry Smith (piano), Joe
Zinken (bass), Willie Ackerman
(drums), Sandy Posey & Priscilla
(Mitchell) Reed (background
vocals).

Recorded at Starday Sound
Studios, Nashville, TN. Produced
by Pete Drake. Personnel: Pete
Drake (steel), Pete Wade (guitar),
Jack Green (drums), Billy
Linneman (bass), Harold Weakley
(drums).

LONESOME CITY: DICK
DAMRON (circa 1969) — Point

Records (Canada), Point 351 (Side One: *Lonesome City, Mirrors Of My Mind, Sweet Dreams Of Yesterday, California Girl, Sharing The Good Life.* Side Two: *Rise 'n' Shine, The Final Hour, Cold Grey Winds Of Autumn, One More Pretty Girl, The End*). Vinyl

Recorded at Korl Sound, Edmonton, Alberta. Produced by Joe Kozak. Personnel: Richard Chernesky (guitar), Al Meroniuk (steel), Ray Norman (bass), Lloyd Marshall (drums).

COUNTRYFIED (1970) — Columbia Records Canada, KHE-90216 (Side One: *Countryfied, When Our Love Was Young, The Clown, Rise 'n Shine, Jimmy Justice.* Side Two: *Goin' Home To The Country, Walk A Country Mile, Jackson Country, Somewhere There's A Mountain, The Long Green Line.*) Vinyl.

Recorded at RCA's Mutual Street Studios, and Sound Canada, Toronto, Canada. Produced by Gary Buck. Personnel: Al Brisco (steel), Al Cherney (fiddle), Red Shea (guitar), John Arpin (piano), Leroy Anderson (banjo), Keith McKay (guitar), Ollie Strong (steel), Bill Gibb (bass), Willie Cantu (drums).

SOLDIER OF FORTUNE (1974) — Marathon Records (Canada) MMS 76069 (Side One: *Mother Love & Country, Backstage*

Ladies, *Soldier Of Fortune, Good Ol' Fashion Memories, Freedom And Time.* Side Two: *Half A Jug Of Wine, On The Road, After All, Lady-O, One Night Stand.*) Vinyl.

Recorded at Nugget Studios, Nashville, TN. Produced by Joe Bob Barnhill. Personnel: Fred Carter Jr. (guitar), Dale Sellars (guitar), Dick Damron (harp, guitar), Tony Migliore (piano), Hal Rugg (steel, dobro), Steve Schaffer (bass), Jim Wolfe (drums). (1973 sessions)

SOLDIER OF FORTUNE (1975) — Westwood Recordings Ltd (United Kingdom), WRS099 (Side One: *Mother Love & Country, Backstage Ladies, Soldier Of Fortune, Good Ol' Fashion Memories, Freedom And Time.* Side Two: *Half A Jug Of Wine, On The Road, After All, Lady-O, One Night Stand.*) Vinyl. Credits same as Canada.

THE COWBOY AND THE LADY (1975) — Broadland Records, BR-1915 (Side One: *The Prophet, All That I Was Living For, Knowin' That She's Leavin', I Remember Love, Eastbound Highway.* Side Two: *Bittersweet Songs, The Cowboy And The Lady, Goin' Home Again, Mama Was A Christian Lady.*) Vinyl.

Recorded at RCA's Mutual Street Studios, Toronto, Canada. Producer: Gary Buck. Personnel same as COUNTRYFIED sessions.

NORTHWEST REBELLION (DICK DAMRON & ROY WARHURST, 12 ORIGINAL INSTRUMENTALS) (1976) — Marathon Records (Canada), MMS 76064, (Side One: *Prairie Grass, Country Express, Pat's Country, Theme From Movie Of The Same Name, Little Britches, Cajun Harp*. Side Two: *Denim And Lace, Countryfied, Twirly, Irish Mist, John Henry, Country Blues*.) Vinyl.

Recorded at Korl Sound, Edmonton, Alberta. Produced by Dick Damron and Roy Warhurst. Personnel: Dick Damron (guitar, harp, banjo), Roy Warhurst (fiddle), Ray Norman (bass), Stu Mitchell (drums).

NORTH COUNTRY SKYLINE (1976) — Condor Records 977-1474 (Canada). (Side One: *Charing Cross Cowboys, Alberta Skyline, Susan Flowers, Waylon's T-Shirt, Country Wine*. Side Two: *Just Another Old Rodeo Song, If You Need Me Lord, North Country Blues, You Can't Call It Country, One More Day Away*.) Vinyl.

Recorded at Nugget Studios, Nashville, TN. Produced by Joe Bob Barnhill. Personnel: Fred Carter Jr. (guitar), Pete Bordonali (guitar), Dick Damron (harp), Hal Rugg (steel, dobro), Steve Schaffer (bass), Jim Wolfe (drums).

A THOUSAND SONGS OF GLORY (1976) — RPA 1015 (Record Productions of America) (Side One: *Charing Cross Cowboys, Alberta Skyline, Susan Flowers, Waylon's T-Shirt, Country Wine*. Side Two: *Just Another Old Rodeo Song, If You Need Me Lord, North Country Blues, You Can't Call It Country, One More Day Away*.) Vinyl. Credits same as Canada with a new title for U.S. release.

A THOUSAND SONGS OF GLORY (1978) — Westwood Recordings Ltd, United Kingdom WRS119 (Side One: *Charing Cross Cowboys, Alberta Skyline, Susan Flowers, Waylon's T-Shirt, Country Wine*. Side Two: *Just Another Old Rodeo Song, If You Need Me Lord, North Country Blues, You Can't Call It Country, One More Day Away*.) Vinyl. Credits same as NORTH COUNTRY SKYLINE with new title for U.K. release.

NORTHWEST REBELLION (DICK DAMRON & ROY WARHURST, 12 ORIGINAL INSTRUMENTALS) (1978) — Westwood Recordings Ltd, United Kingdom WRS102 (Side One: *Prairie Grass, Country Express, Pat's Country, Theme From Movie Of The Same Name, Little Britches, Cajun Harp*. Side Two: *Denim And Lace, Countryfied, Twirly, Irish Mist, John Henry, Country Blues*.) Vinyl. Credits same as Canada.

228

LOST IN THE MUSIC (1978) — RCA Records (Canada) PL 42490 (Side One: *The Minstrel, Whiskey Jack, My Good Woman (That Ain't Right), It Ain't Easy Goin' Home, When Satan Spins The Bottle.* Side Two: *Lost In The Music, California Friends, The Only Way To Say Goodbye, Woman, Sweet Lady.*) Vinyl.

Recorded at Tom T. Hall's Toybox Studios, Nashville, TN. Produced by Joe Bob Barnhill. Personnel: Randy Scruggs (guitar), Gene Rice (guitar), Tony Migliore (piano), Doug Jernigan (steel, dobro), Bobby Dyson (bass), Jim Wolfe (drums).

HIGH ON YOU (1980) — RCA Records (Canada), KKL1-0334 (Side One: *Dollars, We've Almost Got It All, All Night Country Party, If London Were A Lady, The Ballad Of T.J.'s.* Side Two: *High On You, Silver And Shine, Sweet September, Better Think It Over, Slightly Out Of Tune.*) Vinyl.

Recorded at Richey House Studios, Nashville, TN. Produced by Joe Bob Barnhill. Personnel: Pete Bordonali (guitar), Steve Chapman (guitar), Bobby Dyson (bass), Tony Migliore (piano), Weldon Myrick (steel), Clyde Brooks (drums).

HIGH ON YOU (1980) — Westwood Recordings Ltd, United Kingdom, WRS158 (Side One: *Dollars, We've Almost Got It All, All Night Country Party, If London Were A Lady, The Ballad Of T.J.'s.* Side Two: *High On You, Silver And Shine, Sweet September, Better Think It Over, Slightly Out Of Tune.*) Vinyl. Credits same as Canada.

THE COWBOY AND THE LADY (1980) — Westwood Recordings Ltd, United Kingdom, WRS 150. Vinyl. (Side One: *The Prophet, All That I Was Living For, Knowin' That She's Leavin', I Remember Love, Eastbound Highway* Side Two: *Bittersweet Songs, The Cowboy And The Lady, Mama Was A Christian Lady, Things That Might Have Been*).

THE BEST OF DICK DAMRON (1981) — RCA Records (Canada) RCA KKl-0414 (Side One: *Countryfied, Susan Flowers, Waylon's T-Shirt, Whiskey Jack, Just Another Old Rodeo Song.* Side Two: *High On You, On The Road, Mid-Nite Flytes, My Good Woman (That Ain't Right), If You Need Me Lord.*) Vinyl.

HONKY TONK ANGEL (1982) — RCA Records (Canada) RCA KKL1-0446 (Side One: *Honky Tonk Angel & Good Ol' Boys, Reunion, You Don't Know The Lady, Sundown Lady, Rollin' Stone.* Side Two: *The Same Old Songs, The Last Of The Rodeo Riders, Jesus It's Me Again,*

Homegrown, Good Ol' Time Rock 'N Roll.) Vinyl.

Recorded at Ironside Studios, Nashville, TN. Produced by Joe Bob Barnhill. Pete Bordonali (guitar), Don Roth (guitar), John Gully (guitar), Sonny Garish (steel, dobro), Doyle Grissom (steel), Tony Migliore (piano), Jamie Whiting (piano), Jack Ross (bass), Glenn Worf (bass), Clyde Brooks (drums).

LAST DANCE ON SATURDAY NIGHT (1984) — RCA Records (Canada) KKL1-0540 (Side One: *A Little More Country Music, Lover, Tequila Charlie's, Burnin' A Hole In My Heart, Last Dance On Saturday Night.* Side Two: *Don't Touch Him, Ridin' Shotgun, Give It All We've Got, Softer Than Satin, Cozy Inn.*) Recorded at Manta Sound Studios, Toronto. Produced by Mike "Pepe" Francis. Personnel: Mike Francis (guitar), Bob Lucier (steel, dobro), Bruce Ley (piano), Willie P. Bennett (harp), Graham Townsend (fiddle), Kim Brandt (bass), Dick Smith (percussion), Barry Keane (drums). Background vocals: Robert Arms, Shawne Jackson, Coleena Phillips, David Blamires.

NIGHT MUSIC (1987) — RCA Records (Canada), Special Products ST-58068 (8 instrumental tracks), (Side One: *When Love Is Gone, Trivial Pursuit, Chico*

(*Carnival In Mazatlan, Las Vegas Nights.* Side Two: *Street People, Night Music, Sky Channel, Spanish Dancer.*) Vinyl and cassette.

Recorded at Reflexions Studios, Sound Control Studios and Sound Connection, Nashville, TN. Produced by Joe Bob Barnhill. Personnel: Dick Damron (acoustic lead guitar), John Pell (guitar), Walt Cunningham (piano), Rob Hajaycos (fiddle), Bob Burns (bass), Terry Waddell (drums).

DICK DAMRON (1987) — RCA Records (Canada) RCA KZL1-0588 (Side One: *Masquerade, 1955, You'd Still Be Here Today, St. Mary's Angel, Here We Are Again.* Side Two: *Cinderella And The Gingerbread Man, Ain't No Love Around, Hotel Mexico, I'm Not Ready For The Blues, I Stopped Believing In You.*) Vinyl and cassette.

Recorded at Reflections Studios and Richey House Studios, Nashville, TN. Produced by Joe Bob Barnhill. Personnel: Greg Galbraith (guitar), Paul Yandel (guitar), Hal Rugg (dobro, steel), Weldon Myrick (steel), Walt Cunningham (keys), Jack Ross (bass), Clyde Brooks (drums).

THE LEGEND AND THE LEGACY (1989) — BMG Music Canada, Inc. RCA KKL1-0599 (Side One: *The Legend And The Legacy,*

Wild Horses, Mid-Nite Cowboy Blues, Silver Dollars, Superstar. Side Two: *Ain't No Trains To Nashville, The Lady, Rockabilly Days, Baby's Got The Blues, Farewell To Arms.*) Vinyl and cassette.

Recorded at Reflections Studios, Nashville, TN. Produced by Joe Bob Barnhill. Personnel: Michael Spriggs (guitar), Greg Galbraith (guitar), Paul Franklin Jr. (steel), Hal Rugg (steel, dobro), Paul Anastasio (fiddle), Walt Cunningham (piano), Jack Ross (bass), Clyde Brooks (drums).

NORTH COUNTRY SKYLINE, DICK DAMRON (1991) — Oak Canada, Oak 143 (Side One: *Susan Flowers, Just Another Old Rodeo Song, One More Day Away, You Can't Call It Country.* Side Two: *Alberta Skyline, Country Wine, If You Need Me Lord, Waylon's T-Shirt, North Country Blues.*) Reissue: Cassette only.

MIRAGE (1991) — ATI Records, ATICD 0322 (16 instrumental tracks), (*Midnite Lace, Sunday Morning Rain, Coffee Break, Flying To The Sun, When Love Is Gone, Night Music, Sky Channel, Trivial Pursuit, Las Vegas Nites, Chico (Carnival In Mazatlan), Street People, Spanish Dancer, Funny Bone, Fiesta Mexicana, Mirage, Rush Hour.*) CD only.

Additional tracks added to NIGHT MUSIC release were produced by John Pell at Magic Tracks, Nashville, TN. Personnel: Dick Damron (guitar), John Pell (guitar), Walt Cunningham (keys), Sam Levine (flute, sax), Roy Vogt (bass), Terry Waddell (drums).

WINGS UPON THE WIND (THE CHRISTIAN COUNTRY COLLECTION) (1992) — ATI Records, ATI CD 0393 (*Wings Upon The Wind, A Rose By The River, Closer To Jesus, Hiding In The Rock, Jesus It's Me Again, Does The Light Still Shine, Medley: Old Time Religion, This Train, Will The Circle Be Unbroken, Reprise: Wings Upon The Wind.*) CD and cassette.

Recorded at Reflections Studios, Sound Control Studios and Sound Connection, Nashville, TN. Produced by Joe Bob Barnhill. Personnel: Greg Galbraith (guitar), Mark Casstevens (guitar), Hal Rugg (steel, dobro), Tom Morley (fiddle, mandolin), Jack Ross (bass), Clyde Brooks drums.

Jesus It's Me Again was taken from HONKY TONK ANGEL.

TOUCH THE SKY (THE CHRISTIAN COUNTRY COLLECTION VOL. 2) (1994) — ATI Records, ATI CD 0394 and ATIC 0394 (*Glory Train, Touch The Sky, Til The End Of Forever, Mother,*

Love and Country, America's Child, Black And White, A Hole In My Heart Without Jesus, Highway To Heaven, The Gift.) CD and cassette.

Recorded at Reflections Studios and Sound Control Studios, Nashville, TN. Produced by Joe Bob Barnhill. Personnel: Greg Galbraith (guitar), Bobby All (acoustic guitar), Hal Rugg (dobro), Hoot Hester (fiddle), Walt Cunningham (keys), David Smith (bass), John Gardner (drums).

TOUCH THE SKY (THE CHRIST-IAN COUNTRY COLLECTION VOL. 2) (1995) — Coyote Records, Europe CR 5002 (*Glory Train, Touch The Sky, Til The End Of Forever, Mother, Love and Country, America's Child, Black And White, A Hole In My Heart Without Jesus, Highway To Heaven, The Gift.*) CD only.

Released in Holland by GMI Records.

DICK DAMRON — THE ANTHOLOGY (1995) — BMG Music Canada CD 74321-30632-2 and 74321-30632-4 (*Countrified, Hold On Tight, Here We Are Again, Spanish Dancer, Cinderella and the Gingerbread Man, High On You, Mid-Nite Flytes, Susan Flowers, Whiskey Jack, The Last Of The Rodeo Riders, On The Road, The Legend And The Legacy, Jesus It's Me Again (1982 version), Dollars, You'd Still Be Here Today, Cozy Inn, Mother, Love and Country, Sunday Morning Rain, Tequila Charlie's, One Night Stand, Jesus It's Me Again (new version).* CD and cassette. New video version of *Jesus It's Me Again* produced by Randall Prescott at Lakeside Studios, Ontario.

SIGNIFICANT COVER VERSIONS OF DICK DAMRON SONGS

Jimmy Arthur Ordge — *The Cold Grey Winds Of Autumn / Somewhere In Your World* (1967). This cut won the Moffatt Broadcasting Award for best Country Record of 1967.

Lois Davies — *Mr. Tom Cat, Miracle Of Love, Single Girl's Song, Patch Things Up To Make Another* (1967), on the album LOIS DAVIES (produced by Dick Damron), Cynda CNS 1000 (distributed by London Records).

Jimmy Arthur Ordge — *The Cold Grey Winds Of Autumn, Somewhere In Your World, Give That Thought* (1968), on the album THE COUNTRY SOUL OF JIMMY ARTHUR ORDGE, Point Records PS 335.

Brian Sklar — *Reflections Of A Fool / Don't Ask What Love Has Done For Me* (1969), Centurian Records (Edmonton).

Hugh Scott — *Little Old Tavern* (1969), on the album TOWN & COUNTRY'S HAPPY BOY HUGH SCOTT, Banff Records SBS 5305.

Hank Smith — *Sharing The Good Life, Every Mother's Son, Rise 'n' Shine, Sweet Dreams Of Yesterday, Lonesome City* (1969), on the album THE NEW COUNTRY

SOUNDS OF HANK SMITH, (produced by Dick Damron), Birchmount BM 536.

Harry Rusk — *Pineville County Jail* (1969), Apex 77099.

Hank Smith — *Sharing The Good Life* (1969), Quality 1956-X.

Hank Smith — *Sweet Dreams Of Yesterday / Rise 'n' Shine* (1970), Quality 1962X.

Roy Adolph — *Autumn In Her Eyes, Escape, The End, The Final Hour* (1970), on the album ROY ADOLPH SINGS COUNTRY, Point PS 354.

Ernie McCulloch — *Women And The Wine* (1970), Stampede Records S103-B.

The Allan Sisters — *Somewhere There's A Mountain* (1971), Arpeggio 45 ARPS 1021. Also on the Allan Sisters' 1972 album IN SONG, Arpeggio ARPS 10006.

George Hamilton IV — *Countryfied* (1971), RCA Victor 45 rpm 74-0469. This cut went Number 1 in Canada and was a Top Ten hit in the U.S.A. and Europe.

George Hamilton IV — *Countryfied* (1971), on RCA Victor album NORTH COUNTRY.

Hank Smith — *The Final Hour* (1971), Quality 2001X.

Hank Smith — *Where Do We Go From Here* (1971), Quality 2012X.

Hank Smith — *The Final Hour, Where Do We Go From Here, Lady Sunshine, More Than Mexico, The Long Green Line, Take Me Back Into Your World Again* (1971), on HANK SMITH WITH STRINGS 'N' THINGS, Birchmount Records BM588.

Lynn Jones — *Total Destruction* b/w Same Old Song (by Gene McLellan) (1971), MCA 2019 (14764).

Elmer Tippe — *Countryfied* (1971), on I FOUND A SONG. Cynda CNS 1001.

Scotty Stevenson — *Rain Or Shine* (1971), London M.17404-B.

Eddie Chwill — *There Ain't No Easy Way, Love Is All Around You, Somebody On My Mind, Take Me Back Into Your World Again, Rise 'n' Shine, Why Live A Straight Life, Your Kind Of Women* (1971), on THERE AIN'T NO EASY WAY (produced by Dick Damron), Birchmount BM 610.

The Rhythm Pals — *Let My Memory Take Me Home, Goin' Home To The Country, Knowing That She's Leaving* (1972), on THANK GOD WE'VE GOT MUSIC, ARPS 10004.

Hank Smith — *Take Me Home, Once Again, Autumn In Her Eyes, Countryfied* (1972), on COUNTRY MY WAY (produced by Dick Damron), Quality SV 1882.

Hank Smith — *Countryfied* (1973), Quality 2039X.

R. Harlan Smith — *I Remember Love* (1973), on I REMEMBER LOVE, GRT 9230 1030).

Keith Hitchener — *Every Mother's Child* (1973), on STOP, LOOK AND LISTEN, Marathon ALS 385.

Hank Smith — *Everybody's Goin' To The Country* (1974), Quality 2112X.

Orval Prophet — *Countryfied, Rise 'n' Shine, Eastbound Highway* (1974), on MILE AFTER MILE (*Eastbound Highway* was a single).

Keith Hitchener — *Mama Was A Christian Lady, Bittersweet Songs, Knowing That She's Leaving* (1974), on MAMA WAS A CHRISTIAN LADY (produced by Dick Damron), Marathon MMS 76065.

Gary Buck — *Knowing That She's Leaving* (1974), RCA Victor.

Marg Osburne — *Lonesome City* (1974), Marathon Records 45-1129 B-side.

Brian Sklar — *Countryfied / Reflections Of A Fool* (1975), on REFLECTIONS OF A FOOL, Condor Records A977-1453.

Joyce Smith — *Wish The World A Little Love* (1976), on WISH THE WORLD A LITTLE LOVE, Broadland BR 1928.

Bill Hersh — *Good Old Timey Country Rock and Roll* (1977), Maple Haze Records MH7647 (mono and stereo sides).

Jeannie Denver — *One More Day Away* (1978), on WITH LOVE, Westwood WRS128 (released in the U.K.).

Brian Sklar — *Country Rain* (1978), on PROUDLY CANADIAN, Royalty Records 20004.

Tony Goodacre — *Susan Flowers* (1978), on MR. COUNTRY MUSIC, Outlet Records SBOL 4029 (released in the U.K.).

Tommy Goodacre (Britain's Mr. Country Music) — *The Only Way To Say Goodbye* (1979), on YOU'VE MADE MY LIFE COMPLETE, Outlet Records SBOL 4034.

Hugh Scott — *Good Old Timey Rock 'n Roll* (1978), on NOW AND THEN, Snowcan 516.

Bill Hersh & Blue Train — *All Nite Country Party* (1978), Buzzy Frett Records BF001/79.

Mel Hague — *Dollars* (1981), on MERRY-GO-ROUND, Look Records LK-LP6558 (released in the U.K.).

Wilf Carter — *The Last Of The Rodeo Riders* (1981), on CHINOOK WIND.

Ralph Carlson & Country Mile — *Ain't Got Time* (1982), on THANKS FOR THE DANCE, Snocan SCN 518.

Carroll Baker — *Jesus It's Me Again* (1983), on HYMNS OF GOLD, also in the same year on A STEP IN THE RIGHT DIRECTION, Tembo TMT 4324.

Jimmy Lawton — *Jesus It's Me Again* (1983), on CALL ON HIM, Pilgrim Records PM 514 (released by GMI Records in Holland).

Terry Carisse & Friends — *Jesus It's Me Again* (1984), on A GOSPEL GATHERING, Cara Records CR 2001.

Jack Daniel's Band — *Waylon's T-shirt* (1985), on DOWN TO MEXICO, Aktiv Musik Productions HEJ LP-007 (released in Sweden).

Trend — *High On You* (1985), on CHOICES, Bounce Records 3946 (released in Holland).

Ginny Mitchell — *Burnin' A Hole My Heart* (1987), TMC 1002.

Hans de Jong — *High On You* (1987), on STEEL ALONG, Munich Records BV-BM 150.256.

Ray Griff and Dick Damron (duet) — *Movin' Around* (1988), on RAY GRIFF & FRIENDS: HON-EST TO GOODNESS AMIGOS, Warner Music Canada 25-56701.

Lou Paul — *Raining In The Country* (1991), on RUNNING SOUTH ON A NORTH BOUND TRAIN, The Music Connection DMT 91-106.

Brent McAthey & Dick Damron (duet) — *As Far As I Can See* (1995), on WAITIN' FOR THE SUN, Arial Records BRM 00394. Co-written by McAthey and Damron.

Laurie Thain — *Thunder In The Mountains* (1997). Co-written by Damron and Thain.

ACKNOWLEDGEMENTS

Photocredits

Larry Delaney at Country Music News, Don Wise, Maggie Scherf, Samantha Rothwell, Jan Paul, Gordon Davies, Glenys Bowell, Doc Jenkins, The Johnsons at IFCO (International Fan Club Organization), Doug McKenzie, Bob Gardiner, Brent McAthey, Tim Auvigne, Bob Damron, CMA Nashville, CCMA, Hank Smith, Lee van der Ent, Howard Damron, Stacy Green, Vi Campbell, Bill Oja, Brenda Allen, Ken Beaton, Angela Smook, Linda Chomat, Doug Wright, Dee Lippingwell, Country Gazette, Kevin Thomas, and Jim Silverthorn.

Acknowledgements

The author would like to thank the following people for their contributions: Shirlee Matheson, Ruth Andrishak, Maggie Scherf, Gerry Gagnon, Laurie Mills, Glenys Bowell, Bob & Goya Damron, Doctor Harv Haakonson, Larry Delaney, Peter North, John P. McLaughlin, Walt Grealis, Gordon Davies, Bentley Agencies, Linda Haarstad, and the Village of Bentley.

Quarry Press Music Books

☐ *Neil Young: Don't Be Denied*
by JOHN EINARSON $19.95 CDN/ $14.95 USA

☐ *Magic Carpet Ride: The Autobiography of John Kay & Steppenwolf*
by JOHN KAY and JOHN EINARSON $19.95 CDN/ $14.95 USA

☐ *American Woman: The Story of The Guess Who*
by JOHN EINARSON $19.95 CDN/ $14.95 USA

☐ *Superman's Song: The Story of Crash Test Dummies*
by STEPHEN OSTICK $19.95 CDN/ $14.95 USA

☐ *Encyclopedia of Canadian Rock, Pop & Folk Music*
by RICK JACKSON $24.95 CDN/ $19.95 USA

☐ *Encyclopedia of Canadian Country Music*
by RICK JACKSON $26.95 CDN/ $19.95 USA

☐ *Oh What a Feeling: A Vital History of Canadian Music*
by MARTIN MELHUISH $29.95 CDN/ $19.95 USA

☐ *Some Day Soon: Profiles of Canadian Songwriters*
by DOUGLAS FETHERLING $16.95 CDN/$12.95 USA

☐ *Snowbird: The Story of Anne Murray*
by BARRY GRILLS $19.95 CDN/ $14.95 USA

☐ *The Hawk: The Story of Ronnie Hawkins and The Hawks*
by IAN WALLIS $19.95 CDN/ $14.95 USA

☐ *Ironic: The Story of Alanis Morissette*
by BARRY GRILLS $18.95 CDN /$14.95 USA

☐ *For What It's Worth: The Story of Buffalo Springfield*
by JOHN EINARSON $19.95 CDN/ $15.95 USA

☐ *Falling Into You: The Story of Céline Dion*
by BARRY GRILLS $19.95 CDN/ $15.95 USA

Available at your favorite bookstore or directly from the publisher:
Quarry Press, P.O. Box 1061, Kingston, ON K7L 4Y5 Canada,
Tel. (613) 548-8429, Fax. (613) 548-1556, E-mail: order@quarrypress.com.

Name _____

Address _____

_____ Postal Code _____ Telephone _____

Visa/Mastercard # _____ Expiry: _____

Signature _____   Your books will be shipped with an invoice enclosed, including
                                          shipping costs, payable within 30 days in Canadian or
                                          American currency (credit card, check, or money order).